ONE CHOICE TOO FAR

Rod Davison

May your choices reflect your hopes, not your fears.
Nelson Mandela

First Published – 2025
This edition published 2025 by Rod Davison
Brisbane, Qld
Australia

A catalogue record for this
work is available from the
National Library of Australia

The National Library of Australia Cataloguing-in-Publication

Creator: Davison, Rod, author.

Title: One Choice Too Far

ISBN: 978-1-7638980-0-4

Subjects: Fiction
             Australian fiction
             Multi-generational Family Saga
             Searching for Identity
             First Nations issues
             Medical mismanagement

Typeset in Times New Roman 12pt by Donna Munro Book Design.
Cover artwork by Donna Munro Book Design.
Thinking Reader logo drawing by Michelle Davison.
Printed and bound in Australia by Ingram Spark.
Copyright © Rod Davison 2025
Publisher: Rod Davison, Brisbane.
https://thethinkingreader.au

For Sue,
who shares my dreams, my struggles and my joys.

Testimonials

"The plot twists and flow kept me intrigued. It's clear from the writing that the author has deep and close connections with Aboriginal and Torres Strait Islander people and has much lived experience within community life. There are no apparent breaches of Indigenous Cultural and Intellectual Property (ICIP). I loved this story. I know it's given me some healing."

(**Venessa Curnow**, QWC First Nations Cultural Sensitivity reviewer, Cairns, and co-author *Kalaw Kawaw Ya* language book)

"I was walking along our Ruby Bay beach this morning thinking of the novel and the idea came to me that it was like the ending of a symphony. All the themes and characters were crowding together towards a rousing crescendo and a full satisfying finish."

(**Barbara Glass**, Mapua, New Zealand, author of *The Prince and the Dragon*)

"The author got me hooked; I can't wait for the ending."

(**Sharon Barry**, Aboriginal women reviewer, living on Kabi Kabi (Gubbi Gubbi) land, Sunshine Coast)

"A gripping novel of intrigue and mystery and a compelling read for anyone with a keen interest in Australia's intricate relationship with its past and its people. This story of courage and enlightenment explores the complicated journey of a young doctor as he endeavours to find his identity."

(**Ineke van Os,** Brisbane, author of *An Innocent Life*)

"I enjoyed reading my long-time friend's novel - a novel devoid of cultural appropriation. It reflected a cultural sensitivity borne from many years working with, and for, Indigenous peoples."

(**Joseph Murphy**, First Nations reviewer, Canberra)

"A heartrending read for his debut novel. Rod proves his ability to create amazingly real characters. They remain memorable long after the story has ended. My congratulations on a well-researched and culturally respectful Australian story."

(**Graeme Goldsmith**, (Moreton Bay, author of *The Revival)*

Notice for Aboriginal and Torres Strait Islander Readers

Please be aware this story contains fictional references to historic traumatic events, including violent encounters with settlers, forced 'dispersal', sexual violence and removal of children from their families. It also contains references to suicidal ideation.

If you or anyone you know is experiencing suicidal thoughts, 24-hour help is available on the Lifeline Helpline 13 11 14.

For Aboriginal and Torres Strait Islander readers, if you or anyone from your Mob is feeling overwhelmed or having difficulty coping, you can now call **13YARN** [Thirteen YARN] and speak to a Lifeline-trained Aboriginal & Torres Strait Islander Crisis Supporter who can provide crisis support 24 hours a day, 7 days a week.

Acknowledgements

I acknowledge the Traditional Owners and First Nations Elders and Leaders throughout Australia, past, present and emerging.

This is a work of fiction, set in many different locations throughout Australia. In none of these lands has sovereignty ever been ceded.

Cairns City Hospital, Deadend Ridge and Brisbane City Hospital are fictional settings and any resemblance of these settings to real places is coincidental.

The characters, too, are all fictional. Any similarity to real life people is coincidental.

This story was crafted during the years I have lived on Gubbi Gubbi/Kabi Kabi Country and Turrbul/Yagara Country, but the story is not set in southeast Queensland. It is set in the Yidinji, Yirriganydji, Djabugay and Ewamian Countries of far north Queensland, where I have previously worked.

And although the characters in the story are depicted as now living in those lands, they, like many Aboriginal people, have experienced the intergenerational pain and sorrow of their nations being decimated and their forebears being 'displaced' from their own Country to these areas since the arrival of Europeans.

I acknowledge the many First Nations people throughout Queensland, and especially the Bwgcolman peoples of Palm Island, who have shown unfathomable tolerance and kindness to me over the last five decades as I have struggled for understanding.

I extend my gratitude to all those who have helped me mould this story and corrected my mistakes, both literary and cultural.

In writing this story, I have drawn inspiration from many fine novels such as Lucy Treloar's *Salt Creek*, Kate Grenville's *The Secret River*, Andrew McGahan's *The White Earth*, Melissa Lucashenko's *Edenglassie*, Anita Heiss's *Bila Yarrudhangglangdhuray* and Bruce Pascoe's *Blood*.

Chapter 1

An Early Encounter

Cairns, September 1997

"This could be difficult," said Ric, as they swung off Mulgrave Road and headed towards the western suburbs of Cairns. "I might have played footy with a lot of Aboriginal guys, but I haven't ever visited any of them at home."

Ric's decision to come to Cairns with his girlfriend was, in retrospect, somewhat precipitous. In his mind however, there was no other option. He had to find out whether his parents were hiding something from him.

"Ric, your mind's wandering. Are you sure you're up for this visit? We could always turn around and go back," said Cassie, sounding more than a little frustrated.

"Ah, we can't turn back now, Cass. You remember my teammate, Albie? He's the one who insisted we come out here to see his family."

"Why was he so insistent?"

"Albie's a good mate. We look after each other on the footy field if things get a bit rough. And I room with him when we have away games."

"So, is this just a social visit?"

"It's a bit more complicated than that. Before I got injured, the opposition teams were targeting me with dirty tactics, knowing I'd just come up to A grade. Albie took them on. They thought we were both Aboriginal players and then we copped a lot of racial abuse."

"But you're not Aboriginal."

"Albie thinks I might be."

"Oh, I see … Okay, is this the house?"

"Yeah, I reckon that's it," Ric said, pointing to an ageing weatherboard house perched high on wooden stumps. A scrawny kelpie dashed out from under the house and greeted them with barks and growls.

"Git down ya' mangy mongrel!" said a voice from inside.

The dog dropped to the ground, ears lowered, tail wagging. As they looked up, they were greeted by a middle-aged woman with a beaming smile who, despite her weight, appeared to glide down the rickety stairs.

"Hey, you two, I'm Albie's mum. He's told me lots about you both. Come on in. I've put the kettle on."

"Thanks for seeing us, Mrs Watson," Ric said, carefully making his way up the stairs and through to the kitchen where he stashed his crutches against a well-worn red Laminex table.

"You can call me Nora, or Aunty Nora if you like," said their host. "No airs and graces 'round 'ere."

They both glanced around the kitchen. Nora noticed.

"Eh, don' worry, it's not usually this tidy. When you phoned this morning, I raced around and cleaned up. Then I shushed my little grannies outside and told them not to come in and mess up anything."

"Grannies?" asked Cassie.

Right on cue, a small brown face garlanded with rings of curly hair peeked around the doorway, followed by another even smaller one. The smaller one sported long straight hair and a cheeky grin.

"You two, didn't I tell you Nan's having visitors today? You're meant to stay outside and play."

The children eased backwards through the doorway, but Cassie immediately walked over, crouched down on her haunches, and smiled. Soon they were chatting to her, shyly at first, but it wasn't long before they took her hands and pulled her away to show off their toys.

"Mandy, git back 'ere. Now you two have shown your faces, you might as well pull up a chair and have some cordial and biccies with the grown-ups."

To Ric's surprise, each of the kids insisted on sitting next to Cassie, giggling every time she smiled at them.

"Wow Cassie, I didn't know you'd be such a big hit with the kids."

"Maybe there are lots of things you don't know about me."

Ric threw his hands up in mock resignation.

"Righto, c'mon you two. You said on the phone you wanted to talk about what it was like when I was younger and lots of Murri kids got adopted out to white families. But first of all, tell me how Albie's getting on down there in the big smoke," said Nora, as she poured their tea from a large brown teapot ensconced in a knitted tea cozy.

The children stopped fidgeting while Ric told stories about Albie, their favourite uncle. When he turned the conversation back to adoptions, they lost interest and asked if they could leave. Cassie went with them to give Ric and Nora a chance to talk.

"Ay Ric, you wanna look after that one. You gotta treat her with respect, or you're gonna lose her. She's a fiery one, ay."

Ric's friendship with Albie was all that Nora had needed to treat him like family. Their conversation was long and circuitous. It went on for so long that Nora decided they needed another cup of tea.

"Albie used to love sitting around, yarning. He didn't have no milk or sugar in his tea like you do. He always said he wanted it strong and black, like himself."

Ric smiled. "He said some things to me too, after I told him I would be going to Cairns."

"What did he say?"

"He said something like, 'Ay lookout Ric, with your darker skin, you might turn out to be a Murri, yourself. Lots of kids from our Mob got adopted or fostered out to white people in those days.' But then he went all quiet on me."

"Ric, are you thinking you might be one of those kids?"

"Well … um … Aunty Nora. I'm thinking I might have been adopted. And yes, that thought has occurred to me."

"Being a blackfella isn't just about the colour of your skin, you know."

Ric frowned, unsettled.

"There are lots of other things involved. Would you like to talk some more about this?"

"I … I think I would."

"Well, the grannies are at kindy on Fridays. Why don't you and Cassie come for another visit, and we could have a proper talk, while the kids aren't here?"

Ric bit his lip.

"Yeah, okay."

Just then, the children stumbled into the kitchen with Cassie pretending to chase them, which seemed like a good time to say farewell.

"Cassie, I've told Ric that you two would be welcome to come for another cuppa on Friday."

"Oh, okay Aunty Nora."

"But hey, hang on ... I've just had another thought. Sometimes we have a shindig here on Friday nights. I'll invite some of my rellies and friends. They might help him understand how things go with our Mob. They'll probably explain things better than me."

Chapter 2

The Best-laid Plans

Cairns, September 1997

Ric had leased an apartment on the northern beaches, in the hope that the stunning location would give him an opportunity to repair his relationship with Cassie.

"I reckon we should split up," said Cassie at breakfast the next morning.

Ric's jaw dropped.

"Just for today, I mean. The main reason you've come up here is to find out if you were adopted. And you have an appointment to see someone at the hospital, so I thought I'd spend a few hours on the microfiche, see what I can find for you in the old papers."

At the hospital, Ric explained to the Director of Medical Services that he'd been working as a doctor in an Emergency Department in Brisbane, but for various reasons was thinking of coming north to continue his training. This appeared to generate some enthusiasm, so he pressed on with the approach he and Cassie had formulated.

"I've also developed a bit of an interest in medical history now I've got time on my hands," said Ric, indicating his crutches. "And paediatrics is one of the areas I'm interested in. Do you think any of your paediatric staff would remember how things were done up here in the old days?"

The DMS smiled. "I have just the man for you. His name is Dr Ron. He's a paediatrician and he has spent thirty years working in the north, including Cape York and the Torres Strait. He's here this afternoon and he's always willing to help young doctors with their careers. Maybe you'd like to sit in on his clinic and chat with him afterwards?"

That afternoon, Ric introduced himself to Dr Ron. The old paediatrician found space for him and his crutches, then wandered out to the crowded waiting room. Ric noticed the children smiling when he tousled their heads.

In the consulting room, Ron didn't just discuss his patients' illnesses. He enquired about what their families were doing, about their sporting activities, their fishing, and their camping trips. Ric found this approach markedly different from the perfunctory way most specialists related to their patients in metropolitan hospitals.

When the children had all been seen, Ron said he was happy to stay and talk about the old days, and about how children came to be adopted or fostered. Then the old paediatrician surprised him.

"Now Ric, you said you were interested in medical history, and you keep coming back to adoption practices. Is that because you know someone who was adopted up this way?"

Ric stammered out that one of his friends was adopted, and he'd never managed to find his birth parents. Ron looked intently at Ric and, for the first time that afternoon, said absolutely nothing.

Ric's face flushed. "You know what I'm looking for, don't you?"

Ron nodded. He put his hand on Ric's shoulder.

"You suspect you may have been adopted."

"I do."

"Do you have any basis for thinking that?"

"It's a long story, Dr Ron. Some of it is based on facts I've discovered. Some of it is based on dreams I've been having. And as for those damn dreams, they don't just come at night. They come during the day as well."

"I see. These dreams … Do they interrupt you when you're doing clinical work?"

"Yes, that's how things started to go bad for me."

"Ah … yes, that would be a major problem. Would you like to talk about it?"

Ric took some time to reply. Now his cover was blown, he wondered if it would be worthwhile to take Ron into his confidence.

"I'm not sure. It's a long and convoluted story and it would take a fair bit of time to explain."

"The clinic's finished early. All I have to do now is see a couple of private patients in the ward, then I'm free for the rest of the afternoon.

Why don't you grab a cup of tea from the staff room and meet me back here at say, a quarter past four?"

"Are you sure you have time for this?"

"I've always had time for young colleagues struggling with their career. I'd like you to tell me what happened when those dreams interfered with your work. You see Ric, now I'm nearing retirement, I've handed over a lot of my work to younger paediatricians, so yes, I have plenty of time to talk to you this afternoon."

Ron excused himself, leaving Ric alone in the clinic room. How much should he tell the old paediatrician? And if he said too much, would the disclosures become an impediment to his medical registration? He decided to take a leap of faith. But where would he start? His mind flashed back to the most disturbing night he'd had with the dreams. It was back in March …

After making the decision to tell all, Ric's mind plunged into such turmoil, he became concerned it would be impossible to give the old paediatrician a quick summary. When Ron returned, he would have to explain that to him, and thank him for his concern.

But when he returned, Ron was hearing none of that.

"You don't need to give me the short version, Ric. Sometimes it's better to describe the events exactly as they happened and leave it to someone senior to reflect on what you've said. And today, I have all the time in the world."

Ric looked out the window, his eyes on the mountains in the distance.

How did he get to this point? Maybe he *should* tell it all to this kindly old doctor. Tell him more than he'd told the counsellor. Tell him everything. He could begin at the point where things started to go wrong. The night before his first major mistake in the Emergency Department in Brisbane. That was about six months ago …

Chapter 3

Dreams and Disasters

Brisbane, March 1997

All night long, Ric had begged the old man. *Please help me. Make these dreams go away.* As always, the old man had ignored his pleas. He just talked in riddles. And the dreams continued. Night and day.

Ric gasped. Recoiled, horrified. The pings on the nearby monitors offered no reassurance. Beads of sweat dripped down his forehead and into his eyes. How could he have allowed his inner turmoil to endanger the sight of this young man?

Against his better judgement, he'd dragged himself in to work in the Emergency Department. Within minutes, an apprentice panel beater had staggered into the hospital, clutching at his face and yelling, "Help me! There's something stuck in my eye."

The young man had never been in a hospital before. He recoiled from the sensory overload, the unfamiliar sights, sounds, and smells of a busy hospital ED. The pungent smell of sanitiser and the foul stench of blood and pus assaulted the young man's senses. He turned to walk out, but the triage nurse ushered him into the treatment area.

When Ric examined the trembling man's eye with a slit lamp, he discovered a small piece of metal embedded in the cornea. He inserted anaesthetic drops and told him to climb onto a trolley and stay perfectly still.

The tradesman's jaws clenched as he pulled the hi-vis vest tight around his shoulders, mumbling that the eye was still hurting. Ric reassured him it would soon be totally numb. When a child let out a scream in the adjacent cubicle, Ric squeezed the young man's arm and told him to stay calm, he'd be back in a few moments.

He pulled the curtain aside and discovered a junior colleague examining a boy whose arm was obviously broken. The frightened child was protesting that the doctor was hurting him. The boy was wearing a school football jersey and objecting because an intern was attempting to cut it off.

Ric leaned his muscular frame above the boy's chest, distracting him by asking what position he played in the team. The boy barely noticed when the other doctor removed the jersey, inserted a needle and anaesthetised his arm.

"Well done little mate. Now you're not going to feel a thing," said Ric as he gave the boy's other hand a reassuring squeeze. His mother's face conveyed her gratitude.

Ric returned to the tradesman whose eye was now numb. As he set up the procedure, the man's good eye squinted at the equipment. Without warning, the tradesman's hand jerked up to protect his eye, almost upturning the tray of instruments.

"Shit doc, you're not going to stick that thing into my eye, are you?"

Ric was brandishing a needle as long as his finger.

"No of course not. We don't use the needle point to scrape out the metal. We use the side edge of the bevel."

As Ric covered the panel beater's face with sterile drapes, the man wriggled around on the trolley, farting loudly. Ric launched into his best tradie slang.

"Mate, if you could just chill out and lie still, your eye will be as good as gold in no time."

He began scraping the metal off the cornea. It was a procedure he'd done many times before. The tradesman had stopped fidgeting, so Ric relaxed, his hands methodically proceeding with the operation, relying mainly on muscle memory.

Last night's dream invaded his mind.

Bloody hell. Why is it always the same dream and the same old man?

As he lifted the particle of metal from the eye, the tradesman's head moved. Ric's hand slipped, leaving a laceration halfway across the cornea. Sticky fluid coursed from the cut across the eye. The tradesman didn't flinch. His eye was still numb.

On the other side of the sterile drapes, the doctor did more than flinch. He froze, watching in silence as the fluid oozed its way out from the eyeball and across the cornea towards the lower eyelid.

Damn! This poor guy could lose his sight! Maybe this is what the old man meant when he said, 'Your mind isn't listening to what your body is doing.'

Ric's dusky face turned ashen. He removed the drapes and gave the tradesman what he hoped was a reassuring glance. For months, he'd been dreading a disaster like this. Thoughts in disarray, he stumbled down the corridor like a sleepwalker. When he entered the duty consultant's office, his face was still pale. He was relieved to find it was his mentor.

"Dr Claire, I've just punctured a guy's cornea. The poor bugger could go blind!"

"Ric, settle down. Tell me exactly what happened."

"I must have been … distracted. My hand slipped when his head moved, and now this poor bloke's got fluid oozing out of his eyeball."

Ric wondered if Claire could smell his fear.

"All right, I'll come and have a look. We'll put some stain in his eye and see if the cornea has been ruptured. But this is not like you, Ric. What's happened? You look awful. Are you sure you should even be at work today?"

Ric shook his head. After a long silence, he cleared his throat.

"Dr Claire, I know you're the duty consultant today, but you're also my mentor. Can I tell you something in that capacity?"

"Ah … yes, I think that would be alright. But until I go off shift, I will still need to function as your supervisor as well. And as I'm your mentor, we can drop the formalities; just call me Claire."

"Yes, of course … I … probably wasn't concentrating well enough today. My mind has been throwing up images … scenes like in dreams … and they're scaring the shit out of me. I think you're right. I should have pulled a sickie."

Ric's Adam's apple lurched up and down.

"Uh oh, I'm going to chuck." Hand over mouth, he rushed from the room.

When he didn't return nor answer his pager, colleagues searched the bathrooms and the staff rooms, but no one could find him anywhere.

With a heavy sigh, Claire introduced herself to the tradesman. She applied antibiotic ointment and placed a shield over his eye. The tradesman asked in rapidly escalating anger about where the other doctor had gone, and what had happened to his eye.

Claire explained that Ric was one of their best young doctors but when he'd removed the metal, he found the operation had caused a tear in the front of the eyeball. When the frightened man asked whether he could go blind, she explained that was unlikely, but it was still a possibility. The tradesman punched his fist into the thinly padded examination trolley, swearing loudly.

Claire arranged for an ophthalmologist consultation and a daily review until the eye healed. Her explanation that, in most cases, the eye would recover fully did little to reassure the young panel beater.

When she phoned Phil, the Director of Medical Services, he sounded hassled but agreed to fit her in. The Director of Nursing had already handed him the Incident Report.

Phil scowled as he listened to Claire's summary of the incident and the steps she'd taken. The fact that Ric had disappeared caused only a fleeting elevation of one eyebrow.

"I suppose he's hungover after partying all night. These young doctors are all the same, aren't they? Anyhow you'll have to excuse me. I've got another meeting."

"Things are a bit more serious than that," said Claire, as she recounted what Ric had said during his mid-term review the previous week. How he'd talked about quitting medicine as he was hoping to score a contract with the National Rugby League.

"But there was something else, Phil … he seemed … depressed, and he kept saying he had to sort himself out … and now this."

Phil kept glancing at his watch. Claire wound up her report and they agreed on how the incident should be handled. Then almost as an afterthought, he asked, "What's the young doc's name?"

"Ric Castelillio."

"Ricardo Castelillio! Why didn't you tell me that earlier?"

"You already had the Incident Report. I'm sure his name was on the form."

Phil made an obvious effort to calm himself. He picked up the report and read it again, shaking his head and murmuring.

"I'm confused, Phil. As soon as I mentioned Ric's name, you suddenly seemed more concerned about the incident. Is there anything particular I should know about Ric?

"No that's fine Claire. It just … reminded me of something."

Claire frowned as she ventured back into the Emergency Department. Medical staff vied for her attention, buzzing around like blowflies on roadkill, all speaking at once.

"Ric's been drinking a lot lately."

"His girlfriend wasn't too happy at the staff party."

"He's thinking of giving up footy."

"I hope he doesn't top himself."

"Enough!" said Claire. "Everyone who's free, join me in the meeting room. Now!"

"Right. We've got a waiting room full of people, and the paramedics are bringing in a cardiac arrest. We're one doctor short. Leave me to deal with Ric. Concentrate on your own work and get this place cleared."

They filed out, eyes darting, but no one made further comments. An uneasy sense of purpose returned to the ED, punctuated by furtive whispering.

Claire continued to call Ric, but still there was no answer.

Chapter 4

Rainforest

Scenic Rim, Southeast Queensland, March 1997

Ric groaned, trying to recall the dance of the wait-a-while vine. Experienced bushwalkers knew it well. The vine snatches, impedes your progress. You stop, step back and pivot away. The tendrils tear out. You turn full circle and then you have to search for another path through the forest.

A bit like my life at the moment.

Ric performed the dance then checked for damage. A long row of puncture wounds oozed blood down his arm.

A waterfall roared nearby, enticing him to continue. He climbed up the rockface, cleaned off the blood and took stock.

He'd left the hospital in Brisbane and driven to Lamington National Park. He'd stayed in a hostel overnight, woken before dawn and found his mind again throwing up disturbing images. After a quick breakfast in the communal kitchen, he'd headed straight into the rainforest.

As he padded along the track, he found himself struggling to understand what the dream images could mean. He had no idea why he kept thinking the old man could help him. Who was he, anyway? He had a gnarled face, and his skin was dark, similar to his own. Although he looked familiar, his facial features were not at all like his own. Who did he look like? Maybe like some of his teammates, the Murri lads from north Queensland?

His confusion was heightened by a conversation he'd overheard in the common room that morning. Two European backpackers told him about a bora ring they'd been shown the day before, near Tamborine. They speculated about the ceremonies that may have been performed there, in years gone by.

When they asked Ric what happened to those original Australians, he couldn't explain. His reply that the local tribes had probably just died out, clearly didn't satisfy the travellers. Now he wondered why *he* hadn't ever thought about this question.

When he reached the waterfall, cooling spray showered his face as he lifted his gaze to the elkhorn ferns and the king orchids in the rock crevices above. Birds nest ferns clung onto the tree trunks. In the valley below, piccabeen palms and tree ferns competed for prime position on the creek banks. In the distance, a catbird called, it's cry mimicking a baby in distress.

Ric's muscles relaxed. He inhaled the earthy smells of the rainforest floor as he climbed up the side of the waterfall.

The peace of the forest shattered when his heavy mobile phone buzzed into life. He glanced at the screen, intending to turn it off. It was Claire, his mentor, the one who'd had to deal with the mess he'd created.

He couldn't pick up the call, hanging onto the rock face. He searched the cliff. There was nowhere safe nearby. He'd have to climb to the top of the falls and phone Claire from there. He took advantage of the delay, trying to stem the shower of images racing across his mind. He had to present a coherent story to his mentor.

"Ric! Thank God, I've found you. What's that hissing noise, are you in the shower?"

"No, I'm not in the shower; I'm sitting on a ledge above a waterfall."

"What the hell are you doing there? You're rostered on duty, and we need you here."

"I had to get away, Claire. I'm … not in a good place."

"Are you safe?"

"Yeah."

"And is there any likelihood you'll be back at work today?"

"No."

"Why not?"

"I've been trekking since breakfast, trying to escape the confusion in my mind. I couldn't get back for hours even if I tried. The creeks are swollen, and I've got stinging vines slowing me down. And ah, bloody hell! Now I've got leaches bloating up under my socks. There's blood everywhere."

"Ric, I'm not interested in your pathetic adventure. You're absent from duty and you haven't even had the courtesy to call in and advise us. I'm supervisor again today, and I'm trying to cover for you, but the boss is breathing down my neck. What's going on?"

"I don't know Claire, it's just so complicated. All I know is I needed to get away and sort myself out. Hey, how's that guy's eye?"

"Your patient is okay this morning, no thanks to you. His eye is improving, but he's still considering a formal complaint. You made it worse when you didn't come back and explain what happened. I've had a long talk with him, and I've offered him an appointment with the DMS."

"Oh great," Ric said, already regretting he'd picked up the phone.

My whole life's turning to shit, my mind's throwing up scenes and dreams, and I'm stuffing up my patients. I've got absolutely no idea what I'm going to do.

He cast his gaze down the face of the waterfall and focused on the swirling pool thirty metres below.

Maybe that's the answer ...

He could make out the shape of a body floating in the creek, blood streaming from the head and mingling with the torrent.

Hang on a minute. Is that my body?

He'd had this dream many times before. Slowly the shade faded into the spray. His body trembled as he shook the image from his mind.

"Ric, are you still there?"

He leaned backwards, breathing slowly, groaning as he rolled over and forced himself into a goanna crawl across the mossy rocks to another ledge.

"Yeah, I'm here. I'm safe now. I'll make my way out of the forest."

"Call when you're out. Come and see me in my office as soon as you're back."

"No way I'm going anywhere near that bloody hospital today!"

"Well, you're going to have to come and talk with me somewhere, unless you'd prefer to face disciplinary action!"

There was no response.

"Well, I suppose I could meet you at Vino's after I finish work."

"Yeah, that would be good."

Claire phoned her confidante, Lisa, the Director of Paediatrics, an old friend from medical school.

"One of our staff has gone AWOL. He's a troubled young guy. When I managed to get him on the phone just now, he was sitting on the edge of a waterfall, leaning over, and God knows what he was thinking! He says he'll come back and meet with me this afternoon. I know I should update Phil …"

"Well, why don't you?

"You know what Phil's like. He'll just lean back behind that silky-oak desk with a scowl on his face and those bushy eyebrows contracting. Then he'll insist on calling the police and sending out a search party."

"That may be the safest thing to do. You know you're taking a calculated risk here. That young man's life could be in danger."

"I know. But I have a gut feeling he won't let me down. And Phil already has Ric under scrutiny, for some reason."

"That's an even bigger risk for you then, if you don't tell him."

"I just can't deal with his attitude today."

She sent Phil a message.

"I've located Ric. I'm meeting him later this afternoon. I'll brief you tomorrow."

Chapter 5

Deep Water

Brisbane, March 1997

Ric arrived at Vino's in his hiking gear, looking dishevelled.

After they'd ordered food, he grabbed a beer and took a few quick gulps. Claire drank sparkling water. After downing his first beer, Ric signalled to the waiter for another.

"Now Ric, before you get yourself pissed, we need to talk."

"Yeah, I know. Is that guy's eye still okay?"

"Yes, he's on strict bed rest and he's on meds to control the pressure in the eyeball. Oh, and he hasn't lodged a complaint … yet … although he had a fair bit of pain. But he does want to talk with you."

"Poor bugger. He comes to the hospital with a simple problem, and he leaves in danger of losing his sight. I'll have to face up to him, I know. But it's the last thing I feel like doing."

"It's not like you to walk away from trouble, you're usually very responsible. I think you owe him some kind of explanation. I think you owe *me* one as well."

Ric squirmed, trying to remember what he'd rehearsed in the forest. He had difficulty sticking to the script.

"I don't know how to tell you this, but I've been really struggling lately. I've tried to deal with it, but I just can't seem to get on top of things … and I don't know who to turn to."

"Can't you talk to your parents?"

"I wouldn't say I'm close to my mum and dad. They were much closer to the younger kids when we were growing up."

"You have lots of friends though, don't you?"

"I get on alright with the staff in the ED, but apart from my girlfriend Cassie, there's only one other person. That's Mark, my old schoolmate, he's one of the psychiatry registrars here at the hospital."

"Is there anything else? Whatever you tell me as your mentor, you know I'll treat as confidential. This is supposed to be a formal meeting, even though we're here," said Claire, waving her glass at the surroundings.

Ric put his beer down and looked Claire straight in the eye. "Ever since I was a child, I've had thoughts and images coming into my head for no apparent reason. They're kind of like dreams, but I'm not even asleep. They make me think of doing stuff I don't necessarily want to do."

"I see … Have you ever told anyone about this?"

"No, not recently. When I was little, I used to call them my daytime dreams. I told my Poppy about them when I was a preschool kid, but then he went and died on me."

Claire reached over and put her hand on Ric's shoulder. "Why don't you get some of that pasta into you, before you drink any more beer?"

He nodded. After wolfing down the pasta, he ordered triple gelato for dessert and shifted to drinking water.

"Ric, I need to ask you something. Were you thinking of jumping off that ledge?"

"The thought did come to me, but I pushed it away."

"Hmm. I think you need to talk to a counsellor or maybe even a psychiatrist. Although I'm your mentor, there's a limit to what I can do. But as your mentor, I *do* need to be sure you're safe to practise medicine. Will you agree to go and get help?"

"I don't have any other choice now, do I?"

By the time coffee arrived, they'd agreed on a plan. Ric would go to his GP and get a medical certificate for the rest of the week. Then he would book into counselling with the employee assistance program at the hospital. If they had any serious concerns, he would return to his GP and ask for a referral to a psychiatrist.

Ric's phone rang as he walked to the car. It was Cassie.

"Hi babe, how're you going? I haven't heard from you for a couple of days."

"Yeah, I'm not too bad Cass, better now I hear your voice. Could I come over?"

"Of course. You want dinner?"

"No, I've eaten. I'll see you in an hour."

Ric's spirits rose when Cassie greeted him at the door. She smelt so good, he was thankful he'd showered and changed. He knew he looked better than he did earlier, but he didn't feel any better, and it must have shown. His lips quivered.

"Hell Cass, I just can't do it. I can't pretend anymore."

"Ric, what's wrong?"

"We need to talk."

Cassie took his hand and pulled him towards the couch.

"You've been different lately. What's happening? Are you thinking of breaking up with me?"

"What? Why do you say that?"

"You've been really distant, and recently you haven't called much. Now you're saying we need to talk, which is not like you at all."

Ric knew he had changed. Normally, he'd be relaxed and happy as soon as he laid eyes on Cassie. And she was the one who usually wanted to talk, not him.

People used to say his wide smile lit up every room he entered. He often wondered whether it was the contrast with his dark skin. Or maybe it was the gap between his front teeth that people found endearing. But whatever it was, he had to admit that lately, he wasn't smiling very much at all.

"Babe, I can see it in your face. I've always loved your eyes, but lately, they look all dark and cloudy. Please tell me what's going on."

"Um, there's so much to tell you, it's hard to know where to start," said Ric, buying time. He mentioned the problems at work, and his subsequent meetings with Claire, but not why he'd been distracted. He spoke about his escape to the rainforest. He avoided telling her what he'd seen in the creek far below, or what he'd been thinking as he sat on the edge.

"Why do I have the feeling you're not telling me everything?"

"I'm still trying to work out what's happening, Cass."

Cassie took his hands and peered into his eyes.

"Okay babe, you've told me you're going to get a few days off, to work it all out. Can I help?"

"Maybe, but first, I need some time to myself. I have to go and see the counsellor and then the Director of Medical Services."

"You look troubled. Why don't you stay with me tonight?"

"I'd love to," he said, looking at Cassie's anxious face, "but I just need some space. Oh, and I've been meaning to tell you, I don't think we should move in together at the moment."

"That *is* why you came over tonight. You *are* thinking of breaking up with me!"

"Gees Cassie, it's not all about you. I do have other things going on in my life!"

Ric stood and stomped out the door.

"Fine!" said Cassie, slamming the door behind him.

Ric had to talk to someone. He'd let his friendship with Mark lapse in recent months. His old schoolmate was working hard to become a psychiatrist.

Is that why I've been avoiding him?

He decided to invite Mark for a bushwalk. It would be easier to talk when he was doing something.

On the walk, he rambled on about many things. It was hours before he finally blurted out that sometimes he saw scenes, like he was in a dream. And sometimes after the dreams, he felt driven to do things he hadn't planned to do. And he had no idea what was wrong.

"Mate, I don't think I can take it anymore. I've got to work out what all this means."

Mark looked pensive, for what to Ric seemed like an eternity.

"You've never mentioned this sort of thing before."

"I didn't want you to think I was going loopy. And up until recently, it didn't happen very often."

"But now it's happening more frequently?"

"Yeah, it is. When I was a little kid, I told my mum about it, and she dragged me off to see a doctor. I was frightened. I didn't want to be different from the other kids. I thought it'd be best if I never told anyone again."

"Surely you must have told someone though?"

"Apparently when my poppy used to care for me, my eyes would stare into the distance, and I'd go all quiet. He made me tell him about it afterwards, but he never got angry with me, like Mum did. He'd just sit with me until the thoughts went away. He always told me the same thing."

"What was that?"

"He'd say, 'It's okay Ricky boy. You have a special gift. The Old People talk to you. You don't have to tell anyone else about it.' Ever since I was a little kid, I've repeated Poppy's words to myself, like a mantra, whenever those strange thoughts come."

"And you still say those words?"

"Yeah."

"Have you told Cassie any of this stuff?"

"Not yet."

He called Cassie that evening. She didn't answer his call. Nor did she call him back. He called again a few days later.

"Hello Ric," said Cassie, in a tone he'd never heard her use before.

"Ah, hi Cass. Would you like to go out to dinner tonight?"

"Not really."

"You're still pissed off with me?"

"You could say that."

"I've been talking with Mark, and also with the counsellor. I'm feeling a lot better, and I'm going back to work next week. Could we maybe have dinner the following weekend?"

"I don't know, Ric. I'll think about it."

Chapter 6

Staying Afloat

Brisbane, March 1997

Ric returned to his workplace the following week. Some of his colleagues asked how he was. Others avoided him.

I wonder what they're thinking. Maybe they've figured out what's wrong with me.

Claire interrupted his thoughts. "Ric, I'd like to speak to you, in my office."

Ric wandered in, looking as nonchalant as he could.

"Thanks Claire. I'm glad I had that time away from the ED, now I'm raring to go." Ric sat upright in the chair, tapping his fingers on her desk.

"It's not working, is it Ric? I'm thinking you might need more time off."

"Ah, thanks Claire. But truthfully, I feel better when I'm doing stuff."

"I understand why you say that. You're a practical sort of bloke. But I can't advise the ED Director to let you loose on patients until I'm certain about a few things."

Ric winced. "What sort of things?"

"The DMS wants reassurance your mind will be on the job, and you won't be distracted. And I need to know if those images have stopped coming into your head, and whether you're still getting help."

"Yeah, I'm getting help. I'm seeing the counsellor, and my mind's a bit more settled."

"That's good then. But the director won't allow you back in the ED unless you agree to work under strict supervision. That means you'll have to check everything with a senior colleague before you commence any treatment."

"What? Like I'm a new intern? I've never let anyone down before, have I?"

"No, you haven't, but this incident could have been serious, and we owe it to the patients to make sure you're back on top of your game. Incidentally, that young man's eye is going well and he's hoping to return to work soon."

"Ah, that's a relief."

Ric was pleased the ED was busy when he emerged from Claire's office. He proceeded, with some trepidation, to pick up patients, firstly low priority cases and then increasingly more complex ones.

After a couple of days, Claire advised him the reports from the seniors were positive. She would be recommending that supervision be phased out soon, but it would be Phil, the Director of Medical Services, who would make the final decision.

When he presented himself to Phil's office, Ric had no time to make himself comfortable.

"You know your actions could have caused permanent blindness in that young tradesman?" asked the DMS.

Ric nodded.

"We expect better than that from our doctors. If you ever wake up hungover in the future, just stay home and don't put your patients at risk! If this sort of thing happens again, I'll be notifying the Medical Board. Do I make myself clear?"

"Yes."

Should I tell him why I was so distracted?

Phil stood and gestured towards the door.

"You'll remain under close supervision for the next four weeks. Then I'll ask Claire to give me another report from the consultants group before I decide whether or not you can return to normal duties."

Ric returned to Claire's office. He took a deep breath, then shook his head.

"He's not easing up on my supervision. It seems way over the top to me, but it looks like I don't have any choice in the matter."

"Well, you'll just have to deal with it. I'll take full responsibility for your supervision over this period, and I won't make it obvious. Just don't let me down, or we'll both be in trouble."

That night, Ric called Cassie again. She seemed pleased to hear his news. She still didn't agree to go out to dinner.

After another few days, Claire advised him the tradesman's eye had fully recovered, and he'd decided not to put in a formal complaint. Soon, Ric's sudden sick leave was all but forgotten. His colleagues had relaxed with him and returned to their usual banter.

As he began an afternoon shift, a patient in his late seventies presented with stomach pains. He had leathery skin and squinty eyes.

"G'day old mate," said Ric, "it looks like you've spent a fair bit of time outdoors."

"Too right, doc. I was a professional fisherman for most of my working life."

The old man spoke with the broad north Queensland accent Ric knew so well. And even though at times he was in obvious pain, he couldn't help making wisecracks about his life in the north.

Old Mate (which was the way Ric thought of him) said he'd smoked all his life, but he wasn't drinking as much as he used to. Ric noted that the old fisherman was taking tablets for cholesterol and high blood pressure. After recording the history, he did a thorough examination.

All he found was that the man's blood pressure was a bit high, and his stomach was mildly tender all over, although his abdominal muscles didn't tense when Ric prodded them. Nothing seemed to point to a definite diagnosis. Ric was reassured by the man's cheerful conversation, and the alacrity with which he jumped off the bed and dressed.

"Fair dinkum doc, it's probably nothing to worry about. I really only came in 'cos the missus has been nagging me to get these gut pains checked out."

Ric decided to be cautious. He ran the usual pathology tests, X-rays and ultrasounds.

When the old fisherman's pathology results came back, they showed nothing abnormal. Ric checked out the man's imaging which revealed nothing either.

All the consultants were in a planning meeting, but just to cover himself, he phoned one of them to discuss the case.

"His path results are normal, his X-rays and ultrasound look clear, except for some shadows showing faecal impaction – a blocked bowel. The radiologist's reports aren't available yet, but I'm confident there's no bowel obstruction. I really don't think this is an 'acute abdomen'. I think he's just constipated like most of these old guys."

"Would you like me to come down and see him?" asked the consultant.

"No need," replied Ric. "I'm happy to get the nurses to give him an enema, then send him home and review him tomorrow."

"Okay Ric, that's fine if you're sure. If he still has the pains tomorrow, we'll go over the case together."

Old Mate was not too impressed with the idea of an enema.

"What? You're going to stick some stuff up my arse?"

"Not me mate, one of those cute nurses over there."

"Bloody hell doc, is that really necessary?"

"I'm afraid so."

The old fisherman mumbled a lot but eventually consented. After he had the procedure, all he said was, "Well, that should keep the missus quiet."

The nurses reported an impressive result from the enema.

The rest of the day was uneventful, until an ambulance siren wailed. The paramedics had phoned in saying they were transferring a male patient who was in shock, pulse racing and blood pressure dropping through the floor. There was no external bleeding and no evidence of a heart attack, but his abdomen was rigid. They suspected an internal bleed.

Beads of sweat formed on Ric's forehead. The queasy feelings returned. He rushed to the trolley as it was wheeled into the resuscitation bay. It was the old fisherman.

"BP 70/40, pulse 120 and weak, he's losing consciousness," said the paramedic.

Semi-organised chaos ensued. Consultants, nurses, and interns all arrived at once. The administration officer brought in the radiologist's report on the films from earlier in the day. Before Ric had a chance to recount the man's story, the consultant shouted out commands.

"Get that intravenous line into his arm. Call the surgeon urgently, tell him we've probably got a leaking abdominal aortic aneurysm, and we're losing him. This man needs surgery now. Prep him for a central line and notify theatre."

Ric steadied himself by holding on to the trolley, trying desperately to control the churning in his own gut.

Chapter 7

Further Troubles

Brisbane, March 1997

Ric's hands were so sweaty and shaky, he barely succeeded in getting the central line in.

He pulled the consultant aside. "This is the same patient I called you about earlier. I didn't even consider a Triple A."

"Okay Ric, we'll discuss that later. Let's get this man to theatre."

After the patient was wheeled out, Claire called him into her office.

"This is an elderly man with abdominal pains, a life-long smoker with high blood pressure and high cholesterol. Why didn't you consider a leaking aortic aneurysm?"

"Well, all of those things are pretty common in this age group. His path results were okay, and his imaging showed faecal impaction. He had a good result from the enema, so I phoned the consultant, sent him home, and planned to review him tomorrow."

"That history may be common, but it also increases the likelihood of significant pathology, including a Triple A. Why didn't you check with the radiologist before discharging him?"

"I really wasn't worried about him, Claire. Okay, I'll have to admit … my mind may have been on other things. It was such a quiet shift."

"Isn't the counsellor helping you get on top of those 'other' things?"

"The counsellor? Well yeah, I've been getting on well with her. I've been planning what to say tomorrow, about the things I've been seeing … and maybe even about how I was feeling on the ledge, and all that other stuff."

"What! You still haven't told her those things? What's stopping you?"

Ric's head slumped onto the desk.

"I dunno. Maybe I *am* psychotic. Some of the Murri guys in my footy team have said a few things as well. They've sowed seeds of doubt in my mind …"

"You need to sort yourself out, Ric. This kind of mistake could cause a man's death. Let's hope he survives the surgery. But we can't allow you to continue working until you provide us with evidence you're back to full capacity. Go and see your GP, get another medical certificate and get an urgent referral to a psychiatrist."

"Hell, that's a bit harsh, isn't it?"

"Maybe it's not harsh enough. The other option is to recommend you be stood down."

Ric's shoulders slumped. He murmured incoherently.

"Ric, I do care about you. But my first responsibility is the care of our patients. You recall the Hippocratic oath? First do no harm?"

"Yeah, I do."

He made no attempt to stand and leave.

"I don't know, Claire. My whole life's coming unstuck. Do you think I could ask for a few months' leave without pay?"

"You could, but you're not going to. You're going to that counsellor tomorrow and you're going to tell her what you've told me. And then you're going to answer all her questions as directly and truthfully as you can."

Ric remained slumped in his seat, elbows on knees and palms pressed to his temples. His head and shoulders rocked back and forth, and he began murmuring again.

"Ric, you have to tell both your counsellor and your GP what you were thinking about on the edge of that bloody waterfall!"

Ric grimaced. "Gees Claire, I've really got you shitty this time."

"Yes, you have."

Ric followed Claire's suggestions and sought advice from the counsellor. He also arranged for his GP to write a referral to a psychiatrist. For most of his sick leave, he meandered aimlessly around the nearby suburbs, speaking to no one, trying desperately to work out why his mind was throwing up images.

After some weeks, he returned to work, relieved to find the old fisherman had recovered well. His colleagues rallied around him saying they could have made the same mistake. His error hadn't been fatal, but it could have been. He was put on an official return-to-work program. He decided to accept his 'demotion' in good grace, working the remainder of his time in ED, under Claire's direct supervision.

"It's bloody frustrating," he told Mark over a beer several weekends later. "It's so demeaning having to work like a new graduate under close supervision. But Claire's a great doctor and she does care about me. I feel comfortable with her. I suppose I ah … tell her things long before I tell my counsellor. And the GP has given me a referral to a psychiatrist."

"Have you said much to Cassie?"

"No. To be honest mate, I'm struggling to hold it all together. I want to sort it out for myself first."

"Bloody hell Ric, sometimes you close up as tight as a dingo trap."

"Cassie's barely even talking to me at the moment. But at least I've nearly finished my penance, and it looks like I'll get my Emergency Medicine term signed off after all. Hey, would you be interested in coming on a road trip for a couple of weeks?"

"A road trip? Um … I was going to use my leave to get stuck into study for the psych exams. But I guess I could do with a break. Okay, I'll see what I can do."

How am I going to explain to Cassie why I need to get away?

He invited her to coffee, hoping that in a public space, she might stay calm. When they arrived at their favourite café, Cassie's face was blank, and her responses were terse.

This isn't going to be easy.

"Hey babe, thanks for giving me a chance to explain. I really don't want us to split up. And I do want to move in with you as soon as I get myself sorted. But I don't think it would be fair to lumber you with all my problems at the moment."

"Why not? Isn't that what relationships are about? Are you sure you're not having doubts about us?

"No, not at all. I'm doubting myself."

"So, is this the old 'it's not you, it's me' cliché?"

"What? No, I really am having difficulties. As you know, I'm seeing a counsellor, and the GP is referring me to a psychiatrist."

"Okay, but it's nothing to do with us?"

"No, and I promise I will share everything once I've worked it all out."

"Right. And when will that be?"

"Ah, I'm not sure, Cass. Umm … there's another thing. You remember Mark, my old school mate who's doing psychiatry training?"

"Yes."

"I've asked him if he would come on a road trip with me. I think he may be the one who can help me sort things out."

Ric held his breath.

"Okay, if you're going on a holiday with Mark, I'm sure as hell not staying in Brisbane. I'll ask Lou to come on a holiday with me."

"Yeah, fair enough. And maybe we could catch up again when we're both back in town."

"I'll think about it."

Chapter 8

An Unsettling Holiday?

Cape Willoughby Lighthouse, Kangaroo Island, April 1997

"It's definitely not a dark and stormy night," Ric muttered to himself, remembering the trope they'd mocked in high school English classes.

At times, this night was eerily quiet.

He and Mark had flown to Adelaide and driven to Wilpena Pound, where the tour guides had explained both the unique geological features and the ancient rock engravings. Then they'd travelled southeast and caught a ferry to Kangaroo Island.

Ric decided they should stay at the old lighthouse, a lonely but peaceful place, which they would have all to themselves. On the first night in the lighthouse cottage, Ric couldn't sleep. The old man who talked in riddles had re-entered his dreams. He dressed and crept out of the cottage to wander along the well-worn tracks around the rugged cliffs, as a light mist enveloped them.

His thoughts turned to Cassie. He knew this could be the end of their relationship, but there was just no way he could sort things out with her, when he couldn't sort things out with himself. The road trip had been a useful distraction, but now all the unwanted thoughts returned.

There were no lights near the old buildings. The clouds were winning the battle of the night skies, but the moon, though chastened, still managed to produce a luminescent shimmering on the ocean surface as the swell rolled in.

On the knoll behind the cliff face, Ric had no difficulty discerning the narrow path, thanks to the regular bursts of light from above. The Cape Willoughby lighthouse emitted three flashes every fifteen seconds. To Ric it appeared to be alive, especially when the lights across Backstairs Passage flashed in reply.

For more than a century, the lighthouse had been sending out its warning beams to sailors. They hadn't always heeded the warning.

There had been so many shipwrecks, so many deaths. On this sloping headland, the keepers had watched helplessly as wooden ships shattered on rocky shoals. Many times, they'd tried to rescue sailors being torn to pieces on those jagged rocks, their attempts rarely successful.

Tonight, no ships would be wrecked. The seas were too calm. At times when the clouds exposed the moon, Ric looked up, amazed at the number of stars in the Milky Way. The sky was just as clear as it was in Wilepena Pound. He'd never seen the sky like this, even working night shifts. In the cities, there were always lights on somewhere. He caught a whiff of the pungent aroma of the kelp and other marine life on the exposed rocks, mingled with the salty smells of the ocean spray.

The westerlies blew, but only in gusts. The wind barely moved the long thin leaves of the she-oaks. Ric could just make out the fields of pussy tail grasses bending in long waves, mimicking the movements of the ocean swell.

Continuing along the path, he heard a sound. Then something moved. He froze – skin prickled on the nape of his neck. There were only two people on this headland tonight. He was one and Mark was the other, and Mark was asleep in his bed.

He strained to hear the sound again. All he could hear now was the swell breaking on the rocks, the seagulls screeching overhead, and a lone owl hooting in the distance. He tried to relax as he began walking again, convincing himself it could have been kangaroos moving about.

That morning, he and Mark had been transfixed by the sight of whole families of western grey kangaroos, but tonight the kangaroos were on the ground, resting.

As he padded along the path, he heard no more sounds. He breathed deeply, comforted by the stillness of the night and the closeness of the natural world. His eyes adjusted to the dark. His gaze moved from the quiet ocean to the whitewashed lighthouse.

"Shit! What the hell is that?" he said out loud, startling the kangaroos.

The now-familiar deep gnawing in his gut returned. Near the old weather station, shadows moved. Like the pussy tail clumps, they waved in tandem with the wind gusts. But there was no vegetation there. Now the prickling sensation spread over his entire body. Even the hair shafts on his scalp tightened.

The shadows moved towards the cliff face then across to the ocean. He could see them best in his peripheral vision. Their heads were craning upwards, their limbs writhing. At times, they seemed to go into spasms.

Those shadows are people and they're struggling. Maybe they're in the ocean, drowning!

He crept past the anemometer. As he approached the weather station, the shadows disappeared. He looked back to the path. The shadows were there again, more this time, some smaller than others.

He turned his eyes away, keeping his head still, then looked back to where the shadows had been. Nothing. He threw himself to the ground and curled up into a ball.

I must be hallucinating.

He rose to his feet and swore as he stumbled over a rock. In the dull silver light, the shadows could be the ghosts of the lighthouse keepers. His thoughts became morbid, thinking about the keepers' lives, their boring daily routines punctuated by sudden ferocious weather and then frenzied shipwreck rescues.

New sounds interrupted his thoughts. The roos lifted their heads, ears pointing upwards. Once again, the gusts of wind stirred the leaves of the long-suffering she-oaks. The sounds became regular as a shape approached him. Ric froze again, then began shaking.

"Ric, you moron! What are you doing out here in the middle of the night?"

It was Mark cutting across the grassy slope, cursing when his bare feet squelched on kangaroo droppings.

"Mate, you scared the shit out of me. I was fast asleep. I woke when I heard yelling and swearing. At first, I thought we had unwanted visitors, then I worked out it must have been you."

"Well, if you worked out it was me, why didn't you just roll over and go back to sleep?"

Ric was unsure whether he was relieved to see Mark, embarrassed about what he'd been imagining, or just angry that his friend was challenging him again. He settled on angry.

"Bugger off Mark, just leave me alone. I don't need you analysing me again."

Mark's face twitched. "Mate, I'm here now. Why don't we just walk together for a bit?"

"Yeah, that would be really clever. You're in your pyjamas, your feet are covered in roo shit, and you're shivering. Just piss off and go back to bed."

Mark didn't go back. He followed a few steps behind as Ric trudged further down the path. As they walked on, Ric's responses changed from angry retorts to muffled grunts.

"Hey Ric, I'm really sorry about how I've been talking to you. It's just that you haven't been your normal self lately."

Ric started to arc up again, but before he spoke, he experienced a disturbing realisation.

Those shapes couldn't have been Mark. I saw them well before he heard me swear. And the sounds came from the opposite direction to where he was sleeping!

Now confused, he was unsure whether to tell Mark, who was banging on again.

"So Ric, what got you started on this night-time wandering?"

Mark shivered. Ric didn't shiver, his skin crawled. He tried to hold down the panic and focus on Mark's question. His old friend was clearly worried about him, which was why he'd agreed to come on this road trip. But what should he say?

He started off slowly, trying to sound nonchalant. "Yeah, I just couldn't sleep. The wind was rattling my windows and the light beam kept scanning across. I reckoned I might as well get up and go for a walk and enjoy the sounds of the ocean. I thought it would settle me down."

"Settle you down, eh?"

"Yeah … I saw some shadows, which spooked me a bit. You know I was reading that book about the shipwrecks and how many seafarers perished out here. I kept thinking about the lighthouse keepers and …"

"Hang on a minute, you mentioned shadows, why did they spook you?"

"Well, I thought their shapes looked like people moving." Ric stopped. He'd said too much.

Mark shuddered. He put his arm around Ric's shoulder. "You said the shapes were like people moving. Are they still there?"

"No mate, they've gone now."

"Okay, why don't we go back to the cottage. I've found a tin of Milo someone must have left behind. We could make a hot chocolate and add some of that rum we brought."

Ric couldn't reject Mark's suggestions; that would only heighten his concerns. As the clouds began to engulf the moon, he turned to check out his friend's face.

Mark's eyes betrayed his fear.

Chapter 9

Avoidance Strategies

Kangaroo Island, April 1997

The warmth of the cottage stopped Mark shivering; it did nothing to calm Ric's inner trembling. And sitting in the old lounge chairs flipping through vintage books about shipwreck stories didn't help much either.

The windows rattled again as the wind picked up.

"How did anyone ever survive in this place?" asked Ric.

Six ships had gone down in immediate sight of the headland, many on the aptly named Scraper Shoal. Multiple others had perished nearby.

Those writhing forms, were they sailors being sucked down as their ships sank? But hang on. They weren't wearing any clothing. Maybe they weren't sailors. Maybe they were people from a much earlier time?

Ric's eyes closed. Much later, when he looked up, he was surprised to find Mark standing directly in front of him.

"I wasn't sure whether to wake you, but now you've started groaning, I thought I'd better. Here, get this into you," said Mark, handing him a mug of steaming hot Milo and a half-empty bottle of Bundy rum.

Ric poured a generous splash of rum into the chocolate drink and swallowed a gulp before looking up at Mark. "Cheers," he said in mock bravado.

Mark poured himself a smaller nip and sat watching his friend.

"Now tell me, what's up?"

"Whad'ya mean, what's up?"

"C'mon Ric, this is not like you. I've known you since we were schoolkids. I've seen you tackle big Tongan forwards. I've seen you run straight over opposition backlines, and now you expect me to believe that a few shadows are turning you into a whimpering blob of jelly?"

"Yeah well. Life's not a football game."

"But mate, in many ways football *is* a metaphor for your life. When you play full of confidence on the field, you are just the same off the field. Teammates want to be with you, women want to flirt with you. On those rare times in the past when I've seen you down, you're also off your game. You've been down a lot lately."

Ric stood and paced around the room.

"Can't you just leave me alone?"

"Look, you asked me to come on this trip; I'm not sure why. You told me you had to make a choice, and you'd like me to help. But you won't talk about anything now we're here. And you look bloody terrible."

At that moment, Ric had a fit of coughing. "I must have ... put too much rum in the chocolate," he said, with tears in his eyes and a flushed face. "I'll concede I haven't been much fun lately." He grasped for a way to divert the conversation. "Remember that huge bird we saw last week, on the long drive from Adelaide to Wilpena Pound? I think I'm still recovering from that fright."

"Ric, are you sure there was a bird? I couldn't see it even after you stopped the car."

Ric's eyes flashed. "Right. You think I just frickin' imagined it, do you? Or now you're training to be a bloody shrink, have you already decided I'm psychotic?"

"All I'm saying is, I find that story hard to believe."

In their school days, Ric and Mark had spent countless hours studying together at their old boarding school. They'd continued this all the way through medical school, at the same time as Ric was trying to break into the NRL. Mark had always been the studious one. He'd already commenced training in psychiatry.

Mark sipped his Milo. "Hey mate, why don't you settle down and tell me again about the bird."

"Why should I tell you again about the bloody bird?"

Mark's eyes widened. Ric stopped pacing and shrunk back onto the couch.

Mark was the philosopher, the nerd, the quiet one. Ric was always out there, physically strong, the loud one. Yet, all their lives, they'd looked after each other. Ric thought for a while.

"Okay, I'll give it to you again. Your head was down, you were checking the maps, working out how far we had to go. We were doing about a hundred kays. I saw roadkill up ahead, probably a dead wallaby. Birds were picking away at the rotting carcass, maybe crows or ravens. They flew away as we came closer."

Mark said nothing.

"There was one bird still tearing off flesh, sort of brown and black coloured. It flew up, lazily flapping its wings and coming towards us. I never said anything 'cos I reckoned it would fly up over the car. But it bloody well didn't!"

Mark's face was stony. Ric took a deep breath, then continued.

"I could see the legs below its body, and then its eyes. Its wings flapped faster, but not fast enough. It still didn't get much higher, and it was heading straight for our windscreen. As it got closer, I could see its wingspan was even wider than our car, the wings now flapping frantically. I was mesmerized by its eyes which seemed to be looking straight into mine. I couldn't swerve and I couldn't stop."

Mark shook his head slowly.

"I was saying to myself, 'Lift you bastard bird, lift!' but it didn't. Time seemed to slow down. I thought the glass is going to shatter and we're going to get blood and gore all over this hire car and … we're probably going to die. Then the bloody bird lifted at the last second and flew over the top of the car."

Mark still didn't look convinced.

"I saw that massive tail wedge. I think I yelled out 'shit!' Then you looked up and said, 'what the?' You made a big show of looking around and saying you couldn't see anything. Whatever else you were going on about, I didn't hear. I was in shock. I just kept thinking what if we had died right there."

"You really thought we could have died?"

"I did."

There was a long silence in the cottage before Mark spoke again.

"Mate, when you were reading those stories about the shipwrecks, I noticed some tattered old books about Australian plants and wildlife. I'll see if any of them mention large birds down this way."

Ric threw up his hands and rocked back onto the couch.

"I give up."

A few minutes later, Mark shouted, "I found it! There *are* wedge-tailed eagles in South Australia, and their wingspan *can* reach three metres. And they *do* gorge themselves so much they have difficulty flying."

Ric smirked.

"You really didn't believe me, did you?"

"No, I didn't. I know nothing about wild birds," said Mark.

"And I bet you thought I was hallucinating when I told you I'd seen that bird, didn't you?"

"Yeah, I guess I did think that."

Mark swallowed the remainder of his drink in one gulp and slumped down on the couch. The tension eased in the room. The sash windows rattled, the seagulls shrieked, and the possums thumped around on the wooden verandah.

"Mark, can I ask you something?"

"Yes of course."

"Have you decided I'm losing my mind?"

Mark pursed his lips but didn't answer the question.

Ric raised his mug in mock salute. "I think I'll head off to bed with this."

Chapter 10

Conversations

Kangaroo Island, April 1997

Mark woke to a westerly squall battering the shrubs against the cottage windows. It was way past dawn, but the sky was still dark. When he opened the door, the wind slammed it shut.

The noise woke Ric who emerged from the bedroom, rubbing his eyes. He grabbed a glass of water then slumped into an old kitchen chair and stared into the garden. The lavender shrubs had been blown horizontal, and even the seagulls were taking shelter behind the stone wall.

"Nice day for it," said Ric.

"Nice day for what?" asked Mark.

"Nice day to have that chat you wanted me to have."

"Okay Ric, do *you* want to have that chat? I stayed up late last night thinking about things. I figured you may not be ready to talk yet."

"The thing is Mark, I really *do* want to talk, but I don't know what to say. Mate, I really need some coffee. My mouth tastes like the inside of a pelican's beak and my head's pounding. How much rum was in that Milo?"

"A fair bit. And I topped it up when you were pacing the room. I thought it might settle you down."

"Right, and did it?"

"Sort of, at least you went to bed."

"Hmm."

Ric poured the strong coffee, added loads of sugar and sipped in silence while Mark cooked bacon and eggs.

"I think I might stick with toast this morning. I'm not sure my stomach could cope with a fry-up."

"Sure Ric, but gees, this local bacon smells good. And look at the yolk in these eggs."

"Orright orright, I'll give it a go, now I've got some caffeine on board."

After starting gingerly, he wolfed down the bacon and went back to empty the frypan. He winced as a bolt of lightning flashed, followed immediately by loud explosions of thunder.

"Like I said mate, nice day for a chat, especially about the kind of things I need to say."

"Is it about Cassie? Or was it something at work? I know you were off sick for a while."

"All of that Mark, and probably a lot more," said Ric, who then went quiet again.

Mark pottered around the kitchen, brewing more coffee.

Apropos of nothing, Ric blurted out, "We all have to make choices, eh? I've never had to make big choices. Everything seems to have fallen into place for me, until now. You just go along, thinking life's been good, then out of nowhere, it leaps up and whacks you in the face. Then everything starts to come unstuck."

"Ric, I have absolutely no idea what you're talking about."

A burst of sunlight streamed into the room highlighting the stubble on Ric's face as he continued to stare out the windows.

"Hey, that squall looks like it's blowing over, but there's another one building in the west. Why don't we pack up and get out of here? I don't want to get bogged on that gravel road especially if it turns to mud. Anyways, this place is too isolated to hang about in this kind of weather."

"Ah, we're booked in for another night," said Mark. "And I don't want you avoiding talking again."

"I'll cover it mate, and don't worry, I intend to keep talking. I can organise my thoughts better when I'm moving. I haven't got much stuff, so I'll clean up while you pack."

They drove to Penneshaw on the northern side of the island and were lucky enough to score a vacant spot on the car ferry to the mainland. There had been a few cancellations that morning. They soon found out why. As the big ferry left the shelter of the harbour, huge swells rolled under the hull.

They decided against eating on board, which turned out to be a good plan. In the open ocean, the incoming squall added a vicious chop to the swell. The ferry was rolling and then dropping hard onto the ocean surface. Vomit bags were soon in short supply. Ric turned a delicate shade of green before they reached Cape Jervis.

Mark took the wheel on the route to McLaren Vale, driving cautiously as Ric was still pale. After his gut settled, Ric kept his word. He spoke in hesitant fragments about Cassie, about his dilemma in choosing between medicine and football, and about his anger with his parents.

"Stop!" yelled Ric, interrupting his own meanderings.

"What's wrong?"

"Nothing's wrong, mate. You just passed the turnoff to my all-time favourite winery."

"Is this another way for you to avoid talking?" asked Mark as he pulled over.

"No, I'll keep talking. You know our family has always been into wines. It's an Italian thing."

English oak trees lined both sides of the entrance road, and behind these, hundreds of rows of vines, their leaves russet-coloured after harvest. On the scale of wineries, this was a small family-owned establishment, with a rustic cellar door outlet. Under a wisteria vine trellis, a jumbled assortment of wooden tables and an array of old wine barrels enticed guests to linger.

The winemaker appeared from behind nearby vines and wandered across with his dog. They began tasting his wines and ordered cheese, olives and crusty bread.

"Good to see you enjoying the wine mate, but honestly, your story has been all over the place. I'm going to tell you what I think you've been saying. And then you can straighten me out if I've got it wrong."

Ric felt himself tensing. Thankfully, the wine would take the edge off his response.

"Okay, so I think you're telling me you're not sure about how you and Cassie are going, and you don't know how to tell her. And also, you can't keep concentrating on both your medical career and your footy career, so you have to make a choice."

"Yeah, I suppose you're right. But hey, that's a really heavy scene for me," said Ric, first shaking his head then curling his mouth into a smile. "But if you're driving, I can at least pour myself some more wine."

Mark called 'last drinks' and deftly capped the bottle. "No, you can't. Come on, we've got a long drive back to Adelaide," he said, bundling Ric into the car.

As Mark drove, Ric sat in silence, his mind returning to Cassie and their recent tension. She'd never been this angry with him. When they first met, nothing seemed to faze her. They'd met when they'd bumped into each other (literally) in the café on their starting day at the hospital.

Cassie had been standing behind him in a queue when he turned suddenly to greet an old friend. She was holding a tray of arancini balls, three of which ended up on the floor.

He'd apologised and offered to pay so she could replace them. She not only refused his offer, but once she'd secured the remaining food on her plate, she flashed a mischievous smile and said, "You could have caught them for me."

He was so embarrassed; he could think of no suitable retort. She took pity on him and asked if he'd like to join her at the table. They'd been together since.

Chapter 11

A Deliberate Choice

Adelaide, April 1997

After they unpacked in the City of Churches, and before they reopened the bottle, Ric phoned Cassie. He was only slightly irritated when he had to leave a message. He was more irritated when she didn't return his call until late that night.

"Hey, are you all right, I called you this afternoon," said Ric when she called.

"Yeah, I'm fine, and you know what? I've been leaving you messages for days," said Cassie.

Thankfully, Ric had sobered up a little over the last few hours. He lowered his tone.

"Yeah, I'm really sorry, babe. We had no mobile signal; we've been staying at a lighthouse and the weather turned bad."

"Fair enough. But you're okay?"

"Yeah, I'm okay, but what about you, you sound different."

"Yeah, I'm okay," said Cassie.

In the silence that followed, Ric surmised she might have been missing him, so he rattled on about his trip, glossing over the events at the lighthouse. "And what have you been up to, since I've been away?"

"Ah, nothing much, I took some time off and Lou and I went away for a few days. We had a good time."

"Where did you go?"

"Oh, here and there," said Cassie.

Now even Ric began to suspect things had changed.

"Hey Cassie, can I call you again in a day or two?"

"Okay … bye," said Cassie and hung up.

"How was that?" asked Mark.

"Not good," said Ric said, followed by another long silence.

It was about time he talked to Mark. Once he opened the floodgates holding back his stream of thoughts, they all poured out in a torrent.

Ric spoke of the hassles with Cassie, and his difficulties deciding what to do with his career. Then of his despair when he saw the body at the bottom of the waterfall, and his fear when he saw the shadows on the headland.

"There's something else, Mark. I've always thought of myself as an Aussie of Italian descent. Both Dad and Mum are Italian. Dad's family grew cane near Innisfail and Mum's family grew tobacco on the Atherton Tableland. But my siblings have much lighter skin than me."

"So, what are you saying?"

"A lot of the people in these images have much darker skin. I don't know who I am anymore. And I don't know why my mind keeps playing tricks on me. But I do know I'm going to have to find out one day soon. Otherwise …"

"Otherwise, what?"

"Umm …"

Ric let this thought hang for a few seconds, then he stood up. "Hey, now I've got all that off my chest, I think I'll go and crash. Maybe we could talk some more in the morning if that's okay?"

"Yeah, okay."

As Ric walked to his bedroom, he stopped when he overheard Mark muttering to himself.

"If he doesn't get to a psychiatrist soon, someone will have to notify the Medical Board. I hope it doesn't have to be me."

Still in Adelaide the next morning, it was Ric who cooked the bacon. And it was Ric who opened the conversation.

"Thanks for talking with me last night, mate. I think I've made up my mind. Can I run something past you?"

Mark nodded.

Ric paced the room as he blurted out what he planned to do. When he stopped pacing, he burst out laughing.

"Hey mate, you look like one of those porcelain clowns at the annual show; their heads turn from side to side but their mouths stay wide open!"

Mark clamped his mouth shut, then opened it again.

"Did you just say you're going to drop out of Medicine to concentrate on football?"

"I did indeed, my friend. My coach called this morning saying one of the NRL teams wants me. He told me to get a manager to help me negotiate a contract as a pro footballer."

"But you've studied Medicine for so many years, why would you give it all away?"

"Mate, I'm struggling with the two careers. I keep getting pulled in one direction then the other. And I'll only get one chance at being a footy star. I want to give it everything I've got while I'm still young."

"Bloody hell, Ric. I think you're crazy giving up your medical career for a football career, but even more importantly, I think you need professional help to sort out this stuff that's messing up your head,"

"Maybe, but I reckon they'll offer me a pathway back into medicine after I retire from footy. And as for those weird things I've been seeing. I'm hoping they'll just go away when I stop working at the hospital. Maybe it was work stress that caused those things to come into my mind."

"'Hmm. Well, why don't you ask for twelve months leave without pay to see how things go?"

"Yeah, that might work. I guess the first contract will only be for one year, hopefully with options to extend."

"But you really need to sit down with Cassie, to talk her through all this. That kind of decision will affect her life too, Ric."

"True. So can you help me work out a strategy for breaking all this to Cassie?"

"Yeah, sure mate, I could try – but you know I've never even had a girlfriend."

"Ah come on Mark, what dya' reckon? I'll invite her out to dinner as soon as we get back to Brisbane. I'll take her to one of those swanky places, with the starched tablecloths and all."

"That might be a good start, but remember, if she agrees to go to dinner, take it easy on the alcohol and don't just rave at her. Give her a chance to talk about how she feels about it all."

"Okay, I'll call her now."

Chapter 12

Minjerribah

Stradbroke Island, April 1997

While the two lads tripped around South Australia, and unbeknown to Ric, Cassie and Lou travelled to Stradbroke Island, where Cassie enrolled in surfing lessons. After a few lessons, the coach cajoled her into paddling 'out the back' behind the breaking waves.

Suddenly, Cassie turned and paddled straight to shore. She staggered out of the surf, dragging the tail of the fat 'foamy' board along the sand.

"Gees – I thought that thing was going to get me!"

"Cassie, come back out, there's a good swell building," said the coach.

"Luke, are you kidding me? Didn't you see that fin heading for us?"

"Fin? Hey, that wasn't a shark's fin, it was a dolphin's. They're just enjoying the waves like us."

Cassie looked back, astonished to see four black mammals flicking their tails and riding the waves towards shore, mouths open in what appeared to be grins of delight.

"Yeah, dolphins often check out the surfers around here."

"Dolphins like to surf with us?"

"Yeah, they do. But when you see fins, it isn't always a pod of dolphins, so it's good to be cautious. I want you to paddle out the back again but stay with me, until I give you the call to paddle hard for a wave."

To the right was the low headland separating Cylinder Beach from Deadman's Beach. As Luke had taught her, Cassie paddled out just clear of the rocks so she would avoid being caught in the strong sweep. Many times, she tumbled off her board then clambered back on, as she struggled through the never-ending close-outs.

By the time she'd made it out the back, she was exhausted, trying hard to regain her breath while Luke explained what she had to do.

"There's just so darn much to learn," she said.

Luke looked out to sea, assessed the swell, and called, "Now!"

Cassie managed to get to her feet on the board, only to wipe out in the time-honoured fashion of newbie surfers. When the board struck the side of her head, her ponytail came loose. She rolled around underneath the waves, swallowing water, even inhaling some. It was only her buoyancy which brought her to the surface.

"Hey Cassie. You look like a drowned possum."

"Thanks," said Cassie, shaking her head.

Luke paddled closer.

"That was a great effort, but now it's time for you to paddle in."

Lou jogged over to join them when they reached the sand. Salt water poured out of Cassie's nose in a steady stream, landing on her feet.

"Eeuw!" said Lou.

Luke looked concerned.

"Okay Cassie, maybe take it easy for the rest of the day," he said, then he turned to Lou. "If you girls have the energy for it tonight, there's a gig on at the pub."

The two girls trudged up the sand towards their rooms. "So, how was the private lesson?"

"Pretty awful, Lou. I thought I was surfing okay, but I just can't stand up on those green waves. And Luke makes it look so damn easy," said Cassie with a faraway look.

Lou punched her arm and burst out laughing.

"Maybe you're focusing more on Luke than on the surfing?"

"Yeah, he's a nice guy, so gentle and patient with me. And he is cute. It's not just the ripped body and the tangled blond hair, it's those beautiful blue eyes. And when the saltwater drips off his eyelashes … hey, let's grab a smoothie. Do you reckon we should go tonight?"

"Well," said Lou, with a conspiratorial smile. "It does get a bit quiet around here. But tell me honestly, what's happening with Ric? Were you planning to have a bit of fun while he's away?"

Cassie slumped down onto the sand.

"I hadn't planned to do anything like that. But yeah, things have been pretty bad lately."

"What happened? You guys have been going out for years, and you always look so happy together. You met at work, didn't you?"

"Yeah, we started at the hospital at the same time, first job for both of us."

"I remember you sounded so excited when you told me about him."

"I was very excited. I've always wanted to be a sports physio, so when I met this interesting young doctor, a couple of years older than me, who was also a great footballer, I was rapt."

"And it had nothing to do with him being tall, dark and handsome?"

"Maybe."

"And he got on well with your parents?"

"Not really. Dad's always said he's not good enough for me. But Ric's a doctor, for goodness sake. Then Dad goes, 'Yes, but he's from north Queensland. And he's a footballer,' as if that says it all."

"You think he's still in love with you?"

"Oh Lou, he keeps saying he is. But he's gone all weird lately, and he won't tell me what's troubling him. He's hiding something from me. And on top of that, I get the feeling he's not that interested in me anymore."

"How do you mean?"

"He doesn't hear what I tell him, he's not interested in what I'm doing, and he expects me to tag along whenever he asks. It makes me feel like I'm just an appendage."

Cassie stifled a sob. Lou's hug did little to lift her spirits.

"Come on, let's go and get that smoothie."

The banana smoothies lightened the mood.

"You know, Lou. I used to have so many plans. I was going to set up my own practice, employ other physios and then each of us could specialise in the areas we were interested in."

"What area would interest you?"

"I'd love to work with children who have a disability. They often have so much potential, but they just need intensive therapy and someone to work with them to bolster their confidence."

"Would you need to do further study?"

"Yes, lots of further study and I'd need a supervisor to work under as I developed my skills."

"Have you made any enquiries along those lines?"

"I have. And I might just follow them up when we get back to the mainland."

"And you may need to spread your wings a little, in your personal life."

"Yeah, you're right, Lou, I should put my own needs first for a change. And I've got to learn to be more assertive and stand up for myself."

"Remember we used to play netball together at uni? Why don't we go and find a netball team?"

"Yeah, why not."

That evening, they arrived at the hotel just as the headline act was tuning up. The rolling Pacific Ocean was now a sea of black, punctuated by the blinking lights of fishing trawlers. Their most casual clothes looked formal compared to the locals' gear. Dressing up on Straddie seemed to involve finding your best pair of thongs and a T-shirt not yet stained with sunscreen.

Lou smiled as she sat down with her friend. Even wearing a casual summer dress and minimal makeup, Cassie had already turned the heads of most guys in the room.

Her long auburn hair was pulled behind her ears with a simple clasp, and the only other jewellery she wore was a pair of dolphin earrings Lou had bought her in the tourist shop. The dolphins were made of coloured stone which matched her hazel eyes.

The band played original songs interspersed with covers, in a chilled-out surfer jazz style they could best describe as a cross between Jack Johnson and Xavier Rudd. The locals' hips were already moving with the beat, when the lead singer explained that Aboriginal people had lived on this island, which some called Minjerribah, since time immemorial.

A local Noonuccal musician played didge on some of the tracks, although he was keen to explain the instrument was not from this area, as the didgeridoo or yidaki was originally from east Arnhem Land. Two of his cousins were dancers with the band. It didn't take long for other girls to start dancing, followed by Cassie and Lou and eventually, the Point Lookout surfers.

Cassie hadn't realised how much alcohol was in the cocktails until she noticed Lou laughing and flirting, which was way out of character for her. She decided to switch to cola and look out for her friend.

She was sitting at the side of the room when Lou dragged one of the surfer guys over to introduce him.

"Hey Cass, you going to join us this next bracket?"

"Nah, I'll just chill tonight."

"What's up with her?" asked Mikey as they returned to the dance floor.

"She's got a boyfriend, and things aren't going well. I think she's pondering what to do."

"Well, she's got a big smile on her face now," said Mikey as he watched Luke saunter over and pull up a chair next to her. It wasn't long before Luke had dragged Cassie out onto the dance floor.

After a few tunes, Cassie began to move closer to Luke. As the musicians wound up the set and they'd returned to their chairs, Cassie grabbed his hand. "Why don't we go out on the balcony and get some fresh air."

A startled look spread over Luke's face. "Hey Cassie, Mikey tells me you've got a boyfriend. Maybe we should stay inside with the others, I don't want to get you into an awkward situation."

Cassie let go of his hand, head down and lips pursed as they rejoined Lou and Mikey. She looked up when she heard four rowdy guys enter the bar, order beers and lean against the wall nearby. They were big lads, half smashed and very loud.

"Footy jocks," muttered Mikey.

One of them elbowed his mate, pointing as he called out. "Hey Cassie, where's Ric?" As he spoke, his gaze shifted to Luke.

"Ah, Ric and Mark went out bush in South Australia, so Lou and I came over here to relax and learn a bit about surfing."

"So does Ric know you're here?" asked the biggest one, pushing himself between Cassie and Luke.

Luke moved around closer to Cassie.

"Rack off, mate," said the footballer, pushing Luke on the chest. He looked surprised when Luke stood firm.

When Mikey came over, the other footballers held him back.

"Come on Lozza, just leave it, will ya," said one of them.

He pushed Luke again, harder this time. Luke crouched, ready to spring.

"Back off Laurie, don't be a dickhead," said Cassie, coming between the two.

Laurie reached out with both arms, trying to separate Luke and Cassie. "You're Ric's girlfriend, I'm not going to let this guy move in on you while he's away."

Cassie smacked his arms down. "Ric doesn't own me, Lozza. I do what I want."

Local surfers gathered round, moving close to the footballers. A huge Māori security guard homed in, followed by another.

"You okay Luke? And how about you, Miss?"

Cassie was speechless. Her eyes blazed.

"Come on boys, let's get out of here and leave these wankers to themselves," said Laurie, moving towards the exit.

The musicians did their best to lighten up the room with upbeat tunes, but the mood had changed, and the party broke up soon after.

As they walked home, Cassie threw her arms in the air.

"Urghh!"

Chapter 13

Decisions

Brisbane, April 1997

On the flight from Adelaide to Brisbane, Ric had felt content that he now had a clear plan for his future.

When he'd called Cassie from Adelaide, she'd sounded surprised to be invited somewhere different for dinner, not their usual haunts of pubs and clubs. She'd accepted, but only after a few moments silence.

Ric surprised her once again when he arrived wearing slacks, a buttoned-up shirt, a light blue jacket and leather shoes, none of which she'd ever seen before. His usual attire involved shorts, a T-shirt and thongs.

Lou had persuaded Cassie to buy a new dress and wear some bling, but despite her appearance, Ric could see in her face that her mood hadn't improved.

From their table, they had a view across the Brisbane River. It was just before dusk, and the City Cat ferries churned back and forth, leaving the rowing sculls rocking in their wake. Cassie looked so stunning, Ric tried to convince himself that peace and order had returned to his world. He didn't detect the depth of Cassie's reticence.

"It's so good to be back with you, Cassie. And you look great in that new gear."

"Well, I wouldn't say I feel that great, Ric. We have a lot to discuss."

Ric took that as an opening. As Cassie picked at her seafood and sipped on her Riesling, he filled her in on the trip with Mark. When he finished, she made a token effort to tell him about her own holiday on Stradbroke Island but didn't tell him any details.

"I wish I'd been there with you."

"I guess you could join me next time I go to Straddie, if you like …"

"Oh, so that surf coach teaches guys as well, does he?"

Cassie crossed her arms, lifted her head and jutted her chin forwards.

"Yes, of course he does. What are you saying?"

"Oh, just that the footy boys reckoned you looked pretty happy with him at the pub that night."

"Hey, we were discussing the surf lessons … okay, I suppose I did dance with him for a while."

"Yeah, I know babe, I don't blame you for wanting to have a bit of fun," said Ric. When he noticed her flushed face, he moved closer to hold her hand.

Cassie's hand twitched. For a moment, he thought she was going to pull it away. He waited until her hand relaxed before he continued his efforts to re-engage.

"When Mark and I were away, I had plenty of time to think. We talked about lots of different stuff."

"That's good," said Cassie, her voice inflecting upwards.

"Yes, it was good, Cass. And I'm ready to make a decision now, about what I'm going to do with my life."

"You know what Ric? Lou and I had lots of good chats as well, and I'm thinking of making some decisions too."

"Great Cassie. Anyhow, I've been trying to work out how to tell you everything."

Cassie sighed, looked like she was going to speak, then took a long sip of her wine and leaned back in her chair.

Ric chose his words carefully, slowly leading her through his thinking processes, all the while watching her face for clues.

"Cassie, I've been offered a contract with an NRL team. I'm thinking of applying for 12 months leave from the hospital, so I can concentrate on footy."

Cassie took a sharp intake of breath and sent Ric a death glare.

"Hey, what's wrong? I'm not saying I want to split up with you, the team's based in south-east Queensland. And we could move in together if you're still interested."

Cassie let out her breath and threw her hands in the air.

"I *have* been wanting to move in with you Ric, but why would I want to do that now? Lately, you never think about me, all you ever talk about is yourself! I'm not even sure I want our relationship to go on any further."

"Hey babe, I know I've had a lot on my mind lately, but I've been trying hard to sort it out. I didn't know you were feeling that way. Why didn't you say something before?"

"Arghh," said Cassie, shaking her head and pouring herself more wine. "I've been trying to have this discussion for weeks!" Other diners turned as her voice rose. "Just leave it. I don't want to talk about it anymore."

"Aw, come on Cassie, I'm finally starting to get on top of things. Now I can just concentrate on my football, I'll have more time to spend with you. Can't you give me another chance? Surely, you're not going to walk out on me now?"

Cassie glared at him. They finished the meal in silence.

As they walked home along the boardwalk, a full moon rose in the east, but their eyes were drawn to the western sky. Dozens of bats glided across the sky, shrieking and squabbling, and clearly unsettled.

Chapter 14

Escape

Brisbane, April 1997

Next morning, Ric met with Matthew, the Director of Training. He was a general physician with a reputation for being supportive of junior staff. Ric was surprised to find he'd invited Claire to the meeting. Because he'd rehearsed his speech many times, Ric took a deep breath and got straight to the point.

"I've been offered a contract in the NRL, top level. I'd like to take a year off, leave without pay, to give myself a chance to concentrate on footy. If it doesn't go well, I'll return to the hospital next year, and then concentrate on medicine."

"And if it does go well?" asked Claire.

"Then I'll come back and discuss what I should do."

Both senior doctors put up objections. Only Claire knew about Ric's mental turmoil. Although she continued to object, Matthew changed tack and said he was prepared to think about it further. They agreed to set up a meeting with Phil, the Director of Medical Services.

After Ric left the room, Claire accosted Matthew.

"Why did you roll over so easily? This decision could destroy Ric's career. He should be learning from his mistakes and concentrating on his patients, not running around a field playing football."

"I know, Claire. I would normally have put a lot more obstacles in his way."

"So why didn't you?"

"I really don't know."

Phil had a hospital to run. His usual response to this kind of proposal was that you can't establish a precedent with one young doctor unless you're willing to do the same with others. Then you wouldn't have enough doctors to run the hospital. When Matthew had called to arrange the meeting, Phil challenged him.

"Why are you supporting this, Matt? You're usually the one advocating for juniors to complete their training."

Matthew considered the question. Before he could formulate his response, Phil spoke again.

"I know you played footy in your younger days. You were a local hero in north Queensland when I worked at the hospital up there."

"Yes, I did play for a couple of years after graduation, then I gave it away. Hey, did you end up working at the same hospital as I did?"

"Yes, I followed in your footsteps a few years later. It wasn't just footy where you left your mark. People would often tell me about your exploits. But I'm wondering if you're reliving your dreams through your young colleague here."

"I guess that's a possibility."

"Okay, let's get back to Ric. He's been making far too many errors. He needs to sort himself out. I think you and Claire should both attend the meeting, and we should be prepared to hear what he has to say. But I can't see why we shouldn't just make him buckle down and concentrate on his medical career."

Ric continued to call Cassie, but she declined to see him again until he'd met with his seniors at the hospital. Ric was surprised when she gave him specific advice.

"If your boss is going to do you a big favour, his heart needs to be in it. You need to make a play for his emotional response before you come straight out with the proposal."

Ric approached the meeting exactly as Cassie had suggested.

Claire continued to put up resistance, but Matthew supported the proposal.

"Matthew why is football so damn important?" asked Claire. "Are you living your boyhood fantasies through Ric? Would you have made the same decision if it was a female doctor wanting to play netball?"

Matthew said nothing. Ric squirmed. Silence pervaded the room.

Phil sat looking at Ric, a stern expression on his hardened face.

"I think this young man is going to follow his own mind whether we support him or not," said Phil, with a resigned scowl. "If we approve his request, we may have a chance of getting him back to working as a doctor after he's followed his sporting dreams."

Claire said no more.

Ric suspected the pre-planned strategy may have helped, but there was more to it than that. He had no real idea why either Phil or Matthew caved in. But that didn't matter now. He had approval from the hospital to take a year off to concentrate on football.

After the meeting, Claire pulled him aside. "Ric, none of us wants you to drop out of Medicine. You need to stay in touch and keep up your professional development. I'd like to set up a monthly meeting with you, as your ongoing mentor."

After he agreed, Claire decided she would also set up a mentoring arrangement for herself, with Matthew.

Ric spent the next couple of days carefully sorting and filing his textbooks, journals, and online resources. Preseason training was due to commence in ten days' time, so he picked up the courage to invite Cassie to join him on a short holiday.

"No discussion, Ric's idea and I'm meant to agree again," said Cassie to Lou the next day.

"You could always say no."

"Yeah, I know I could, but I'm thinking I will just say yes. I'll have his undivided attention, and this time, I plan to sort him out once and for all."

After they returned from their holiday, Cassie immediately phoned Lou. "Honestly Lou, that holiday didn't change a thing. All Ric talked about was football. He didn't listen to a word I said. I can't put up with it much longer."

"I thought you said he was still madly in love with you?"

"He says he loves me, and he keeps telling me there will never be anyone else. As far as I can work out, he never strays with any of those women who throw themselves at him. But whenever I try to talk about what I need from our relationship, his eyes gloss over."

"Hmm. That's not good at all. Oh, I've been meaning to tell you. Mikey said he'd love to see you again. I'm having lunch with him tomorrow. Why don't you join us, instead of hanging around waiting for Ric?"

When Cassie walked into the café the next day, three people were waiting for her. The third one was Luke, pretending to look nonchalant. It didn't take long for Cassie to relax as he and Mikey entertained them with stories of life on Straddie.

"Well, how was that?" asked Lou, when the guys had left.
Cassie smiled and thought for a while.
"Good thing they had that ferry to catch."

Chapter 15

Thrills, Dreams and Despair

Brisbane, July 1997

Ric had been training hard for the last couple of months. The more he threw himself into footy, the more his mind settled down. No more uninvited thoughts, and no time to think about his identity.

He started off in reserve grade. Halfway through the season, he graduated to the A grade bench. He sat on the sideline throughout the first game, nervous but excited. One of the halfbacks was taken off the field for a head injury assessment.

Ric was sent on to replace him. The opposition started sending big forwards straight at him. Thankfully, he now had mates in his team. Albie, one of his second rowers, was a tall Aboriginal lad from Cairns. He put in a big effort to help Ric with the tackles. Between them, they nullified the opposition tactic.

The opposition shifted their attack to the open side of the field. They kicked a high bomb, which his fullback muffed; the ball dropping backwards to the ground. Ric still had enough energy to get back onside to support the fullback. He scooped up the ball and managed to step his way around the opposition halves, palming off players who were much smaller than him.

He managed to bring the ball back fifteen metres before he was tackled. His team regrouped with newly found energy after the quick play-the-ball. As the game re-commenced, the referee called a halt in play. The trainer was out on the field as there was a player on the ground.

It was Ric.

He'd fallen to the ground, swearing and holding his leg. "It's my knee. It won't hold my weight when I walk. It's not painful, it just feels loose."

The team doctor examined his knee after they carried him to the sideline. "I think you've torn your anterior cruciate ligament."

Ric waved him away, his head dropping to his chest as he punched the ground.

"Yeah, I know about ACL injuries, I'm a doctor myself. Shit! My season's over."

Scans the next day confirmed the diagnosis. On the day after, he had surgery to reconstruct his knee. He woke to find himself recovering in a private room six floors above the Emergency Department in his old hospital.

A few of his teammates came to visit. Albie stayed on after the others left.

"Hey brother, you'll be out of action for the whole season. How're you gonna manage?"

"Ah, the club will have insurance cover, and I've got some money saved from my hospital work."

"Yeah, that's good, but I wasn't thinking about the money. I was thinking you'll need your family around you. Aren't they all in Cairns?"

"Yeah, but I'm not real close to them."

"I reckon you might need them now. I would, if this sort of thing happened to me."

Albie sat beside the bed, staring at the ceiling.

"So, your family is pretty close?"

"Yeah. Us mob stick together, especially when we're in trouble."

"Albie, can I ask you something?"

"Course."

"When I nicked off for a bushwalk up near Tamborine a few months ago, I stayed in a backpacker hostel and met a couple of Swedish girls. They asked me to tell them what happened to the local Aboriginal people."

"Hey brother, those Swedish girls are hot! Did you string them along?"

"Not really. I told them some cock-and-bull story that the tribes just died out. They didn't look too impressed. But the truth is, I just didn't know."

"Well, you're not alone in that. Most people don't know. Or maybe they don't wanna know."

"Yeah, you could be right. But how could I learn about what happened? Are there any good books I could get, so I could learn all this stuff?"

Albie laughed.

"There's plenty of books alright. Most of them are written by white fellas. Our Mob don't usually write this stuff down. They yarn about it though. You'd be better off getting to know our families, especially our Elders."

"Yeah, maybe I could do that."

"Tell you what. I reckon you should go and see your family in Cairns when you're allowed to travel. And my Mob are all up there, so you could go and see them as well – they'll make you feel welcome."

"Why would your family look out for me?"

"That's just the way Murris are. Family is everything to us Mob," said Albie, giving Ric a meaningful look.

Ric grabbed Albie's arm.

"Yeah. Thanks mate, I might just do that."

Ric had many hours to think before his next visitor arrived. It was Mark, who'd come to ask how he was going. He replied that he was coping well enough with the post-op pain. However, the disturbing visions had returned.

Chapter 16

Discoveries

Brisbane, August 1997

Ric was not a happy lad hanging around alone at home. Lying on a couch with his leg elevated might reduce the swelling, but it didn't reduce the frustration.

The surgeon had been firm. "You'll need a fixed brace for a month or two, and when we remove it, you'll have to follow the physiotherapist's instructions for the following six months. If you don't follow instructions, you'll tear the ligament again, and you'll be back having more surgery."

Ric groaned. By the time he would be allowed to train again, the footy season would be over. At that point, he would have to decide whether to try football again, or to return to work as a doctor.

When Cassie came to visit, he tried showing some interest in her work as a physiotherapist, mainly asking about physio treatments for the knee. Cassie had other ideas.

"Now you're not able to do anything Ric, maybe this would be a good time for us to talk about our future?"

Ric studied her face. Multiple thoughts whirled around his mind. He tried to focus, knowing Cassie wanted reassurance about their relationship, but he knew any form of commitment was impossible until he'd resolved his mental state.

"Cassie … I've been hiding things from you … One night on Kangaroo Island, I saw strange shadows moving near the lighthouse. Those shadows have come back over the last few days. I've got no idea what's going on."

Cassie inhaled a deep breath.

"The shadows looked like people. Mark thought I might be developing a psychosis. I got angry with him at the time and told him to back off. But now I'm wondering if he was right."

Ric pushed himself upright on the couch, trying to get comfortable. "I never told you why I walked out of work and escaped to the rainforest either, did I?"

"No, you didn't. To be honest, you didn't tell me much at all."

"Yeah, I know. I just couldn't cope with making any more medical mistakes. Sometimes it all seemed too much. When I was in the rainforest by myself that day, I was sitting on the side of a waterfall. I … I found myself thinking of jumping off."

Cassie gasped and flung her arms around his neck.

"I'm so glad you didn't do that, Ric. And I am glad you're telling me these things now. But what took you so long?"

"I just wasn't ready."

On her way home, Cassie phoned Lou. "I'm thinking of taking some time off work just to be there with Ric; he's starting to talk a bit. It sounds like he's been suicidal. I think there's something else troubling him as well."

"Are you sure he's not just sucking you into his vortex again? And weren't we going to join that netball team?"

"Sorry Lou, but I think this is serious, I can't just leave him like this."

Next time Cassie came to visit, Ric had more surprises for her. "My parents must have lied to me all these years. I'm starting to think I was adopted. And the worse thing is, my parents still haven't told me." Ric's face was racked with anguish.

"Ric, whether you're adopted or not, it won't make any difference to me. But slow down and tell me. Why are you thinking you were adopted?"

"You know how you have to provide your birth certificate when you get a driver's licence, or complete your medical registration?"

Cassie nodded.

"Well, I've only ever glanced at the birth certificate, and then submitted a copy attached to the forms."

"So, doesn't it say who your parents are?"

"Yes, it says Mum and Dad are my parents. But you know what Cassie? That doesn't mean a bloody thing! When kids were adopted back then, they changed the name of the baby's parents and issued a new birth certificate."

"Are you telling me you found your previous birth certificate?"

"I wish, if only it was that simple. But I think I'm going to have to try."

"Okay, so your birth certificate lists your parents' names, and you haven't found a previous birth certificate, and your parents haven't told you anything, so why are you saying you were adopted?"

"It's just that the location of birth is listed as Cairns."

"Right, and isn't Cairns the place where you grew up, and don't your family still live there?" asked Cassie, rolling her eyes.

"All that is true Cassie, but my mother and father were both teachers in Townsville. Mum was teaching right up to a couple of weeks before I was born."

"Okay …"

"And Mum wasn't pregnant in Townsville. Then the next month they move to Cairns, and she has a baby!"

"How do you know that?"

"You remember I told you about our shit-scary boss at the hospital?"

"Yeah. Didn't you say his name was Phil?"

"That's him. Well, the thing is, he wasn't so shit-scary with me when I made those medical mistakes, nor when I asked for a year off. He was really calm and supportive the day I was dragged in to meet him. I couldn't figure it out at the time."

"Okay, but what's he got to do with all this?"

"Well, I bumped into him a few weeks later in the staff canteen. For some reason, I just came straight out and put it to him. I'll play back the conversation for you. See if you come to the same conclusion as I did."

"I asked him whether he's a rugby league follower, He replied that he couldn't stand the game, and wanted to know why I asked. I told him that he'd been pretty easy on me, giving me a year off to play football."

"He told me that he'd probably been too damn easy, but he couldn't bring himself to be hard on me. He said my mother taught him at high school, and he had a lot of respect for her."

"He said that Castelillio is an unusual name, but he knew it from his younger days. My Mum had put in lots of extra time tutoring him to help him get top marks, so he could get into medical school. When he saw my name on the rosters, he decided to keep an eye on me."

"He kept going, saying that the last time he saw my mum was when he came down to attend his brother's graduation in Townsville in December 1970, a few months before he left Cairns. I started doing the mental calculations."

"He told me that, after graduation, Mum told him she was leaving Townsville that week as her husband had scored a promotion to deputy principal at one of the high schools in Cairns. He was really sorry to hear she was going."

"Phil stopped there; he looked embarrassed about sharing all this personal stuff with me. But something made me follow up, and I made some comment that she must have been very pregnant at the time, as I was born in January 1971."

"Phil looked startled, then he frowned and said that she definitely wasn't pregnant at Clem's graduation. Then he looked even more awkward, saying he may have got the year wrong, then he just rambled on for ages about working in Cairns."

Cassie had been listening intently to Ric's replay of his conversation. She thought about it for a few more moments then said, "Okay, now I can see how you came to the conclusion that you might have been adopted."

"Good, I'm glad you agree. But just to confirm my suspicions that he was trying to cover up what he'd said earlier, I went to the library and searched out his bio details. Sure enough, he'd left Cairns to become a registrar in Brisbane a few months after I was born."

"Ric, you must have been thinking about this for a long time. Why haven't you told me anything about it?"

"I didn't know how you'd take it, Cass. I didn't want to lose you, so I put off telling you."

"Sounds like you don't trust me."

"Well, you do seem angry now."

"Yes of course I'm angry now! But not about whether you were adopted. I'm angry you haven't told me until now! I bet you've told lots of other people already."

"Not really. I have hinted at it with Mark, but I haven't come straight out and said it like I just did with you."

Cassie's eyes were still shooting daggers at him, but eventually she softened.

"So, have you asked your mum and dad about all this?"

"Yeah, like as if I'm going to phone them up and ask if they're my real parents. No, I haven't done that, but I did phone Mum to tell her about my knee injury. Then I mentioned I'd met someone she'd taught in Townsville, who said she was a great teacher."

"Your Mum would have been pleased about that."

"Yes, but then I asked what years she taught in Townsville. Mum must have suspected something, because she started off saying it was in the early seventies, but she couldn't remember exactly. Then she said she had an appointment and had to go."

Cassie nodded and then looked away. After what seemed like ages, she turned back to him.

"Okay babe, I think I have a plan. Let's book a trip to Cairns to see your family. You can say you want to catch up with them, now you have time on your hands. And maybe, just maybe, you might track down some information on your real parents if they're still living up that way."

Ric had been dreading doing the exact things Cassie was now suggesting. But he knew he had to try to resolve the issue or put it out of his mind altogether. It could be difficult, maybe even impossible. And if he did succeed, he may not like what he found. Then another thought occurred to him.

"Hey Cassie, you told me you may not want to continue our relationship. Have you changed your mind?"

"Why would I change my mind? Our relationship hasn't progressed at all. I'm only coming because you're going to need help with the driving while you sort out your situation. I'm hoping once you've done that, you might be able to focus on us again."

As Ric stared at Cassie's scowling face, he detected none of her usual cheerful disposition. His hopes for an easy resolution of their conflict were dashed by her cold response. He decided the only choice was to go along with her suggestion.

"Maybe you're right. I can hobble around just as well in Cairns as I can down here. I'll clear it with the club and then we can get organised."

Chapter 17

Does Ric Want to Know?

Cairns City Hospital, September 1997

For the last hour, Ric had been dredging his mind for memories of what had happened up to the point when they arrived in Cairns. He'd recounted the first part of his story while staring at the wall. When he pulled his gaze away and looked around the room, he was startled to find Ron still listening.

Ric shook his head, trying to clear his mind. The old paediatrician waited patiently for him to continue.

"I'm sorry, Dr Ron. I don't know much about what happened with Cassie on Stradbroke Island, but her friend Lou has had a long conversation about it with my friend Mark, the psychiatry registrar. If you want to know any more about how that trip affected her attitude to me, you'll have to speak to Mark. She hasn't told me much about it."

"Would you be comfortable if I called him?"

"Yes. I'll contact him now and ask him to speak with you."

"And I also don't know why Matthew and Phil so easily agreed to release me from the hospital."

"Well, Ric. It just so happens that I've known both Phil and Matthew for a very long time. They worked up here, at different times, in this very hospital. Would you mind if I spoke to them as well?"

"Ah, so long as you don't tell them anything about the … dreams … or anything about my possible adoption. Could you just say I'd come to visit my parents in Cairns, and while I was here, I came to enquire about possible future employment?"

"Yes. As that's all true, I'd be happy to say that, without mentioning anything else."

"Thank you. This whole thing seems like a bad dream, Dr.Ron. Can you make any sense out of what I've shared with you so far?"

"I've had some thoughts, however before I share those thoughts with you, I need to hear what Mark has to tell me, and I need to understand the reasons behind Matthew and Phil's uncharacteristic decision to release you. Then I want you to tell me what happened from the moment you arrived in Cairns until you came to my outpatient's clinic. But perhaps you've had enough today?"

"Yes, I do feel a bit washed out."

"Okay Ric, I understand why this is all so important to you. We've had many adopted children tracing their birth parents in recent years. It's always a difficult time for them, and I should warn you, many of them go away unhappy. Are you sure you want to know?"

"I think so."

"Well, you'll need to finish telling me what has happened, especially since you've been in Cairns. And only after you have done that, will we talk about the possibility you were adopted."

At that moment, Cassie's text came through, saying she was in the carpark, waiting.

Unsure what to say next, Ric stretched out his hand to say farewell. Ron took his hand and held onto it.

"Don't be embarrassed, Ric. It's important that we talk more about this. Would you and your partner like to come to dinner one evening next week?"

After some hesitation, Ric agreed.

"So, until we speak again, continue on with whatever you've planned to do in Cairns this week. Then we can review it all if we have a chance to speak privately when you come to dinner."

Ric looked into the distance. It had been hard enough to remember everything that happened in Brisbane, but at least that had happened over a period of almost five months, and he'd had time to digest it all. Since arriving in Cairns, everything had happened so quickly. He suddenly felt overwhelmed. He knew he'd have to concentrate hard to remember what had happened in those last few weeks.

"Oh, and I'll speak to Mark as soon as I can," said Ron, waking Ric from his reverie.

Ron made contact with Mark about half an hour later. He was happy to relay everything Lou had told him regarding Cassie's time on Stradbroke Island.

Meanwhile, Ric made his way back to the carpark, where Cassie was waiting.

"So how did it go?" asked Cassie, after he'd scrambled up into the big Toyota, using his arms to haul himself in.

"Yeah, okay, I think. What about you?"

"Well, it was boring at first. I started off looking at the birth notices for the week or two after you were born. Then it hit me. If a mother was giving up her baby for adoption, she wouldn't pay money to put a notice in the paper, would she?"

"Of course, I never thought of that," said Ric. "So, what *did* you do this afternoon?"

"Well, I thought I should read the headlines and some of the opinion pieces, to try to get a sense of the issues being discussed. I started to lose myself reading about how things were in those times before we were born."

"How do you mean?"

"The editorials were really patronising and insensitive on lots of issues, including single mothers and neglected children. The Aboriginal and Torres Strait Islander mothers were especially singled out for criticism."

"Really?"

"Yes. And there were some activists arguing that the children should not be adopted out to white families. Then I found some sneering comments from politicians about doing what is best for the kids, and saying the Aboriginal mothers were hopeless. Did you remember that Joh and the Nationals were still in government at that time?"

"Ah no, I'd forgotten. Yeah, interesting. I've spent the afternoon sitting in on a clinic with Dr. Ron, a lovely old paediatrician. He's been working in Cairns and Cape York for over thirty years. He's invited us to dinner."

"Oh really? Would you like to go?"

"Yeah, I told him we would come. Hey Cassie, I'm meeting my new physio early tomorrow morning. I need some time alone to digest all this information we've been gathering. Why don't you head into the city and check out the shops?"

Cassie agreed to have a lazy afternoon. Ric tried sitting on the beach and thinking through everything, but he found his mind distracted again. At least this time, there were no unwanted images.

Next morning, the physio found his knee stiffer than expected. Ric had to admit he'd slackened off on his rehab. She gave him a stern lecture, then strict instructions for daily exercises. Ric accepted this as a wake-up call. He would have to work harder on his rehabilitation. He decided to put a proposition to Cassie.

"Why don't we have a whole day off tomorrow? I know a beautiful waterfall. You could drive us there for a picnic."

"No Ric. If we're having a day off, I'm going out to see the reef. You can come too if you like, but you may have to stay in the boat."

Ric still hadn't got used to Cassie directing their movements. He realised he couldn't drive himself and also, Cassie *had* put up with a lot from him lately.

"I'm not sure about me sitting around in a glass-bottomed boat while you go snorkelling in your bikini with all those backpacker dudes."

Cassie looked at Ric with a quizzical smile.

"It's okay Cass. You go. I'll hang around our apartment and spend the day on the phone. I need to catch up with my rellies."

Next day, he managed to contact most of his aunts and uncles, together with a couple of younger cousins. He left his call to his parents to the end, uncertain how to approach them and concerned about how his mother would respond. It turned out his concern was well founded.

"So why *have* you come to Cairns, Ric? With that knee injury, wouldn't you be better off in Brisbane?" asked his mother.

He rambled on about how bored he'd been in Brisbane, stuck at home with his injured knee. His mother sounded unimpressed, displaying little enthusiasm about his proposal to visit them.

Chapter 18

Why did they agree to Twelve Months' Leave?

Brisbane, September 1997

Mark was able to provide Ron a detailed account of Cassie's trip to Stradbroke. He asked Ron not to tell Ric about her trip, as Lou had said it was up to Cassie whether or not to share it with Ric.

It was late evening before Ron made the call to Phil in Brisbane.

Although Phil was at home with his wife, he was delighted to take the call from his old mentor. After Ron told him the purpose of the call, Phil became cautious. He only agreed to speak when he found that Ric had given his consent.

Phil began by describing the actions he'd taken prior to the meeting about Ric's football proposal.

He'd asked the HR department to retrieve Ric's personnel file. He'd checked the details of medical registration, located the birth certificate, and noted the date of birth. At home that evening, he'd rustled through the dusty boxes in his storeroom and discovered the diary he'd kept during the last year he worked at Cairns City Hospital. He described how he had been interrupted in his search by his wife, Julie, saying "What on earth are you doing out there? Your dinner's almost ready." He replayed the conversation for Ron.

"Something's been gnawing at my mind, about one of our young doctors. You remember I've often told you I would never have got into medicine if it wasn't for a special teacher who helped me through high school? And she assisted my brother Clem through his troubled youth as well?"

"Yes, I recall she had an Italian name."

"Mrs Castelillio. Did I ever tell you much about her?"

"It was one of the things you talked about a lot when we first met. I think you had driven down to Townsville the month before, for your brother's graduation."

"Yes, my family had invited Clem's special teachers to dinner to thank them for helping him. It's incredible you remembered that."

"Not so incredible, Phil. It was the main reason I agreed to go out with you."

"Really?"

"Yes, you were such a nerd. So obsessional and serious, all the girls found you hard going. But when you showed me your softer side with your respect for this female teacher, I thought you might be worth getting to know."

"Really, I never knew that. Anyhow, it turns out that Ric, this young doctor who's having problems at the hospital, is her son."

"It really is a small world, isn't it? Now, are you ready for dinner?"

"Not quite. I remember spending a lot of time talking to Mrs Castelillio at the dinner. And she definitely didn't look pregnant at that time."

"Why is that important?"

"Well, she told us she was transferring to Cairns the following month. And Ric's birth certificate says he was born that month in Cairns!"

"Mmm … Hang on a minute. So you think this young man might have been adopted?"

"Yes, but I don't think he knows. And I'm not going to be the one to tell him, especially now he's having so many difficulties."

"You remember we first met in the postnatal ward. We may have even looked after him as a baby before he was put up for adoption."

"Yes."

"Ah, now I know what you're worried about," said Julie, her eyes fixed on her husband. "Are you going to ask someone to search the hospital records to see if it was you who filled out the forms?"

"No, I can't do that. It wouldn't be ethical. Did you just say dinner is ready?"

When Ron called Matthew, he'd responded in a similar way to Phil. He began by talking about exactly the same evening. He said he'd been pacing around the house, muttering to himself. Bec, his long-term partner, had busied herself in the kitchen, but then she interrupted him. He relayed to Ron what he remembered of the conversation.

"What's up doc?" Bec had asked with a silly smile.

"Ah, sorry Bec," he'd said. "I'm a bit unsettled tonight. I've just been thinking of some of the things I did when I worked up in north Queensland."

"Are you just? That was way more than twenty years ago, well before you met me."

"Yeah. I suppose we were all a bit young and foolish in those days. I was talking to Phil today about one of our young doctors. He reminded me of what I used to get up to."

"Did he now?"

"Yes. This young doc has made a few mistakes in ED, but he's a really good doctor. He's also an emerging elite footballer and he surprised us all when he asked for a year off to follow his football dreams."

"Wow, that's a big call."

"Yes, it is. And it may impact on his career choices later on. But the biggest surprise is that I found myself supporting his decision."

"That's not like you, Matthew. You're usually the one who persuades the young ones to get support and keep going. I've met so many who've later told me they're very grateful you did."

"I know Bec. But there's something different about this fellow. I'm not sure what it is. Phil even challenged me about why I supported his request. But then he reminded me about my own footy reputation up north. And he mentioned a few other things I had done in my younger days."

"Oh, what sort of *things*?"

It took a few moments for Matthew to answer.

"Oh, just some of the things I did at the hospital. Apparently, I made a good impression. Phil worked at the hospital after I'd gone. He said I left big shoes for him to fill."

Matthew wound up his conversation with Ron in his characteristic indecisive way.

"To be honest Ron, I'm still not totally certain about why I decided to support Ric's request."

Chapter 19

What *had* happened since they left Brisbane?

Cairns, September 1997

After he'd left Ron to follow up with Mark, Phil and Matthew, Ric decided he would take the old paediatrician's advice and carry on doing what he and Cassie had planned to do in north Queensland.

He would have to put some time aside to sort out his brain. What *had* happened since he'd arrived in Cairns? He grabbed a biro and a notebook from the hospital gift shop, ordered a coffee and found a quiet spot in the café where he could make some notes to help him recount the story to Ron. His mind returned to the plane journey more than a month ago. He'd had no idea how much and how soon his thinking would be challenged.

As their plane had approached Cairns, they'd gazed out the windows, each lost in their own thoughts. Ric detected the brown outline of the Barrier Reef in the turquoise waters of the Coral Sea below. On the other side of the plane, the deep green forests of the Great Dividing Range soared into the sky.

Cassie had never ventured into north Queensland. As they alighted from the plane, she moaned. "It's so hot and steamy up here, I'm having trouble breathing."

"It's worse in the wet season," said Ric, who'd been subjected to the silent treatment for most of the flight. He was beginning to wonder why Cassie had bothered coming.

Her face tightened then softened as she watched Ric trying to hobble around on his crutches and pick up the luggage.

After picking up their hire vehicle they headed to the northern beaches, where they'd booked an apartment. Palm Cove was aptly named, picture-postcard perfect. Ric had insisted on hiring a 4WD vehicle, knowing Cassie was comfortable with off-road driving.

Before they'd left Brisbane, Ric had investigated the legalities of adoption. He'd discovered that some years previously, Queensland adoption laws had changed. From the late eighties onwards, parents giving up their child for adoption would know their identity could be made available to the child on request. For children adopted prior to this date, the identity of the birth parents could only be disclosed to the child if both sets of parents agreed. Ric realised that if in fact he was adopted, he would be in that group of children.

He knew he might end up searching a lot of 'dry gullies', but he had to try, although he hadn't yet decided whether to submit a formal application.

When he'd told his footy teammates he was going to Cairns, some of them shared how homesick they were, especially the Aboriginal players from north Queensland. They asked him to visit their Mob, giving him contact details and saying their families would make him welcome.

Ric had often found himself hanging out with the Murri boys. He usually roomed with one or other of them in the team hotels. They told him he was like a brother to them. When he confided that he was going to try to find his birth family, they teased him about the possibility he may be Aboriginal. On one occasion, Albie, the oldest one, studied Ric's face and became uncharacteristically serious.

"Ric, maybe you're not Italian after all. Some of my true cousins are even lighter-coloured than you. Your face reminds me of them sometimes."

Ric felt the familiar shivers travelling up his spine. This possibility had occurred to him already. He wasn't sure how he felt about probing too far into his family background, but he knew one thing for sure. He wouldn't just be contacting his family and his old friends. He would make time to meet the families of his teammates.

On their first night in the north, Cassie and Ric walked along the moonlit beach under the swaying palm fronds, just like regular tourists. Ric's crutches dampened the romance of the occasion – an omen for what was soon to come.

They sat on a driftwood log, allowing their eyes to adjust to the dark.

Cassie froze. The next log on the beach had moved closer to them. "Ric, do you reckon there could be crocodiles around here?"

"Maybe," said Ric light-heartedly, then following Cassie's line of sight, he noticed the other log for the first time. He began to register how tense she'd become. "Ah, let's head back now. If you like, we can check the beach for croc tracks in the morning."

Ric was familiar with the habits of the salties; he'd seen them many times. He knew if you were sensible, you had no reason to fear the big reptiles. Cassie had no such familiarity. She was still wide-eyed and trembling when they returned to their room. Even when she slept, Ric could sense her tossing and turning all night.

It wasn't the fear of crocodiles that disturbed Ric's dreams. It was the shapes he'd seen as they walked back. Those shapes were not writhing this time. They were running. Some appeared to be screaming, others falling. Each time he managed to sleep, the dreams returned. He'd wake again with his heart pounding and his body soaked in sweat.

At breakfast they feasted on lychees, papaya, dragon fruit and mango with toasted muesli. They washed it all down with fresh juice and half-decent cappuccinos, all of which helped to soothe their frayed nerves.

"C'mon Cass. Let's go back to the beach to see if your 'logadile' has moved any further."

"Yeah, very funny. So you think *I'm* imagining things now?"

"Hey, I'm only trying to lighten things up."

Cassie stormed off down the beach. Ric paid the bill and hobbled down, only catching her when she stopped to sit on the first log. "Gees Cass, take it easy, will you?"

"Have a look at that other log now," said Cassie.

Ric turned to look. The beach was empty. "Shit, maybe it was a croc," he said. "Or … maybe it was a big lump of driftwood, and it got carried out on the high tide?"

"Yeah maybe. Let's go and ask the locals."

Sure enough, locals had seen the tracks of a big croc in the area recently, but there'd been no definite sightings. As they wandered back to their lodgings, they were both quiet. Ric saw the shadows again, this time in the full light of day.

He slumped into a deck chair. "Cassie, I admit I didn't take you seriously last night, when you thought there was a crocodile."

"You treated me like a child Ric, so damn patronising. You do that all the time."

"What do you mean?"

"Ric, I know you think you love me. But you're always shielding me from things, not wanting to worry me. If we ever do live together, we won't be just shacked up together, we're supposed to be building a long-term relationship, at least that's what *I* thought we were doing. But if it's going to work, you've got to start treating me like an equal."

Ric frowned, shaking his head.

Cassie's eyes flashed. "You doctors act as if everybody else is somehow less intelligent than you."

Ric couldn't see how his doubts about the crocodile could have prompted this tirade. His first thought was to defend himself and his behaviour, but he wasn't a quick thinker in these situations. By the time he had half organised his thoughts, Cassie was speaking again.

"Anyhow, you didn't come here to have a holiday, or even to sort out our relationship. You came here to verify you were adopted. Let's just sit down and see if I can help you work out your strategy."

Ric suspected that Cassie's newfound forcefulness might be a cover for her frustration, but he couldn't work out how to respond. The sun was half-up in the sky and the shimmering morning glare had faded away.

Maybe that old croc is out there now, hunting for food. Or maybe the driftwood has floated off to some other beach, to create disharmony with another couple. Or maybe I'm a clumsy oaf.

With a deep sigh, he decided this may not be a good time to deal with Cassie's accusations. She had offered a change of tack. Attempting to display some good grace, he decided to follow her lead.

Cassie took charge. "Okay, so you've suggested to your parents we visit them on Saturday morning. That gives us a few days to do other things. You wanted to meet up with your teammates' families, right?"

Ric nodded.

"You also wanted to see some of the older doctors at the hospital, those who were around at the time of your birth?"

More nods.

"And you wanted to see if anyone from the Families Department would speak to you, or let you see old departmental reports.?"

"Yeah."

"Oh, for Chrissake Ric, you look like the proverbial dog that's lost its bone! I've only got a few weeks off work, and I don't want to waste my time. I can't cope with that hangdog look much longer."

Ric inhaled deeply. "Okay, if you help me make a list of contacts, I'll get on the phone to arrange some meetings."

He suggested they start with the Aboriginal families, then the doctors, then the departmental people. As an afterthought, he threw in the local newspapers, thinking they might have retained old editions on microfiche. To his surprise, he found that the newspaper office had archival records going back fifty years.

Chapter 20

One Gathering – Nora's Party

Cairns, September 1997

As Ron had advised, Ric decided they would carry on with what they had planned to do in North Queensland. They accepted the party invitation from Albie's Aunt Nora. Her old house was already buzzing by the time Ric and Cassie arrived that Friday evening. Most of the guests wanted to ask about their relatives in Brisbane, but some wanted to know why Ric had come up to Cairns when he was having such difficulty getting around.

"Well, I grew up here," said Ric. "I've come to catch up with my family and introduce my girlfriend to them." As Cassie was already a big hit with the children, this reply was met with indulgent smiles.

Ric soon became aware of an older man with a squint in one eye, looking at him intently with his other eye. He was introduced as Uncle Wilbur.

He said, "I hear you bin asking Nora about the old days?"

"Yes, I've heard so many stories and I've been reading that report on the Stolen Generations. After I talked with Albie and his cousins, I wanted to find out for myself how things were in those days."

Wilbur looked at the ground then glanced sideways at Ric and Cassie. He motioned with his lips to two tree stumps at the back of the yard. "You reckon you could drag yourself away from this lovely lady 'ere so we could have a bit of a yarn?"

Cassie smiled and went to join a group of children setting up a game of touch footy.

"You can play on my side, miss," shouted children from both sides.

Cassie laughed, and said, "How about I play at being the ref?"

"We don't always like the refs, miss," said one cheeky girl.

"But we know we're all gonna like you," said a pre-teenage boy, a comment which resulted in a 'wooh' from the other kids, as they pointed out the size of her boyfriend.

Ric found that, even with crutches, he could walk faster than the old man could amble. He held up his beer to Wilbur with an enquiring glance.

Wilbur replied, "No, I don't touch that stuff no more. When I was younger, it nearly got the better of me."

As they sat down, Ric placed his beer on the ground. At first, he looked intently at Wilbur then, intuitively, he realised that might not be proper protocol with this gentle old man. He turned his eyes away to look towards the outlines of the trees in the distance. At first, there was a long period of companionable silence. Ric had a feeling the old man would speak when he was ready.

"You get on well with your parents, Ric?"

"Yeah, mostly I do, but I wouldn't say I was close to them. I haven't actually seen them for a couple of years, but I do call them now and then."

Wilbur nodded. "Those things you been asking Nora about, have you asked your parents all that stuff as well?"

"No, not yet," said Ric, shifting uncomfortably on the stump. "I'm thinking I'll ask them when I go over this weekend."

Wilbur nodded again, then shifted his glance to the ground. "When you grow up, you find out lots of things your parents never told you; it's a bit of a shock when that happens."

"Did you know my oldies in those days, Uncle Wilbur?"

"Not really. But your father taught some of our nieces and nephews when he first came to Cairns as a deputy principal."

"Wow, small world," said Ric. "What was he like?"

"The kids said he was stern, but they thought he was alright."

"What about my Mum?"

"No, she stayed home with her baby. Ay, that must have been you," said Wilbur, as if this possibility had only just occurred to him.

Ric suddenly had a thousand questions shooting around his brain. He tried hard to remain silent, but he couldn't help himself.

"I've recently found out something I want to check with my parents."

The old man pursed his lips and nodded.

"Your Mum wasn't pregnant when she left Townsville," said Wilbur in a low voice.

Every hair on Ric's head stood on end. "How long have you known this, Uncle Wilbur? And how on earth *did* you know?"

"You ever heard of the Murri grapevine?"

Ric shook his head. Wilbur smiled.

"It's pretty fast. Some of our Mob have relatives down in Townsville. By the first week of school term, we'd worked out you must have been adopted. But your parents never mentioned it to anyone as far as we knew, so we kept it quiet."

Ric waited. There was an obvious question welling in his mind. To mask his trembling hands, he reached for his beer.

Maybe he knows my real mother. I wonder if I can ask him.

"So did anyone ever work out who my real mother was?"

"Not really," said Wilbur.

For some reason, the old man didn't answer the question directly. As he talked, Ric concentrated on every word. The sounds of the party and the screams of the children faded into the distance.

"You said you'd read about the Stolen Generation."

Ric nodded, leaning closer.

"In them days, so many of our kids got taken away. When the government people saw they were light skinned, they thought they'd be better off in white families. Some of us used to try and track down where the children had gone. Sometimes we found them, sometimes we didn't."

Ric was transfixed.

"Yeah, it was the same thing for the kids who got adopted. Those ones were the hardest to track down ... I always find it hard to talk about these things," said Wilbur, his voice cracking.

Ric knew he should have remained quiet. Still, he couldn't do so.

"You reckon I could have been one of those children?"

Wilbur flinched, feebly raising his palms.

"That's just the thing, Ric. When we saw Mrs C with her baby, we did think maybe you were one of us. But we never found any of our girls had a bubby who could have been put up for adoption in Cairns around that time. And by then, we had links with all the Murri services around Queensland."

"Uncle Wilbur, my birth certificate says I was born right here in Cairns."

Wilbur's eyes opened wide, but still, he didn't speak.

Ric guessed he was processing the information, trying to fit it in with something he already knew.

Wilbur looked down, shaking his head slowly.

Ric heard a commotion. He looked up to see Cassie running towards them, with screaming children in pursuit. "They all want to sack the ref," she said, puffing.

Things now began to move far too quickly for Ric. Aunty Nora beckoned them over to meet a well-dressed middle-aged woman. This time, there were no pleasantries.

"I suppose you're one of these fellas who's hoping to discover his Aboriginal ancestry," said the woman with an unsmiling face.

Ric wasn't sure how to respond. He introduced himself and Cassie. There were no introductions from this woman.

Nora took the lead. "Nadine, these 'ere fellas are my guests. Don't start on them with your political stuff!"

Ric watched as the two women exchanged stern glances.

"Nadine's my sister. She's on the board of our Community Care Agency up here, and she's involved with a lot of other community groups. I wanted you to meet her 'cos most times, she's pretty helpful to people," said Nora, regarding Nadine with a baleful look.

Nadine still refused to look at Ric and Cassie. "Yeah, you're right, Sis. But I'm getting fed up with these Johnnie-come-latelies who keep popping up. It's a trendy thing these days for people to say they've traced some Aboriginal ancestry. Then we never see them again, and all they do is talk about it at their posh dinner parties!"

Ric stood, leaning on his crutches, slack jawed. It was Cassie who spoke up.

"Nadine, we didn't mean any disrespect. Ric's been struggling a bit lately, and we've come up to see his parents. It was Albie who put us in touch with Aunty Nora and your family."

Nadine continued to glare. Nora turned her back on her sister.

"Come on over here then, there's other people I'd like you to meet," said Nora. Then with a flick of her head back to her sister, "And I'm pretty sure they're not gonna be real hard heads, like this one."

Chapter 21

Emergency

Cairns, September 1997

As Ric and Cassie walked away, they heard screams from behind the food tables. "Come and help Uncle, he's fallen down," shouted one of the women. As Nadine rushed across, everyone moved aside to let her pass. They knew she'd done a couple of years of nursing training, and she'd kept up to date with her CPR.

Nadine knelt on the ground and said gently, "Hey Uncle, what happened?" When there was no response, she felt his neck. "I can't feel a pulse. Call the ambulance, quickly! I need someone to help me with CPR. Now!"

Cassie raced over and Ric hobbled behind. Nadine looked up and shook her head.

"We don't need you two. Hey Rocco, you've just finished your First Aid training. You do the chest compressions and I'll do the mouth-to-mouth."

"But Aunty, I've never done this before. I've only ever practised on a dummy," said Rocco, wobbling at the knees.

"It's called a mannequin Rocco, and you'll be the dummy if you let your grandfather die!"

The onlookers gasped.

As they began CPR, Nora turned to Ric, asking what she should do.

"You could make sure the ambulance is on its way. Your sister seems to know what she's doing." For this he got another filthy look from Nadine. "And Aunty, could you please get someone to bring a pillow?"

Nadine glared at Ric as she did the mouth-to-mouth resuscitations. In between breaths she spat out her responses.

"We don't need his head on a pillow, we need it flat on the ground, so I can get air into his lungs," said Nadine, her voice full of venom.

Then she shouted at Rocco, "Brother, you're not pumping his chest properly!"

Cassie spoke gently. "Nadine, I'm a physio and Ric's a doctor. We can help with chest compressions. Ric has done this many times at the hospital."

"So why didn't you say so earlier? Anyway, he won't be any use to us with that gammy knee."

One of the older kids came up to Ric clutching a pillow.

"I'll be right with my knee on this, I'd like to help."

Before Nadine could reply, Rocco stepped aside. Ric immediately dropped his injured knee onto the pillow and started compressions. "Bloody hell!" he blurted out, "I didn't know it was Uncle Wilbur."

In between breaths, Nadine hissed, "Does it make any difference?"

Ric winced. "No, of course not."

But to me, it could make a big difference if this old man doesn't survive.

Ric was still fit, so he didn't need anyone to relieve him with the compressions. Wilbur's colour began to improve. If Nadine was pleased Ric was helping, she didn't say so.

She did manage to utter in a tremulous voice, "Uncle Wilbur is my true uncle. He's an Elder in our Mob. Everyone loves this old fella."

"I understand," said Ric.

Nadine had tears in her eyes as she looked away.

An ambulance siren blared. Two young paramedics arrived and quickly attached the defibrillator. After checking the trace, they called, "Stand back!" and hit the button.

Adults gasped and children shrieked as Uncle Wilbur's body convulsed. When they resumed the compressions, Uncle Wilbur inhaled a deep and noisy breath. Ric stopped compressing Wilbur's chest as he came around.

When the paramedics asked for the history, Ric inclined his head toward Nadine, indicating she was in charge. After hearing the story and assessing the situation, they transferred Uncle Wilbur to the ambulance. Sirens blaring again, the ambulance left with Nadine in the front passenger seat.

Everyone wanted to know whether Uncle Wilbur would recover. Ric pondered how to respond. He tried to give the family some hope, without sounding too confident.

"He's in good hands. Thanks to Rocco helping Nadine so quickly, he only had a few seconds without blood circulation, so if he recovers, he should be okay."

Ric found he had to rely heavily on his crutches now. His knee had swollen. He stood in silence with Cassie, while Nora comforted her relatives.

The party quietened down as people began to drift away. Ric could tell they were not completely reassured. When he enquired why, he was told that Uncle Wilbur was an old man and so many of their people had died of heart attacks in their forties and fifties, much younger than him. And worst of all, they took him to the hospital. That was the place where Aboriginal people go to die.

As Ric and Cassie said farewell, Nora tried to apologise for her sister. "Nadine has fought a lot of battles for our people. She's not always a bitch like she was tonight. She probably couldn't say it, but I reckon she was grateful you helped with Uncle Wilbur."

On the drive home, Ric told Cassie that Uncle Wilbur had concluded he was adopted.

His fervent hope for the old man's recovery was not all altruistic. Instinctively he knew this Elder may be able to help him understand many things.

"I'm not sure I'm ready to meet my parents after all this," said Ric, his lips compressed into a grimace.

Chapter 22

The Ground Shifts

Palm Cove, September 1997

That night, Ric's sleep was disturbed. Each time he woke, his mind replayed the events of the previous evening. He knew Uncle Wilbur had been trying to tell him something. *But what? And where is the old man now? Is he in Coronary Care, or is he laid out flat on a cold slab in the morgue?*

Ric shivered. He recalled the resuscitation procedure and the interactions with Nadine. She had radiated so much anger, and most of it was aimed at him. And he had no idea why. His heart began racing as his mind went into panic mode. The unwanted thoughts were intruding again. He lay still, trying not to disturb Cassie.

Are these just bad dreams or are they something more sinister?

Fear rose in his throat, like acid bile. The sense of dread returned. Ric knew he couldn't face his parents with his mind in such turbulence. And he wasn't yet ready to confess all these things to Cassie either. He eased himself out of bed and moved to the front room.

The sun's rays were fingering the clouds in the eastern sky. He tried to calm himself and rehearse a plan. The plan would need to give him time to sort out his confusion without freaking out Cassie. He remembered the fear in her eyes when he'd told her about the shadows he'd seen moving on Kangaroo Island.

Is she afraid for me? Or is she afraid of me?

Her manner had changed in the last few weeks. He couldn't put his finger on it, but she wasn't the same easy-going Cassie. Ric had just managed to lean back on the couch and elevate his leg when Cassie came into the room.

"Your knee giving you grief?"

"Yeah, it's so swollen, it's become stiff."

"So, was that what was disturbing your sleep? I heard you cry out a couple of times."

"Yeah, it was. Hey Cass, I'm going to need to keep my leg elevated today. I'll have to let my parents know I won't make it out to see them. Maybe we could postpone our visit until tomorrow?"

"You know they'll be disappointed; they're expecting to see us. Shouldn't you at least try to explain things to them?"

Ric scowled. "Okay I'll try. And apart from elevating the knee, I want to call Nora and see how Wilbur is. I also need to get some advice from the physio, and with any luck, get a bit of sleep. Why don't you take yourself off and check out those trendy shops around here?"

Cassie organised breakfast, brought cushions to elevate his leg, and packed ice around his swollen knee. "Call me if you need me," she said as she headed off.

Ric was relieved his ruse had seemed to work with Cassie. He would phone his parents and Nora and the physio, but he didn't intend to sleep. He planned to call his counsellor in Brisbane, and then catch up with Mark.

Ric worked his way through the calls. His mum was edgy when he cancelled, but she did agree to shift the lunch arrangements to the next day, saying it would give her time to invite the rest of the family.

The physio talked him through some knee movements and gentle exercises, then reassured him it was unlikely he'd caused any serious damage. "Just keep it elevated and iced, and when the swelling reduces, take it easy for a while."

The counsellor didn't answer, so he left her a message asking for a phone consultation.

When he called Nora, she reported that Uncle Wilbur was in Coronary Care. They'd had to shock his heart several times in the Emergency Department. He'd had a heart attack, and he was on the critically ill list. However the nurses had told her that despite his fragile state, he kept asking what was for lunch. Nora thought that may be a good sign.

When the counsellor didn't call, Ric phoned Mark. He spoke openly about the dreams and the intruding thoughts. When Mark pressed him, he admitted to the other episode of 'dreams' which occurred when he was wide awake, walking back from the log.

"Hey Mark, have you got any idea what all this means?"

There was silence at the other end of the phone.

"Okay, I'll be blunt. Do you think I have a mental illness?"

"I'm not sure. I think I need to seek advice from someone more experienced than me."

"Any chance you could get some more time off? It would be good if you could join Cassie and me in Cairns."

"Ah … okay. I'll check with my supervisors."

Mark phoned soon afterward saying he would join them in Cairns. This was such a relief to Ric; he leaned back on the couch and fell asleep.

Cassie returned, crept across the room and located his phone. The log showed he had phoned both Mark and the counsellor.

When she dropped her shopping bags on the table, Ric woke with a start.

Cassie said she'd phoned her friend, Lou, and told her she was worried. Apparently, Lou had raised the possibility of schizophrenia and had also offered to join them in Cairns. And she'd said she would talk with Mark.

Chapter 23

A Very Different Kind of Gathering

Cairns, September 1997

By the next day, Ric's knee was much less swollen, and he was walking more freely, albeit with crutches. He and Cassie had already experienced an incident-filled gathering at Albie's aunt's place. Ric knew that visiting his parents and his extended family could be equally disturbing, but for very different reasons.

When they arrived at his parent's place, he decided on formality.

"Cassie, I'd like to introduce you to my Mum and Dad."

His father gave a mirthless laugh. "You can call us by our first names, Cassie. I'm John and this is Margaret."

John then drew Ric aside, asking him not to upset his mother in front of the whole family.

"Why are you asking me that, Dad? We've only just got here."

"I think you know why. Your mother has been terribly upset since that phone call. You asked exactly what years she was teaching in Townsville. She thinks you're doubting her honesty, and you're angry with her."

"Well, I am angry, and not just with her. I'm angry with both of you. I don't think you've been honest with me."

"That's enough Ric. Just leave it until everyone else goes home. We'll sit down with you and have a talk afterwards."

Ric was about to respond when Cassie came over to see if everything was alright.

"Dad has just asked me to stay cool during the BBQ. Apparently, he and Mum are going to sit down with us and have a talk when everyone's gone."

"Oh, that will be good," said Cassie, leading him off to join the rest of family.

There were so many relatives, all wanting to reminisce about Ric's childhood. But when he introduced Cassie to Cecilia, his favourite aunt, she barely acknowledged him, and cast a long glance towards his mother.

Cecilia had always been close to his mum. She'd lived with them for years before she'd married and had children of her own. *Has Mum already told her about my phone call?*

Uncle Steven intervened. "Ric, the only one missing today is Harry. He's still living in Western Australia. You must remember your uncle Harry, you used to spend hours with him and his mates, kicking a football around?"

"Yeah, I sure do. He was the one who got me interested in football," said Ric, turning towards John. "You didn't have much time to play with me, eh Dad? You were always working."

His father's sour look and his mum's silence put a dampener on the gathering, which petered out earlier than expected. As they said their farewells, some of his relatives suggested further gatherings, but Ric was careful to be vague in his responses, not knowing how things would progress with his parents.

After the guests had gone, Ric and his father skirted around each other, not addressing Ric's issue at all, so Cassie offered to help clean up in the kitchen. Margaret wrapped leftovers, tidied dishes and discarded rubbish, all without saying a word to Cassie.

Finally, she asked, "You know what Ric wants to talk about, don't you?"

Cassie nodded.

"You might as well be part of the conversation then. He probably tells you everything anyhow."

"Well, we do talk about most things, but maybe not everything," said Cassie, prompting a brief enquiring look.

"Okay, the dishes are finished, let's get this over and done with," said Margaret, as she moved to join the men sitting on the back deck. Cassie pursed her lips in a grimace towards Ric. Margaret came straight to the point.

"Ric, when you called, you kept asking me about the year I finished teaching in Townsville. You said you'd met someone I'd taught down there. Was he sure about the year I taught him?"

"Mum, his name is Phil, he's the Director of Medical Services at our hospital. He's obsessional. He was quite sure of the dates you taught both him and his brother Clem."

Margaret and John exchanged glances.

"You finished teaching Clem in the month before I was born. Phil was a doctor in Cairns at the time. He came down for his brother's graduation and you spoke to him there. When I quizzed him, he said you were definitely not pregnant at that time."

Margaret's body jerked backwards in the chair. Her face went pale. She turned to John, who walked over to put his arm around her shoulders. She buried her face in his chest, sobbing. John gestured to Ric to stay silent.

As the sobbing eased, John spoke. "After your call, we realised you'd worked it out. We knew … we should have told you a long time ago."

"So why didn't you?"

"When you were little, we didn't want you to be any different from the other kids. We were going to tell you that first Christmas when you came home from boarding school, but you'd brought Mark with you."

"You still could have told me then."

"You boys were inseparable, and you were so happy together, we just couldn't bring ourselves to do it. We know we were wrong, Ric. We are terribly sorry."

Margaret started sobbing again. Ric saw his parents through a red mist. His face distorted. This time it was Cassie who stood and moved over to comfort her partner. She whispered into his ear. "Babe, you aren't going to get anywhere if you get angry. They'll just clam up. Try to understand what your dad's been saying. Maybe let me speak first?"

Ric remembered the counsellor's words: 'Stay in the moment, concentrate on your breathing. You can't change the past. You can't predict the future. Focus on the now.'

Yeah, as if that's going to be easy.

Tears welled in his eyes as he held Cassie tight. "Fair enough, you speak to them. I'll try to stay calm."

"Is it okay if I say something?" asked Cassie. His parents nodded.

"Thanks. I've been worried about Ric. He's been thinking about this for a long time. I know you're seeing him looking angry here now, but when he worked it all out, he was really upset no one had told him."

Margaret gulped, struggling to hold back her tears. When she finally found her voice, she said, "We'd been having trouble getting pregnant for many years. When you came along, Ric, we were so happy, we wanted you so much. All the family loved you.”

“Ric’s been telling me it feels like he doesn’t know who he is anymore, or even who his family is,” said Cassie.

Ric interrupted. “What about my brothers and sisters. Were they adopted too?”

“No Ric. We were surprised when the other babies came along, because we’d been told I would never fall pregnant. You were the only adopted one, but we loved you all just the same.”

Cassie squeezed Ric’s arm as his jaws clenched. With an obvious effort, he maintained his silence.

His mother continued. “You *are* part of our family, Ric. You will always be part of our family, even if you don’t feel that way at the moment. Our intentions were not to hurt you, just to protect you.”

Ric balled his fist and punched the palm of his hand. His face flushed as he opened his mouth to speak. Then he registered his mum’s distress. He forced himself to breathe slowly.

“Yeah, okay … thanks Mum, I … understand it must be hard for you too. It’s good to finally have it all out in the open. I don’t think there’s anything more we can say at the moment. How about we talk about something else for a while?”

“Yes of course,” said Margaret.

She invited Cassie to join her in the lounge, where they leafed through the photo albums from Ric’s childhood. Ric found himself sitting with his father, who was once again speaking in a strained voice.

“Your mum has been quite unwell these last few weeks. You know you will only make her worse if you go around trying to find your birth mother. Why don’t you just let sleeping dogs lie?”

“You can’t ask me to do that, Dad. If I need to find my birth mum and dad, it doesn’t mean I’m rejecting you both. Could you at least *try* to explain that to Mum?”

“I suppose I could try. But don’t say any more today.”

Ric glared at his father. It was a long moment before he could bring himself to agree.

Cassie and his mum returned to the room smiling, holding embarrassing pictures of Ric as a toddler. He took this as a cue to leave.

On the return trip to Palm Cove, Mark called. Ric tried to sound surprised. "Hey Cass, Mark's on the phone. He's got a couple of weeks off, and he's thinking of coming up to Cairns to see his folks. He's asking if he can spend a bit of time with us while he's here."

"Sounds like a good plan. He might help you sort out a few things," said Cassie without hesitation.

How much does she already know?

Chapter 24

Ric's Confusion Deepens

Palm Cove, September 1997

"Hey, you two, what's been happening?" said Mark, as he walked in the next day.

"Not much," said Ric. "But it is good to see you. Hey Cassie, did I tell you I mentioned to Mark we've been struggling to get anywhere with this adoption thing?"

"That's not the only thing we're struggling with," said Cassie. "The truth is things have been a bit rough between us. In fact, now you're here Mark, I'm thinking I'll head back to Brisbane."

"What? You don't have to leave just because Mark's here. I've been looking forward to ditching my brace after all this time on these bloody crutches. We could do lots of things together."

"Maybe Cassie's right," said Mark. "You two could have a break from each other. And I could be your chauffeur for a week."

Not for the first time, Ric was wrong-footed. Before he could protest, Mark spoke again.

"Yeah mate, I've been looking into my family history as well. I've arranged to go and see my grandpa to talk about the old days. You remember grandpa's station and how we loved going out there when we were kids?"

Ric smiled vaguely, doing his best to work out what was going on. Cassie went off to call Lou.

"Mark, was all this a setup? I knew Cassie was a bit pissed off with me, but I had no idea things were this bad."

"Hey sorry, mate, it's no setup. I had no idea she was going to take off the moment I got here, either."

There was an uneasy silence in the room, punctuated by the noise of drawers opening and bags being zipped in the bedroom.

Cassie came bustling back. "I've booked this afternoon's flight to Brissie. And Lou's going to take some time off over the next few days. I better keep moving."

Mark walked with her to the patio as she collected her things. They spoke quietly for a few minutes.

"What was that all about?" asked Ric.

"She just needs a break, mate. She reckons it's all been pretty intense."

Ric sat, shaking his head.

"Do you want to talk about it?" asked Mark. "I gather you haven't been telling her everything."

Ric slumped in the chair, muttering in disbelief.

"Bloody women, you never know what they're thinking. And anyhow, when did you get into this family history stuff?"

"Well, it was all your talk about finding your birth parents that got me started."

Neither Mark nor Ric was keen to lead the conversation, each wary of the other. After Mark resorted to small talk, Ric began to chill. Cassie interrupted with an airy farewell, and gave Ric a quick peck on the cheek, saying she'd be in touch in a few days' time.

Ric frowned, thought for a moment then decided to accept the inevitable. He cracked open a carton, hoping the beer would settle his unease. Much later, they ordered a pizza and a bottle of wine. The awkwardness between them settled a little. Mark stayed over, sleeping on the pull-out bed.

Next morning, they woke seedy and sorry. They both jumped when Ric's mobile rang. It was Nora.

"I'm really worried about Uncle Wilbur. He's been asking for Nadine until today, but now he's asking for me. He's had another heart attack. Hey Ric, do you think we're gonna lose him?"

Ric tried to clear the fog in his brain. "It's hard to say, Aunty. But you better not muck around, anything could happen. You should get up there as soon as you can."

"Would you come with me? They said his mind is wandering, but he keeps talking about you."

"Me? He keeps talking about me?" Ric's brain cleared suddenly. "Sure Aunty, I can come but you know they won't let me in. I'm not family."

There was silence for a few seconds, then Nora said, "Could you come anyway, even if you have to stay outside in the waiting room?"

Mark drove Ric over to pick up Nora. When they arrived at the ICU, she was ushered in but as expected, Ric was told to wait outside. Mark went off to organise things with his grandpa.

Ric spent the time thinking. Cassie had clearly wanted time away from him, and he wasn't sure what he should do about that. But the man in the room nearby was his main concern today.

Why does he keep talking about me?

Nora came out, a nurse steadying her as she walked.

Ric looked up, expecting the worst. "He's lapsed into a coma," said the nurse. "Nora's distressed. We've suggested she go and have a cuppa, but we need her to stay nearby. We'll call if anything changes."

Nora slumped into a chair; her head bowed. She motioned with her lips. Ric had picked up some of her non-verbals. She and her family seemed to have whole conversations without actually speaking. They walked outside and found a bench under a flame tree. Red bell-shaped flowers had carpeted the ground around the bench. The sight of the flowers seemed to settle her down.

"Uncle Wilbur came around a few times, but really, he just talked in riddles, then he faded away again. I told him Nadine wasn't keen on talking to you, so I asked if there was anything I could tell you. He shook his head really hard, saying it was you and Nadine who had to talk."

Ric couldn't think of anything to say, other than, "Why?"

Nora didn't know why. She phoned her family, leaving Nadine until last. Her sister wanted to know why Uncle Wilbur hadn't wanted her to visit today.

"Nadine, I don't know why he asked for me today. And I don't know why he always wanted you the other days. You've never looked after him like I have." This sparked harsh words from Nadine.

"Anyways, he's now unconscious most of the time. But when he came around, he kept saying one thing over and over."

"What was that?"

"He said Ric and Nadine have to talk to each other."

"I've got no intention of speaking to Ric. Just because he was good at CPR doesn't mean I've changed my opinion of him. Listen Nora, I've got to go."

"Hold on tidda. Uncle Wilbur was insistent. You can't just ignore a dying man's wishes. Ric and his friend brought me to the hospital. He's here with me now."

"Wait, did you just say he's going to die?"

"Haven't you been listening? He's unconscious most of the time. He's on the critically ill list. What else can I tell you? You need to get that bony arse of yours up here quick smart."

"Sorry. I was … concentrating on the bit about talking to Ric. I'll come up straight away. Just keep that young Migaloo out of my way."

"You really are a nasty piece of goods," said Nora. Nadine had already hung up.

Nora relayed the conversation to Ric. He called Mark and arranged to meet him in the carpark.

Just as he was backing his body into the front seat, Nadine drove in. His wave was met by a glare and a flick of the head.

"Who was that?" asked Mark.

"You don't want to know, mate. Hey, you take the 4WD and go catch up with your folks. Just drop me home. We can catch up later."

"Will you be okay?"

"Yeah, I think so. I'll keep in touch with Nora, but I want to call my mum, and make some other calls as well. Oh, and would you be interested in substituting for Cassie on a dinner invitation tonight?"

"Sure Ric, I could be your date for the evening."

"Not likely," said Ric looking wistfully into the distance.

The day passed slowly. When Ric called to ask if he could bring a friend to dinner instead of Cassie, he was surprised to hear the old paediatrician had also invited someone, mentioning seemingly as an afterthought, she was a psychiatrist.

Why would he invite a psychiatrist? Has he decided I'm mentally ill? Maybe that's why Cassie's gone back ... Yeah, maybe that's why Mark's here too.

His heart thumped in his chest. *Like a wild bird trying to escape.*

"Gees mate, calm down!" Ric told himself. "You're turning into a pussy." He concentrated on his breathing, repeating the mantra he'd learnt. *In through the nostrils, down the windpipe, into the lungs, feel the diaphragm moving.* Eventually the bird in his chest stopped flapping.

The phone rang. It was Nora. "Uncle's still unconscious. They said he's stable, but he's critically ill."

"Well Aunty, it could be worse. He's stable now, and hopefully he'll have a full recovery. How are you feeling?"

"I'm coping, Ric. Hey, I talked to that bloody sister of mine."

"Good, how did that go?"

"She wouldn't tell me anything about what Uncle Wilbur's been saying. But she eventually agreed to talk to you. She said you could call her tomorrow at the Community Care Agency. It's the best I could do."

Ric reasoned Nadine had probably only agreed to talk to him out of respect for Wilbur. He didn't want to speak to Nadine on the phone. He contacted the agency and asked for an appointment.

Chapter 25

Evening at Ron's

Cairns, September 1997

As Mark drove him over to Ron's place for dinner, Ric mentioned that a female colleague was coming too. "She's a psychiatrist, apparently. So, if I can get Ron talking about all this adoption stuff, you two shrinks can go off and talk about us crazies!"

Mark shot a glance at Ric, eyebrows raised.

So much had happened since Ric had last spoken to Ron, he'd decided to bring along the notes he made to help him recount his story.

They found Ron's house to be a ramshackle old Queenslander on the side of a hill, facing east towards Trinity Bay inlet. The gardens were lush but haphazard. The house was the same, with books and journals scattered everywhere.

Ric introduced his friend Mark, and Ron welcomed them both. He then showed them around the house and pointed out the photos of his family, including one of his wife, who had died in her early forties. "Breast cancer," he said, his gaze lingering on the image.

Ron's psychiatrist friend arrived. He gave her a perfunctory hug, then introduced her as Sophia. As they settled in, he produced a spicy Middle Eastern dish from the slow cooker, later followed by a spectacular *Tarte Tatin*. "From the patisserie," he said.

The conversation that evening ranged over a variety of topics, during which the two experienced doctors shared insights into their work in north Queensland. Many of the tales related to interactions with First Nations people. At one point, Ron rose from the table and spoke directly to Mark.

"I think it's time we left you and Sophia to talk."

He then led Ric out to a wicker chair at the far end of a wide verandah. The heady perfumes of the tropical garden percolated upwards. Flying foxes squabbled for food in the trees below.

"Now Ric, Sophia will keep young Mark talking for hours about cross-cultural psychiatry, so you'll have plenty of time to tell me what you've been up to since you arrived in Cairns."

"Yes, I will."

Ric proceeded to recount in detail, all the events that had happened since they arrived in Cairns. He was surprised to find he didn't need the notebook much at all.

"So, Dr Ron, now you know everything that's happened from since we arrived in north Queensland until we arrived here tonight."

After Ric finished talking, Ron told him to stay in the wicker chair, while he went to check on Sophia and Mark. He returned soon after to report they were engrossed in conversation. He handed Ric a glass of port.

Ric took a long sip of the port, followed by a deep sigh.

"Ric, recounting all those happenings must have been exhausting, and some of it must have been quite distressing. Are you sure you want to talk about your possible adoption tonight?"

"I do indeed."

Their subsequent conversation was long and circuitous. They hadn't noticed how many hours had passed until Sophia and Mark arrived with a pot of tea and a box of chocolates. Ric recognised this as a signal the evening was drawing to a close. They drank their tea and bade farewell, thanking Ron for his hospitality.

Ron's parting words were intriguing. "I haven't told you this yet, but I know Uncle Wilbur. I hope he recovers. You may be surprised to find out how much that old man knows."

Ric wondered if that statement was meant to be a hint. But for what?

Both Mark and Ric were quiet on the drive home, each mulling over what they'd discovered. For Ric, it was the realisation he may never discover his true identity. Ron had confirmed that in the early eighties, not only were fewer and fewer children being adopted, but there was growing antagonism to the concept of Aboriginal children going to non-Aboriginal families.

Ron had added, "No mother willingly gives up her baby, unless she's desperate. You may eventually find your mother and if so, you will want to know she loved you. But that's not a fair question to ask her. She may not have had time to get to know and love her baby. The authorities made sure of that."

Ric realised this was the first time he'd considered his birth mother's situation. Up until then, he'd been focused on why his mother hadn't loved him enough to keep him. He'd had no cause to think about how she felt. He wondered if this was how Cassie saw him – insensitive and uncaring about others' feelings. Sadness permeated into his mind. Ric choked back tears.

"How was your chat with Sophia?" he asked, in an effort to lift his spirits. Mark obliged him by rattling on and on.

"Absolutely fascinating. She's into cross-cultural psychiatry. You know there are still some old Clever Men practising in remote areas of the Cape? Sometimes the folks down here ask them for help. The whole thing is kept very quiet. Apparently, the missionaries tried to stamp it out, but there's still a deep spirituality among many of the older people."

"What, you're telling me they still have these old guys who point the bone and all that stuff?" said Ric, attempting to be light-hearted.

Mark shook his head. "Mate, that's just a white man stereotype. I think you've had far too much wine to follow what I'm saying."

Ric choked up again, knowing the two psychiatrists would have discussed other things, including his mental state. He'd recently become acutely aware that psychiatrists had the power to authorise involuntary treatment of people suffering certain types of mental illness.

Chapter 26

One Challenging Woman

Cairns, September 1997

"I don't recall agreeing to meet both of youse fellas. *You* can piss off," said Nadine, jabbing her finger at Mark. She stood at the door with hands on hips, wearing a torn Land Rights T-shirt and a pained expression. Although Ric had mentioned she could be edgy, he hadn't expected her to be this rude. She had told Nora she was happy to talk to him, but apparently not Mark, who scowled as he walked away.

"Come in Ric. For some reason, Uncle Wilbur's taken a shine to you. He said you were looking for your birth mother."

No small talk with this lady.

Ric wasn't sure if his head could cope with an angry articulate black woman after while his mind was still trying to integrate the discussions he'd had with Ron. "Yeah, we wuz yarnin' about my mum and dad …"

"Don't treat me like a Myall! I've got university degrees, you know."

Ric's head jerked back.

Wasn't that the way she'd spoken to Mark?

He tried again, choosing his words carefully. "When I told Uncle Wilbur my parents were teachers in Cairns, he said he knew them when I was a baby. He told me the Old People knew all along that I was adopted, which I myself hadn't realised until recently. So, I asked him how he knew, and I also asked did he know my birth mum."

"What was his reply?" interrupted Nadine.

"He explained how Aboriginal kids got taken from their families in those days. He told me how the Elders used to try and find out where the children ended up. He said they'd thought I might have been a Murri … ah, sorry."

"That's okay Ric. 'Murri' is fine."

"Uncle Wilbur said they had links all over Queensland, but they couldn't locate any of their women who'd had a baby who could be adopted in Cairns. When I told him my birth certificate showed I was actually born in Cairns, he went very quiet. But I don't think he ever really answered my questions."

Nadine's eyes narrowed. "So why have you come to see me?"

"Ah, your uncle can be very persuasive."

Nadine smiled for the first time. "He can indeed. But maybe it's the fact that I run a Community Care Agency?"

"Yeah, that too."

"And we sometimes get involved with Link Up, helping children find their birth mothers?"

"That did occur to me."

"Alright Ric, let's fill in these forms and we'll see what we can find. By the smell of your breath, I suspect you've had a big night out. I suppose I should offer you a coffee."

"Yeah, that would be good, thanks. Things haven't gone too smoothly since I saw you last. Cassie's gone back to Brisbane and my mate Mark has come up. He's the one who dropped me over to your office today. We did have a few drinks after dinner last night."

Ric completed the forms while drinking the coffee, which tasted like mud. He hoped his face didn't show it.

"Maybe I'll make tea next time," said Nadine. "Yeah, the Old People's network was good, but the young women got wind of it. Sometimes they'd go interstate to have their babies."

"Why would they do that?"

"You really have no idea, do you? Put yourself in their shoes! Sometimes they didn't want their family to know they were pregnant, because they'd had a stupid affair with the wrong guy, and they were ashamed. Or maybe they'd been raped."

"Oh. Sorry, I hadn't thought of any of that."

"Seems there are many things you haven't thought of. There was a lot of pressure on young Murri women to keep their babies and bring them up in our culture. There still is."

"Right," said Ric, trying for the first time, to focus his thoughts on what a young Aboriginal mother might feel. "Your nephew Albie ... I asked him if there were any books I could read, so I could better understand Aboriginal people and their culture."

"What did he say?"

"He said there were some books, but they were mainly written by white fellas. He said your Mob had lots of stories, but they were mainly passed on by yarning, especially with the Elders. Hey, are you an Elder?"

Nadine laughed.

"Not yet. Not old enough. Not wise enough either."

"Sorry. So, aren't there any books written by Aboriginal people?"

"There are some Aboriginal writers, Kath Walker and Archie Weller are two of them. And there was the legendary Aboriginal writer, David Unaipon."

"Ah, the man on the fifty-dollar note."

"Yes, funny that. You white fellas always know about anyone associated with money! That man also compiled books about our myths and legends, and he was a scientist, an inventor and an activist as well."

"I'll see if I can get hold of some of those books."

"And I'll arrange for some of our Elders to talk with you. If you're going to go poking around in Murri families, you might want to learn a bit of respect."

"Nadine, it seems like I'm always upsetting you. Why would you go to all that trouble when you keep getting so angry with me?"

Nadine pulled a resigned grimace and rolled her eyes.

"Uncle Wilbur?"

She nodded.

When Mark collected him, his face showed he was still angry.

"That woman had no right to treat me like that," said Mark. "Our family always tried hard to look after the Aboriginal people on our station. But despite all that, most of them just walked away, no thanks and no goodbyes. Seems this woman has the same attitude."

"Hey mate, that's a bit harsh. We don't know all the difficulties they've had to deal with in their lives. For one thing, how would we feel if we lost access to all our traditional lands?"

"Yeah, I'll have to think about that. Hey, we're half way to your family home, so you'll need to concentrate on what you're going to ask your mum."

"Yeah, my mum."

"I'm looking forward to seeing her again. She was always so good to me."

"Yeah, she was pretty good in some ways. But I never felt close to her. And she's been really upset since I brought up the adoption thing."

"What? You didn't anticipate that?"

"Well, I expected she'd comfort me, seeing me in such a bad way. But she's been so defensive. It's almost like she's had this big secret all her life. Now the secret's out, all she wants to do is round it up and put it back in its box."

"Yeah Ric. You've always been huge and fast and strong."

"What's that got to do with anything?"

"It's probably what kept you out of a lot of fights, mate. That and the fact that deep down, you're a decent bloke, who doesn't really intend to hurt anyone."

"Nup," said Ric shaking his head. "You've totally lost me this time. Exactly *what* are you talking about?"

"You want me to come straight out and say it?"

"Of course," said Ric, without any idea what was coming. "Hold on. Are you thinking I'm going mad?"

Mark hesitated.

"It's not that Ric. It's like you said before. Ever since I've known you, you've been putting your foot in it, saying the first thing that comes into your mind. You don't ever put yourself in the other person's shoes. You don't think about their background, or their personality, or how they'll react, or whether they'll be hurt. You just go ahead and say it."

"You think that's what I've done with Mum?"

"Maybe."

"And with Nadine?"

"Yeah."

"And Cassie?"

"Probably."

"Mark, stop the car."

They'd been travelling on a road above a cliff. There was a sightseeing lookout ahead.

"Why do you want me to stop the car?"

"Just stop the bloody car!"

"I'll stop as soon as I can."

Ric thumped the dashboard. "You could have pulled off at the lookout."

"Mate, take it easy. This road's a bit tricky."

When Mark pulled off the road, Ric opened the door and hobbled off.

"Ah, that went well," said Mark to the windscreen. "What am I supposed to do now?"

Ric was already out of sight, moving fast despite his walking stick. Mark closed his eyes and rested his forehead on the steering wheel.

A few minutes later, he jumped when a loud thump shook the car. Ric's face appeared at the driver's side. "Got ya!" he mouthed through the window, then walked around to the passenger side. Mark pulled himself upright.

"So you reckon I've got a lot of work to do?" asked Ric.

Mark said nothing.

"I'm glad my dad's at work today. Do you think I should go easy on my mum?"

Mark started the motor and drove slowly to Ric's family home.

"Yeah, that may be a good plan."

Chapter 27

And Another ... At His Parents' Place

Cairns, September 1997

Margaret opened the door with a startled look on her face. "Mark! It's so good to see you," she said, giving him a huge hug, followed by a half-hearted one for Ric. "Where's Cassie?"

Ric explained. Margaret invited them to join her on the shaded patio where tea and biscuits were laid out. Ric tried hard to keep himself under control all through the afternoon tea, as Margaret reminisced about their adolescent years. The conversation veered into small talk about their medical careers, and on to Margaret's dim views about Ric's decision to take a year off.

"So now you've had a major injury, can we assume you'll give up football and go back to practising medicine?"

"Maybe. I just need to sort myself out first. I still can't believe you didn't tell me I was adopted."

"I thought we explained all that the other day ... didn't we?" asked Margaret, her voice shaky.

"Well, you did confirm what I'd suspected, which I suppose I have to be grateful for," said Ric, earning himself a scowl from Mark, which he ignored. "But I don't know if I'll ever be able to trust you again."

Margaret inhaled deeply. "I don't know what to say, Ric."

"There's probably nothing useful you can say, Mum. But maybe you could tell me how it all happened? And could you tell me anything you know about my real mother."

Margaret responded with a pained look and a deep sigh. She followed this with an exasperated look towards Mark.

Mark took the hint. "I think Ric understands you would have been desperate for a baby, Mrs C. He knows you always intended to tell him about it."

He's speaking for me! I don't want to let her off that lightly.

Mark continued. "But I think what he's really trying to find out, is whether you know anything about his birth mother, or why she gave him up for adoption."

Ric would have raked his mother over the coals before he got to this point, and Mark had deprived him of that satisfaction. But now the critical questions had been raised, he decided to listen to Margaret's response, at the same time trying to calm his inner fury at Mark.

"Why do you want to know all this Ric? Whoever your mother was, and whatever her circumstances, she must have decided she wouldn't be able to keep you."

Again, Mark intervened. "It's quite natural, Mrs C. They've taught us in our psychiatry training that people are usually desperate to know their origins. Some people even become emotionally unbalanced, trying to deal with this sort of thing."

Ric's face contorted, initially with anger then with fear.

Is he implying that I'm mentally ill?

"I really don't know what circumstances made your mother feel she had to give you up for adoption. I just know she wanted the best for you."

"And do you know her name?" asked Ric, his tone still aggressive.

"She never wanted you to know her name, even when you grew up."

"What? She told you this?"

"No, she gave me something. The social worker who took the adoption papers said your mother was crying all the time because she didn't want to give you up. They encouraged her to write a little note for her baby, to give him if he ever wanted to know how she felt about him."

Ric's face paled as he swayed on the chair. Margaret put her arms around him. He stiffened, then gradually unwound his muscles, even leaning into his mother, sobbing.

Eventually Margaret said, "Would you like me to get the letter for you?"

Why would my birth mother never want me to know her name? Why would she just want me to know how she was feeling?

Mark's words rebounded in his ears. *You never seem to be able to put yourself in the other person's shoes.*

Mark gestured to Margaret that he would wander out to the garden and give them some space. Margaret looked alarmed, but as she looked at Ric, still sobbing and leaning into her arms, she softened.

"Have you read the letter?" asked Ric.

"I've read it many times, especially when you were little."

"Do you think I should read it?"

"I think you should, but only when you're ready."

"I'm not sure I am ready, at least not yet. But I would like to have it, I think."

Margaret went to the study, opened a locked filing cabinet and took out an old envelope and handed it to Ric. It was light brown, with a Queensland Government logo and the words 'To my baby boy' hand-written in capital letters on the front.

Ric choked up again. Margaret gestured to Mark through the window, indicating he should come back in. When Mark saw the envelope, he nodded to Margaret, who moved away from Ric.

"It's been a big day mate; I reckon we should head back to Palm Cove. Maybe we could grab a couple of beers at the beach before dinner."

Margaret gave Ric a pleading look.

"Ric, I want you to know this is still your home. Even though you're upset at the moment, you will always be welcome here."

"Yeah ... thanks Mum."

As soon as they were in the car, Ric exploded. "You don't have to speak for me Mark, I can speak for myself. You can be so bloody patronising!"

"Hey settle down mate. I could see the situation getting out of hand, I was just trying to defuse things."

"Don't I have a right to be angry?

"Sure Ric. But when are you going to get over it?"

"I don't know if I'll ever get over it."

Ric turned his body away from Mark and stared out the car window. "How about you put yourself in my shoes for a change?"

Chapter 28

To Put Things Aside and Move On

Cairns, September 1997

The atmosphere in the car was icy. And it wasn't due to the air conditioner. Finally, Ric spoke. "I'm going to call Cassie. I want her back here with me when I read the letter."

"Have you spoken to her recently?"

"No, I was trying to give her some space. And I had hoped I could rely on you to help me through all this. But I'm pretty sure Cassie will want to be here with me now."

Cassie didn't answer his call. Ric left a terse message. There was silence in the car again until Nora called.

"Can you come up to the hospital, Ric? Uncle Wilbur's taken a turn for the worse. He's just lying there with a frightened look in his eyes. He keeps saying that Nadine and you have to come and see him together."

"Why does he want me and Nadine to see him together?"

"I've got no idea."

"Okay Aunty, hang in there. I'll come straight to the hospital."

In the hospital carpark, Ric stowed the frayed brown envelope in the glove box, swung himself out of the 4WD and readied himself for what was to come.

He was ushered straight into the ICU, leaving Mark in the waiting room. Nora explained to the Intensivist that Uncle Wilbur had asked for him, and that Ric was a doctor. The Intensivist had just begun discussing Wilbur's new medications with Ric when Nadine bustled in.

Nora moved to the door.

Nadine shot a bleak look at Ric who stood, offering her the chair.

"I'll stand thanks."

As Nadine gazed at her uncle, her face softened, and she took his hand. The Intensivist raised his eyebrows to Ric as he left the room.

Ric stood quietly, feigning a professional interest in the monitors.

Wilbur's eyes opened. When he realised it was Nadine not Nora who was squeezing his hand, he squeezed back. He didn't smile though, until his eyes focused on Ric. Still gripping Nadine's hand, he used his other hand to beckon Ric to the bedside. Nadine scowled.

The old man closed his eyes and said nothing. Ric could tell he wasn't asleep, as he could see him squeezing Nadine's hand. His two visitors stood in uneasy silence.

"You two bin getting on?" asked Wilbur, with his eyes still closed.

For once, Nadine didn't take control. She merely looked at Ric.

Ric cleared his throat. "Umm, Aunty Nadine has been helping me, Uncle. We've had a long yarn. She's uh … checking her records and she's going to introduce me to some Elders."

Uncle Wilbur let go of Nadine's hand and waved his arms around. "What, you still haven't told him, Naddie?"

Nadine flushed. "I'm getting around to it, Uncle," she said, attempting to squeeze his hand again.

He pushed her away. "It's not just for 'is sake. It's for your sake too," said Wilbur with all the vehemence he could muster.

As Ric watched, Nadine's face betrayed her irritation. Then her eyes widened, and her nostrils began to flare. Ric glanced back at Wilbur.

His arm had dropped, and his breathing had become laboured. The nurse who'd been reviewing the monitors pressed the emergency button and asked Nadine and Ric to wait outside.

Doctors rushed in and commenced their emergency response.

Nadine told Nora what was happening to Uncle Wilbur. She didn't mention what he'd said.

Nora wouldn't have heard anyway. She was keening, her maudlin wailing evoking a sense of dread in all who heard it.

Mark grabbed Ric's arm. "Hey mate, maybe we should wait downstairs."

Nadine put her arm around Nora and hugged her tight.

After a long wait, one of the doctors came out to speak to the two sisters. Wilbur was still unconscious, but his heart had stabilized. They could come in one by one to see him – but only for a few minutes.

Nadine went in first. The nurse who'd pressed the alarm walked out to speak to Nora.

"Your uncle seemed angry with your sister for not saying something to Ric. It seemed to stress him a lot and then he collapsed. It may help if you could all sort this out before he wakes up again."

Nora looked up, her eyes betraying a glint of hope which didn't last long as the nurse said, "Of course, that's if he ever does wake up."

Nora called Ric and told him what the nurse had said. She asked Ric to leave his phone on in case she needed to call.

On the drive back to Palm Cove, Ric explained to Mark what had happened.

"Can you help me figure this out? Uncle Wilbur wants Nadine to tell me something. Either it's something he's told her, or something she already knew. If it's something he's told her, why can't he tell me himself? And if it's something she already knew, why is she not telling me herself?"

"Yes, they are the questions, I agree. But there's another clue. Remember, you told me the old uncle said, 'It's not just for his sake, it's for Nadine's sake too.' So, he thinks not only do you need to know, but that it would be good for both you and Nadine if *she* was the one who told you."

"Right, so what does that mean? This old man could be on his deathbed, and he's not at peace because something is troubling him about Nadine. But how on earth could it involve me? He only just met me last week." The hairs on the back of Ric's neck began their now-familiar response.

"But Ric, he said he saw a bit of you as a baby, and remember, he said he thought you might be one of them."

"So, are you thinking Nadine knew my mother when I was little?"

"Maybe it was even more than that?"

"Huh? What could possibly be more critical to me, than her knowing my mother?"

Finally, Ric worked out what his friend might be saying.

"What? No way, mate. That's just not possible. I mean I know it's theoretically possible, she's about the right age, but I'm nothing like her!"

"Well, I don't know about that. You can be just as pig-headed!"

Mark held Ric's gaze for a few seconds. "Just kidding, mate. Of course, there are lots of other possibilities."

"Yeah, I'm not sure I want to know any more. I don't want my life to be this complicated."

"You really think that's possible now?"

"That's what I'm hoping for. If only I could share all this stuff with Cassie. But she hasn't called me back. Hey, you said you were going to talk to me about her."

"Not tonight mate, you've already got too much going around in that big boofy head of yours. We can talk about all these things on the drive out to see my grandpa."

Ric found himself yearning for the simplicity of a football game, or even a night shift in ED, though he knew he couldn't manage either at the moment.

He checked his phone for messages, but there were none from Cassie. He thought about calling her again but decided to wait. He realised she may have found someone else, but tonight, he really didn't want to think of anything that painful.

Chapter 29

Flirtations

Brisbane, September 1997

When Cassie arrived at Brisbane airport after her flight from Cairns, Lou was there to meet her. "Hey girl, it's so good to see you. You been having a rough time with Ric?"

"Hey Lou. Nah, I wouldn't say it's been rough. It's just that he's so obsessed with his big search, nothing else seems to matter to him. And he's still getting those thoughts or visions or whatever. I'll fill you in later but first, how have things been for you?"

"Yeah, good thanks. Mikey's been coming over from Straddie. He's hoping to score part-time work on the mainland. We're having lunch together today, why don't you join us?"

"Hey, that's great Lou. But are you sure you want me along?"

"Yes of course, I want you to meet him properly, and help me decide what to do."

"That serious, eh? Okay, I'll come. When's lunch?"

"Soon. You can leave your stuff in my car, and I'll drop you home afterwards."

"Okay. Come on then, tell me all the goss."

Lou had always been the tall gangly girl everyone liked but no one had fallen in love with, and now it was obvious – she was in love, and blossoming. Cassie was still urging Lou to tell her more when they walked into the café.

"G'day Cassie," said Luke.

"Oh … hi Luke," said Cassie, turning to Lou.

"You didn't tell me Luke would be here."

"Why, is that a problem?" asked Lou in a loud whisper.

"Of course not," said Cassie, in a loud voice. This brought on laughter from Mikey and Luke. "Well Mikey, I've been hearing lots about you too," she said.

Mikey replied, "Yeah, and Luke never stops talking about you either," which earned him a thump on the shoulder from Luke.

"Well, now we've got all that out of the way, let's go and order lunch," said Lou.

The light-hearted banter continued until mid-afternoon. Before it became awkward for Cassie, Mikey and Luke wound it up. "Hey, we're really sorry ladies, but we've got to catch the next ferry. There's a big swell rolling in this afternoon."

Mikey managed a quick kiss and a hug for Lou. Luke gave Cassie a friendly, but platonic hug.

"Luke's really hot," said Cassie as the boys walked away. "And really uncomplicated!"

"He is hot, but I wouldn't say he's uncomplicated, Cass. His coaching business is struggling, and he's trying to get part-time work in his old job as a physical education teacher. The trouble is, there's only limited work on Straddie, so he may have to work on the mainland."

"I think I could handle that kind of complication."

As Cassie checked her phone, she saw Ric had called. She listened to his message, then groaned.

"Lou, have you got time to talk some more about Ric? He's left a message and wants me to call back."

"Yeah sure. But first, tell me what you thought of Mikey?"

"He's great. I think you should go for it, Lou."

"Excellent! Okay, let's talk about Ric."

Despite talking about him for hours, Cassie still didn't call Ric. And as she drifted off to sleep that night, it wasn't Ric who spiced up her dreams.

Back at the hospital, Claire continued mentoring Ric by regular phone conversations. She sought advice from Matthew when she realised the long-term injury had done nothing to induce Ric to recommence his medical career.

Despite Matthew's best efforts, they couldn't find any way to influence Ric. Claire reported that it wasn't just his interest in football, it was the search for his origins which now consumed Ric's thoughts. Matthew promised Claire he would keep working with her on the issue.

He requested a meeting with Phil to discuss his concerns about Ric.

When he arrived, Phil posed an unexpected question.

"How is Bec these days?

"She's fine," said Matthew, with a frown.

"Do you ever find yourself thinking back to your young and carefree days?"

Matthew studied Phil's face. "Why do you ask?"

"I suspect you may have been a bit like me. Perhaps you also did some things you would now regard as … irresponsible … Anyway, I've been meaning to tell you. I think I may have caused Ric's problems."

"What?"

"I did some unfortunate things up north when I was young."

"Phil, I have no idea what you're talking about."

Phil pursed his lips and leaned back in his director's chair, slowly nodding his head.

"Matt, it's late in the day. Would you be interested in a whisky?"

"Ah, yeah, I could manage that. How about we adjourn to the club and find a quiet corner?"

Phil's grimace morphed into a smile. "Now you're making sense."

The club reeked of old money. It engendered a sense of refuge from the world, with its wood-panelled walls, dark green carpets and full-sized billiard tables. The butler greeted the two doctors by name and indicated a quiet corner. He presented the whisky in a crystal decanter, placing the matching crystal water jug nearby.

They sank into the leather armchairs, drawing deeply on the single malts, each lost in their own thoughts, until Matthew broke the silence.

"You asked about Bec. Are there rumours circulating that I'm spending a lot of time with Claire?"

"There are some. I suppose it happens to all of us when we reach late middle age. We begin to look back on our lives, thinking about what we could have done differently. Young Ric has made a couple of serious mistakes but it's still possible for him to learn from those, to make amends and have a good career."

"Yes, I suspect it was too easy for him to escape into football."

"You know Matthew, it's good you and Claire are giving him plenty of support. My mentors certainly helped me when I got into trouble. But in the end, it all falls back on yourself. Sometimes you can ruin people's lives when your mind is on other things."

"You're right about that. And earlier you asked me about Bec. Lately, my thoughts keep going back to the women I used to hang around with, one in particular. Yeah … we were both moving pretty quickly, but then she had to go away for a while. I had another fling – then she just refused to take my calls."

"Yes Matthew, I remember your reputation well."

"Hey, I wasn't that bad. And I wasn't always like that. But after she'd gone, it was like I needed to prove myself. I kept having more and more … dalliances. I wasn't too careful either. But, when I moved back to Brisbane, I met Bec. And we're still together after all those years."

"Do you have any regrets?"

Matthew took another slug of whisky. "Maybe. What about you?"

Phil glanced at his watch.

"I'm sorry Matthew, I have to go. We have people to dinner tonight. Maybe we could meet here again, say next Friday night?"

"Yeah, okay," said Matthew.

"And yes. I too, have regrets."

Chapter 30

On the Road Again

North Queensland, September 1997

Back in the north, Mark had organised the trip out bush to see his grandfather. Ric helped load the 4WD with fruit, vegetables, prawns, and several cartons of beer. Grandpa would at least be delighted with the last two items.

They headed out on the Gillies Highway. Mark concentrated hard on negotiating the bends and the inclines, swearing often.

"Some of these bloody drivers! I'm not sure which ones are the worst – the grey nomads trundling along in their Winnebagos, the fat-bellied Harley riders escaping their mid-life crises, or the European backpackers in their rented campervans!"

"I'd be looking out for those tattooed truckies slugging wakey-wakey pills if I were you."

"Yeah true. Hey Ric, have you got that letter with you?"

"Locked in the glove box."

"Good. I've been thinking you may never get to read it with Cassie, you may have to read it with me."

"Why is that?"

"I'm not sure how to say this. But Cassie is starting to have doubts."

"What? I knew she needed a break, but not … has she told you something?"

"She's been saying a lot of things to Lou. It was Lou who pressed me to come up to see if I could help, while Cassie sorted herself out in Brisbane. Yeah, so … here I am," said Mark with an extravagant arm gesture, which Ric interpreted as a guru readying to pontificate.

Despite his panic, Ric couldn't suppress a laugh. "Well come on, share your wisdom, oh great one. Are you saying she wants to break it off with me?"

"Gees Ric, do you always think of everything in black and white? No, she hasn't come right out and said that. But when I walked her out to the car as she was leaving, she seemed exasperated and upset, and maybe also a little fearful."

"Shit," said Ric.

They arrived at the station in a cloud of dust, to the sound of barking dogs and the sight of grandpa working on his tractor engine.

Grandpa's King Gee shorts had once been olive green, but they'd faded to a mottled brown. His elastic-sided RM Williams boots were scuffed at the toes. The sleeves on his flanno were rolled up to his biceps, which bulged when he pulled on the wrench. On his head was a wide-brimmed Akubra with a ragged hole in the crown.

"G'day you two. Can I get you a beer?"

Mark walked over to shake his grandfather's hand and give him a hug, but the old man was having none of it.

"Get off with ya, blokes up this way don't hug each other. Gawd strewth, what's the world coming to? Hey young fella, you must be Ric. Cripes, you've grown a bit since I saw you last. Played a bit of footy I heard?"

Ric smiled. Mark's grandpa hadn't changed much.

"Yeah. I was going well until I busted my knee. Hey Grandpa, is it all right if I still call you 'Grandpa'?"

"Nah Ric, you can call me Bill now you're bigger than me."

"OK, listen Bill, we've brought you some supplies, including some cartons, but it's a bit early for a beer. Wouldn't you prefer a cup of tea?"

"I s'pose so. I must be turning soft," said Bill, walking bandy-legged to the back of the 4WD. "Cripes, you did bring some stuff." He heaved a carton onto each shoulder and walked towards the house.

Mark finished unloading while Bill prepared the tea in yet another large brown enamelled teapot. He served the tea in half-pint tin mugs, accompanied by corned beef and pickle sandwiches.

"Righto Mark, what's all this rubbish about researching your family tree? Trying to find a few skeletons in the cupboard, are ya?"

Mark's eyes opened wide. "No, I hadn't even thought of that. Ric's been looking into his family, and Mum said if I wanted to do the same, I should talk to you. But hang on. Do we have any skeletons in the cupboard?"

Bill laughed. "Yeah, your mum probably thought I'd be carking it soon, so you'd better come and talk to me while I've still got me marbles."

Mark was about to protest when he saw his grandpa smiling. The old man had lost a bit of weight and the creases on his face had deepened, but his brain was still sharp.

After settling them into their rooms and catching up on all the family news, Grandpa began to talk about his family history. Mark scribbled notes and started drawing the family tree. They had only gone back two generations when the sun dipped below the distant hills, lighting up the rock faces with red and ochre toning.

"Time to go and get some tucker. I cooked a stew in one of those new-fangled slow-cooking pots, so all's we need is some mashed spuds. I'll go and boil them up while you boys sort out your gear."

"Can you throw in some carrots and beans?" asked Mark, to disgusted grunts from the old man.

The meal was surprisingly good. They ate on the verandah, mosquito coils on either side, cans in the Esky nearby. Grandpa insisted they didn't need any lights. As the meal progressed, the two city lads began to appreciate the astonishing profusion of stars in the Milky Way, and the luminescence of the gum leaves under a three-quarter moon.

"No more talking about the family tonight. We're going fishing tomorrow. You boys should hit the sack early. You'll be up way before daylight."

Bill roused the boys to the sound of the crows. Bleary-eyed, they washed down breakfast with more mugs of tea, loaded the fishing gear and set off before sunrise. They soon arrived at a muddy brown creek.

The old man rowed them along in his tinny until the creek widened. He glided the boat to a stop and pointed. "You need to cast out towards those tree roots opposite, but make sure you don't cast too far. If you snag your lure, you'll be wading over to get it with the crocs checking you out."

They soon realised he wasn't joking when they saw a crocodile slide from the muddy creek bank into the water and disappear, barely making a sound.

The morning wore on. Ric had done very little fishing out bush, always preferring to kick a football, but he was the first to get a decent tug on his line. He jerked his rod upwards. The fish swam straight for a tree root. Ric wound in quickly, wrenching his rod vertical. The line snapped and Ric stumbled backwards. Grandpa grabbed him and eased him onto the cross seat.

"Well, at least you didn't snap the rod," said Bill with a grimace. "You've got to play with these barra, Ric. Give him a bit of line when he pulls, wear him out, reel him in slowly then let him drag you again. They're big fish, and they don't give in easily."

Ric tried to recover composure. "Ah, do I really have to go over there and retrieve the lure?"

Bill looked him straight in the eye for a few seconds, then smiled. "Maybe not this time."

They had a few more bites, but only grandpa managed to land a fish. It was at least five kilograms. "That'll be your dinner tonight," he said, hitting the big fish on the head with the back of a small axe, and then dropping it into an Esky filled with ice slurry. They returned to the old wooden jetty, where Bill instructed them to drive towards the distant hills.

"Good thing this is a proper fourby, I'm not sure how the tracks are holding up this year," said the old man.

Ric didn't respond. He found his eyes staring at the locked glove box, fighting back tears as the implications of Mark's remark that he may never get to read his mother's letter with Cassie, finally set in.

Chapter 31

Grandpa's Surprise

Out Bush in North Queensland, September 1997

Mark shifted into low range to negotiate the washouts and potholes scarring Grandpa's bush track. Several times they had to shift fallen tree branches. In other places, shrubs were growing in the middle of the track, some three feet high.

"You've got a bull bar and a sump guard, just drive over the bastards," said Bill.

"Maybe," said Mark. "But Ric will have to pay for any damage to the vehicle, so I might just drive around the bigger ones."

His Grandpa shook his head and scowled. "I was hoping to get there in daylight."

Ric had been quiet all morning. He pushed away any thoughts of Cassie as he reflected on the events of the day. He'd relished the peace of the river, punctuated by the occasional nibble on his line and the intermittent small talk. Even the bumpy ride soothed his mind and slowed the stream of uncertainties which had cluttered his brain over the last few days.

"Do ya' think you could drive any slower?" asked Bill.

"Where are you taking us Grandpa? You never took me out this way before."

"Damn right, young Mark. You wouldn't have appreciated it. Turn down that track on the left."

The 'track' was a barely visible wallaby path between the gum trees, heading towards a cliff face.

"We're not driving up that cliff, are we?"

"Nah, from here on, we're walking. Good thing you boys wore those fancy hiking boots. Grab your sandwiches and water bottles, we'll be gone for a while. Ric, you okay walking on uneven ground with that knee of yours?"

"Yeah, I think I'll be right with this stick, so long as there's not too much climbing involved."

They walked up a gradual slope, pushing shrubs aside and allowing startled snakes time to move out of their way. Bill located an overhang on the side of the cliff face. Mark and Ric followed him in under the rock. Their eyes took time to adjust to the change of light. Bill waited, gazing at the upper wall.

They could just make out markings, painted shapes. Coming from life in an urban streetscape, their first thoughts were graffiti, then realisation dawned. These were not recent paintings. These were old, some already deteriorating. Some shapes had been painted over others. There were symbols, lines, wallaby shapes, human shapes, fish, spears and something that looked suspiciously like a horse.

Grandpa's tone was now almost reverent. "These paintings are many thousands of years old, most of them anyway, maybe not the horse. They were painted by Australia's original people. I think of them as our ancestors too. Those anthropologist fellas reckoned these paintings were like signposts for the people."

Mark and Ric stared, saying nothing, their eyes moving slowly around the gallery.

"But it wasn't just food they were showing. The anthropologists said this area held special significance for the people."

Bill's voice continued, but for Ric, it seemed to fade away. Soon Ric could no longer hear him.

What he could hear was a roaring sound. And he could see young men gathering, painting their faces and bodies. He could feel their excitement and their anticipation. He sat down on the ground and closed his eyes. Bill noticed first.

"You orright mate? Maybe the heat's getting to you. Hey, pull out your water bottle and grab some tucker."

Ric did as he was instructed, trying to clear his mind.

"I grew up with a lot of Aboriginal lads, probably descendants of these people. They used to live in a camp on our station and help with the mustering," said Bill. "My old man used to give them rations, but he never paid them much."

"What happened to them?" asked Mark.

"They moved into a mission, nearer to the coast. I haven't seen them for ages. If they're still alive, I'd like them to come out here again and have a good look around."

Ric still hadn't said anything.

Bill thought for a while then said, "Come up to that big rock and I'll show you the view. But then there's a razorback ridge and a gorge on the other side that I definitely won't show you. Those Aboriginal fellas reckoned they were forbidden to go there. I think it was a special place for their people."

"So you never went there?" asked Mark.

"I used to go to the top of the ridge with the Aboriginal boys, then the bigger ones would scare us with stories of kids who'd gone down and never been seen again. None of us ever tried to climb into that gorge."

"Can I see it from that rock?" said Ric.

"No mate, you have to climb right up onto the razor back and then along some exposed bits of cliff face. It's too late in the day to start, and besides, with that knee of yours, it would be dangerous. You could miss a foothold and go over the edge."

The blood drained from Ric's face. His body crumpled as he fell to the floor of the cave.

Ric groaned as he pressed his hands to his ears. The roaring noise grew louder, accompanied by tapping sounds and thumping noises. The human forms were indistinct, their features blurred by smoke.

Ric was aroused by the touch of Mark's arm around his shoulders, and the sound of Bill speaking with authority.

"Righto, that does it then. We're getting you home, Ric. You can put your feet up in the shade and have a cold drink. I'll clean and scale the fish and bake it in the oven. Mark, you can do the veggies and the spuds. We'll just give your mate a bit of time to himself."

After they arrived home, the others unloaded while Ric dozed in an old squatter's chair on the verandah. Mark and Bill prepared the meal, speaking only of trivial things, each immersed in thought.

While the meal was cooking, Bill dug out some salted peanuts and cracked open a stubby for each of them. The familiar pffsst was enough to wake Ric. The others joined him on the verandah. They leaned back in their chairs, yarning about the day they'd had, laughing about the boys' attempts at fishing.

"Ric, I saw your face go pale when we were in the cave. What was that all about?" asked Bill.

"Ah Grandpa, Ric's been through a lot lately. It's not just his knee injury. He's had some other … issues," said Mark, uncertain how much to tell.

"It's all right Mark. I'm happy to talk about it. Bill, how much do you want to know?"

"Well, it's up to you, my young mate. We've got plenty of beer, and we've got all night."

"Okay," said Ric, who then proceeded to give what he hoped would be a back-of-envelope summary of what had been happening to him over the last year or two.

"Ric, I don't get much company out here, so I tend to talk a lot when I have guests. But I'm also a fair hand at listening. Do you mind if I ask you some questions?"

Ric didn't mind.

Bill opened the Esky and passed around more beers. His questions were surprisingly insightful. He became concerned when Ric explained what happened in the cave.

"Our fish must be ready by now. Mark, come with me while I check if everything's cooked. You can help me bring it out."

As soon as they reached the kitchen, Bill said, "Okay Mark, you're training to be a shrink. Those things Ric's experiencing, do they mean he's going a bit off?"

"I'm not sure Grandpa. People with psychosis do experience things like that, but there's nothing else to go on. I talked to a psychiatrist, and she reckoned we shouldn't jump to conclusions. It may just be all the strain he's been under."

Grandpa nodded.

"She reminded me that many people have premonitions or thoughts which are somehow related to what's happening in their lives."

"Yeah. I used to know someone like that. He seemed to know when things were happening, long before anyone told him. Also, my old mum was Irish. She used to say some people had a gift."

They brought out the meal and settled down to eat, washing down the food with even more beer.

"You boys up for a bit of local history?"

They nodded.

Bill leaned back, talking about his family and his ancestry. "My grandpa's name was Warwick. He used to sit me down on this very verandah and he'd often tell me the same story about this station. I never got tired of hearing it. Funny thing was, the people who had the station before him, never ever mentioned this story. It was told to him by a young Aboriginal stockman. Are you sure you'd like to hear it?"

Ric and Mark were enjoying the company as well as the beer, so they both agreed.

"The local people lived in the black's camp down by the creek. The men helped with the mustering. The women helped around the house. In exchange, they got rations of food and tobacco."

"Only rations Bill, didn't they get any pay?"

"No mate, just rations. The young stockman's name was Jimmy, and he was a natural storyteller. He could imitate the English accents, and he could imitate the voices of his Old People and the way they strung their words together. Warwick would always try to copy Jimmy's voice when he told me the story, so I'll do the same for you boys."

Chapter 32

Jimmy's Story About Jambulyama

North Queensland, September 1997

"*Wha'dya want me working on today, boss?* That was what Jambulyama, my grandfather, said. The white fellas usually called him Jammy, it was their way of making fun of him.

Well Jammy, you know that new yard we fenced last year, out near the rocky outcrop? The grass should be good after the rains we've been having. You ride over there and check it out for me. See if we can move this mob of cattle to that yard so we can fatten them up

Jammy looked sideways at him. *Ya reckon, boss? Maybe that grass not too good for cattle, ay.*

Jammy, are we gonna have one of those irritating roundabout conversations again?

What you talkin' about, boss?

Jammy – just bloody well go and check it out for me!

Ah boss, I heard from one of my Mob, all that fencin's bin' burnt out.

Bullshit! There haven't been any fires out that way.

I reckon there must ha' bin, boss.

Bloody hell, it's no use arguing with you today, Jammy. Saddle up and I'll ride out there with you.

After an hour or so in the saddle, the ole' fella and his boss came to the new yard. Boss man shook 'is head. The fencin' was all burnt out and not only that, there wuz plenty of roos hopping around, eating all 'is grass.

Jammy, why didn't you tell me about this before?

Eh, you never asked me boss. Jammy turned his head away like this as he talked, so he wouldn't have to look at the boss.

Jammy, how do you reckon these fires got started?

Dunno boss. Maybe lightning, eh?

Yeah, right. Come on, let's go and check out what's left of the fencing.

Not that way boss, I reckon we oughta go this way. Jammy led him away from them big rocks. He made a big show of looking at what remained of the fencin'.

Them fires started over this side of the yard, boss. Maybe best if I do some tracking, ay?

He got down on his haunches and looked all around the place. He must have taken too long with the tracking – way too long for the boss, who couldn't see any of the signs Jammy showed him. The sun was getting high, and that boss man kept wiping the sweat off his face and flicking the flies out of his eyes.

Bugger it, Jammy, let's just go back to the station and get some lunch.

You go boss, I've got more trackin' to do. I'm a bloody good tracker, you know that, eh? I found those kids of yours when they got themselves lost.

That boss fella went back to the station. He didn't miss Jambulyama until late in the day. By then Jammy had already put the stockhorse back in the yard and asked his brothers not to say they'd seen him. That boss was real wild that afternoon!

Jambulyama had jumped into the creek and made his way along until he found a rocky slab he could use for climbing out. That slab had no plants, no dust and no ants crawling over it either. It was in full sun as well, so when his footprints dried, even the best trackers wouldn't be able to follow him.

He kept hopping between rocks until he got to the big boulder that blocks the gorge. There were no footholds on that boulder, but he'd climbed it before, and he knew exactly how to get over to the other side without leaving any prints on the creek bank. Then it was real easy for him to swim further up the gorge and climb all the way to the top of that razorback ridge.

After that, he camped out in the high country for a couple of weeks. When he came down, there wuz still plenty of roos hopping around that paddock. He snuck back into camp and had a good feed of roo meat before the boss realised he was back. The boss must have cooled down while he was away, 'cos he came into camp real reasonable-like and asked if he could talk to Jammy.

So, where have you been, Jammy?

I bin campin' out, boss.

Up in those hills?

Yeah, it's real good up there.

There's something special about that country, isn't there?

Jammy didn't answer, just squinted his eyes a bit.

I've been talking to your Elders while you've been away. They go all quiet when I mention that paddock up near the escarpment. One of them said maybe you'd tell me about it if you ever came back, so can you tell me this? Are some of your people still living up there on that escarpment?

He'd caught Jammy by surprise with this question. Jammy didn't tell him nuthin' that day. He needed to sit down with the Elders and have a long yarn with them. Bye-and-bye, the Elders agreed they should take a risk and put their trust in this boss fella. Next time he came down to the camp, the Elders spoke to him first, then they went and sat on that big log nearby, smoking their baccy and watching the two of them talking.

Eh boss, last time you came down 'ere, you asked me if any of our people still live in those hills.

Boss man nodded. Jammy looked far away, facing into the hills.

All our Old People still there, boss.

You're kidding me.

No gammin, boss. They there alright, they'll always be there.

Ah Jammy, is that where your people had their ceremonies?

Maybe.

And they still do that?

Jammy didn't answer. He just kept looking up into the hills.

Jammy, I've had a lot of time to think since you've been away. I've worked out there may be a few things I don't understand. When the Elders talked to me just now, I told them I was prepared to find another paddock for the cattle, and to check with them before I fenced it, if they would just explain to me what was so important about the area. They said you might be able to help me.

Jammy looked over to the Elders. They gave him the sign with their lips. He had their permission to share his ancestor's story, about when the white men first came to our Country."

Chapter 33

Jambulyama's Ancestor's Story

North Queensland, September 1997

Bill's eyes had been gazing into the distance as he recounted the first part of Jimmy's story. He turned to check out the two lads and found they were watching him closely.

"Are you boys right if I tell you Jammy's ancestor's story?"

Ric and Mark nodded.

"Can I get you another beer?"

The young doctors accepted the beers, but neither was in a hurry to open them. They were both impatient to hear Bill continue to tell the story in the same style that his own grandfather had used when he mimicked Jimmy's voice.

"Okay boss, I'm gonna tell you directly about things that happened when your people first came to our Country. This was a long time ago, before I was born. Even my father was only a little picaninny at the time.

So that would have been around the 1870s or 1880s?

Dunno boss, we don't work it out that way.

Sorry Jammy. I'll stop interrupting.

When them white fellas first got here, our people watched their strange-looking animals eat all the grass. Soon, there wuz no more kangaroos for us to eat. The Old People speared one of those big animals, and our whole Mob had plenty to eat that night. Everyone went to sleep with full bellies, but in the morning, the settlers rode over to our camp and started shooting at us. They killed one of our men.

Boss man screwed up his face. *No Jammy, that can't be true. I never heard about anyone getting shot.*

It happened, true as God. You can ask any of the Elders, they'll tell you.

The boss looked over to the Elders, and they all nodded their heads.

That's shocking, Jammy, I find that very hard to believe. I'll ... have to look into it. But anyhow, why don't you tell me the whole story.

Jambulyama began again. *Our warriors threw their spears at the settlers and made a big racket, so the women and children and all them Old People could get away. The warriors kept on taunting the white men while they were running away through the trees. They led the settlers up the tracks into those hills. At one stage, they speared two of their horses.*

Our Mob heard one of them say, '*We're going to have to teach these boys a lesson.*' The settlers tethered their horses and followed our warriors a lot more carefully now, further up into the high country.

Every now and then, one of our warriors would show himself, but when the settlers fired their guns, he would be gone. Our people knew every rock and every tree in those hills. They led the white men over a big hill, down into a gully and then up to the bottom of a cliff.

As the settlers turned to go back, spears scattered the rocks at their feet. The settlers fired shots, but the warriors had already hidden, and all those bullets just bounced off the rocks. They kneeled down on one knee and aimed their guns, waiting for our warriors to show themselves.

Spears came at them from behind, closer now to their heads. When they turned around, there was no one to fire at. Then spears came from another direction. The settlers dropped their guns and put their hands in the air.

Them whitefellas looked real foolish, stuck out in the open at the bottom of the cliff, with their hands stuck in the air. Some of them tried to climb up the cliff, but they kept falling back to the ground when our warriors threw their spears between their legs. They still couldn't see our warriors hidden high behind the rocky outcrops all around them.

When our Mob finally showed themselves with spears ready, the white men got real scared. There was no way out. The warriors drew back their spears, but their leader talked softly to them. He told them, *True, payback is the traditional way if a warrior had been killed. But the law is that the leaders must sit down with the Elders and work out the best way to carry out any punishment.*

As the warriors kept on pointing their spears at the settlers, their leader signalled to the white men they should climb back down the ridge.

When they began to pick up their weapons, another spear struck, pinning one of the men's trouser legs to the ground. Our Mob made it clear to the white men they had to leave their weapons on the ground.

The settlers walked back down those cliffs, watching the warriors out of the corners of their eyes. No more spears were thrown.

Later on, the station people gave this place a name. They called it Deadend Ridge.

As time went on, the settlers started to show our Mob a bit more respect. And we worked out there were some benefits in making peace with them. We told them which parts of the country they could safely run the cattle on, and they shared their meat with us when they slaughtered the animals.

Our people were good station hands, though they never got the pay they deserved. But the settlers did still 'allow' us to go hunting. For some reason, we could never get the white fellas to understand, it wasn't so much that we owned the Country, it was us that belonged to the Country.

But on this station, we still had our culture and our ceremonies. And when the ceremonies and the serious business was over, we used to have some fun. One of our all-time favourite dances was the one about Deadend Ridge.

The dancers would pretend they were settlers climbing up the ridge, getting angry when our warriors kept taunting them. They'd show how confused they got, up against the cliff face. Our people would sit around the ring, cross-legged and watching every move. No one would say a word.

Even though they knew the story, there would always be screams when the warriors jumped into the ring with their spears ready. Other dancers would show how scared the settlers were. Everyone would chuckle at that. Then they'd show the warriors allowing the white fellas to come back down the mountains, without their weapons.

This dance was always done at the end of our gatherings. And each year, we'd have a gathering with nearby Mobs, and the stories got passed down through generations. As the years went on, our people became sad when we'd hear the stories from the other Mobs, 'cos most of their stories didn't have happy endings. We got really scared when we heard how many of our people were killed up near Yungaburra and Cooktown and some of them other places.

They told us the settlers killed lots of people in their families, except they stole the young women. They destroyed lots of sacred sites and burial areas too, and the people who were left behind didn't have much food to eat. The gatherings became smaller and smaller. Our Mob couldn't understand why our brothers and sisters had been treated this way.

After Jammy told him his grandfather's story from long, long ago, the boss man just sat there looking at him. He didn't know what to say. There wasn't really anything he could say. Jammy took over again, seeing as how he knew the boss still wanted to fence a new paddock for the cattle.

We didn't burn no fences out there, boss. But maybe it was the spirits of our Old People who stirred up the lightning.

Fair enough, Jammy. So you reckon we ought to respect the agreement your people made with the original owners of this station?

I reckon, boss. And you must be a lot smarter than those early settlers. We didn't need to chuck any spears between your legs!"

Mark and Ric had been listening so intently, their beer was warm.

"That gorge you showed us behind the razor back ridge, was that where they had their big gatherings?" asked Ric.

"No, they would skirt right around the base of the outcrops and set up their gatherings on a grassy area on the other side. That gorge was where they had men's ceremonies. No women or children were allowed to go there, and no men, unless they'd been initiated. It was like it was a sacred place to these folks."

Mark moved his chair in closer. "And what happened to those Aboriginal families then?"

"They carried on living in the station camp and their living conditions improved a bit, but their pay didn't. Some men started making better money in the towns. Then in the mid-sixties, the government passed a law which said everyone had to be paid award wages. The station could only afford a few workers on award wages, so most of them were laid off. They drifted into the missions and the reserves."

"So, were there any Aboriginal people still on the station when you were young?" asked Ric.

"Yeah mate. There were quite a few families still here. In fact, when I was growing up, most of my mates were Aboriginal kids. But by the time I was in my twenties, even they had all gone. Those games we played as kids, they're still the memories I treasure most. But gees boys, I'm stuffed, it's been a long day. I'm off to bed."

Ric remained sitting on the old squatters' chair. "Why didn't we learn any of this stuff at school?"

Chapter 34

Events Move Quickly Now

North Queensland, September 1997

As Mark and Ric drove back to Cairns, Ric's phone lit up. He'd missed a call from his mum and another one from Nora. He'd also missed two calls from Cassie.

He listened to his mother's message. She sounded different, less defensive. She told him the family was organising a picnic at his favourite swimming hole. All family members were invited, and Uncle Harry might come over from Perth. Then she confused him at the end of the message by saying, "Ric, are you sure you'll be up for all this?"

Ric returned the call. "Hi Mum, yes of course I'd love to come. I have great memories of Crystal Cascades. And I haven't seen Uncle Harry for years."

"I know Ric, but will you want to share the news of your adoption with the whole family?"

"Why not? No sense in hiding it any longer, is there?"

"I suppose not. But I'm not sure I want to be there if you do. By the way, have you read the letter from your birth mum?"

"No, not yet. I wanted to get Cassie back up here to read it with me. But tell me, why wouldn't you want to come?"

"I've hidden that information from the family for so long, Ric. And depending on how they all react, it may not be very pleasant for me."

His mother's voice cracked. Ric wasn't sure how to respond. He couldn't bring himself to be empathetic with his mother. He was still angry with her.

Mark glanced at Ric, who was now squirming in his seat.

"Ric, could you let your mum know we're about to drive behind a long line of hills. We may lose the phone signal. Ask if you can call her back later."

Ric conveyed Mark's advice to his mum. She seemed grateful.

"I don't need to talk any more. Can I tell the family you'll come?"

"Yeah, sure Mum, I'll be there. And I'll call you tomorrow."

Turning to Mark, he said, "How did you get so bloody clever at handling these situations? You used to be a quiet, timid little kid, who never said much at all."

"It's a bit easier when you're not so emotionally involved, mate. Anyhow, you'd better see what Aunty Nora wants."

"Yeah," said Ric, clenching his jaw as he steeled himself for news about Wilbur.

Nora reported that Uncle was now back in the Coronary Care Ward. He was still asking to see Nadine and Ric, but Nadine didn't think that was a good idea.

"Aunty Nora, I have no idea what this is all about."

"Me neither. But there's something you should know about Uncle Wilbur. He makes out he's just a simple old man and it's true he never had much schooling. None of our people did in those days. But he seems to know things long before other people know. When we were kids, we used to think he was a Cleverman, a Medicine Man or something."

"Really?" said Ric, at once interested, but curious about where all this was going.

"I don't want you getting a big head or anything, but he's seen something in you, Ric. He said, 'That young feller's gonna be good for our people, but he's got so much to learn and he's so damn cocky as well. I want Nadine to help me with him, but she just won't do it.' Then he became all vague and wouldn't say any more."

"Thanks Aunty, he could be right about me being too cocky. But I'm not sure what to make of all that other stuff. I will go and see him tomorrow, though. Hey, did you get any information out of Nadine?"

"I tried, Ric. She reckoned she'd been through a lot of hard times, and she hadn't had much support from the family. When I pushed her a bit more, she clammed up."

"What did you make of that?"

"I know my sister, she's hiding something, and Uncle Wilbur must know what it is. And she's scared of something in her past life. What I can't understand is how it's got anything to do with you."

"I did tell Uncle Wilbur about my adoption, but he already knew, because my dad taught his nephews and nieces. They knew my mum wasn't pregnant as people had seen her in Townsville a couple of weeks before she showed up in Cairns with a new baby. They even thought I might have been one of you, but they could never prove it."

"What, you mean one of our family?"

"No, I don't think he meant that, just that I had some Murri features. He had thought I must have been born somewhere else and adopted here in Cairns. He said the Old People used to have links all around the state, but no one could ever find an Aboriginal woman who had given up her baby anywhere else in Queensland at that particular time."

"When were you born?"

Ric told her.

"Hey, that was the first year Nadine was in Sydney. Maybe she'd had a baby and not told us! But hang on, if she'd had a baby in Sydney and adopted it out, the baby would have been adopted in New South Wales. Were your parents living in NSW at any time?"

"No way Aunty, we're all Maroons, through and through."

Nora chuckled. "Well, so much for that theory. Maybe Nadine has come across something at the Community Care Agency. Maybe she's discussed it with Wilbur 'cos she often discusses her work with the Elders ... But Uncle is usually very careful with these sorts of things," said Nora, her voice trailing off again.

"It sure is a mystery, Aunty. But thanks for all your help. I reckon I'll go by myself to see Wilbur tomorrow. Maybe he'll tell me something, even though Nadine won't be there."

"Don't hold your breath," said Nora.

"Well, that puts paid to our first theory, for which I'm really grateful," said Ric, after finishing the call.

"How do you mean?" asked Mark.

"You know those way-out theories we had that maybe Nadine was my birth mother? Well, she can't be. She was away in Sydney at the time I was born. And babies born in New South Wales stayed in that state when they were adopted out."

"Yeah, that must be a relief," said Mark.

"For sure mate. If she did have a kid there, he would have ended up being a Blues supporter!"

The football allusion settled the matter for Ric.

"I wonder if there'll be any clues in my mum's letter. If only I could get Cassie to come back and read it with me. Have you had any more hints from Lou about what she's thinking?"

Mark pursed his lips. "Nah mate, and I'm not going to be your go-between either. You need to talk to her yourself. And if you've learnt anything in the last few weeks, you ought to change the way you talk to her, if you don't want to lose her altogether."

Ric jerked his head up. "What are you saying? Has she found someone else?"

Mark didn't answer.

"Hang on a minute. Has she been seeing that surfer dude from Straddie?"

Mark raised his eyebrows. "Why don't you listen to her messages, then just give her a call."

"Umm, I usually don't bother listening to her messages. I usually just ignore the message and call her back."

"Have you ever asked her how she feels about that approach?"

"No, not really."

"Have you ever asked her how she feels about other things?"

"Yeah, I sometimes ask her how she feels about me."

"Okay, but any other things?"

"Uh, I'm sure I must have, I just can't think of any at the moment. Hey Mark, haven't I asked you that sort of thing?"

"You have, Ric. When you arrived at boarding school, you asked me how I felt about football. That was the first time you asked me about my feelings. I think that may have been the last time too."

"Oh really? Shit … that's pretty bad, eh? Well, um, could you help me work out what to say to Cassie?"

"Ric, for Chrissake! I've never had a girlfriend, I'm probably the last person you should ask. Okay … maybe you could ask her about the things that are troubling her, or the things she'd like to do with her career, or something like that."

"Well, I thought I already knew how she felt about those things. I thought we were going to have a life together. But you're right, maybe I didn't actually check out what she wanted. But she never said anything different."

"Romance 101 Ric, or more likely, Relationships 101. Maybe you could start by putting yourself in her shoes and thinking about how you'd feel if your partner related to you the way you relate to her."

Chapter 35

Ric Tries a New Approach

North Queensland, September 1997

Ric slumped back into his seat, stunned by Mark's response. He spent the rest of the journey in quiet contemplation, punctured occasionally by a curt question to Mark. Just before they arrived back in Cairns, he listened to the messages from Cassie. As he hung up, he frowned at the phone. "She didn't say much, and she sure wasn't very warm in the first message. But she did sound a bit concerned in the second one."

"There you go Ric. You're not just listening to her words; you're listening for her feelings. Maybe there's hope for you yet!"

"Yeah, thanks. Now who's being arrogant? Maybe that's why you've never had a girlfriend. Sorry. Okay, when we get back, I think I'll just wander down to the beach and grab a bit of space. Then I'll put in a private call to Cassie."

As soon as they arrived in Palm Cove Ric walked away, cursing his knee as he limped down the path between the coconut palms. The sand would be even more challenging, but he needed to find a quiet spot, away from the backpackers and their constant chattering – like courting magpies, and just as annoying.

He eased himself onto the sand. An afternoon sea breeze blew on his face, soothing the tension in his body. He turned the handset away from the wind to make the call.

Cassie didn't answer. Her voice on the message bank was full of sparkle, which cheered him for a moment until he realised she'd recorded that message months ago. He thought about what sort of message he should leave. He tried to raise the tone of his voice.

"Hey Cassie, it's just me. We're back in Palm Cove. I'm sitting on the beach, thinking of you. Could you give me a call when you get a chance?"

Hey, that wasn't so hard ... well, it didn't come naturally either. Maybe Mark's right. Maybe I am a bit self-centred and egotistical. Maybe she is avoiding me. Maybe she's found someone else.

Ric tried walking around to calm himself. He wasn't looking down. He stumbled and overbalanced as he heard a small girl scream, "Daddy, that man kicked my sandcastle over!"

He fell, apologising to the girl and her father. As he tried to help them rebuild the sandcastle, the phone rang. He crawled away and dug out his phone.

"Hi Ric, how's it going?" Cassie's voice was back to its usual sparkle. His spirits lifted.

"Yeah, pretty good Cassie. I've got loads to tell you, but first, how are *you* going? Have you been getting a bit of peace without me there, harping on about my problems?"

Cassie hesitated. "Yeah, I guess I'm okay. I'm back at work and catching up with a few people in my spare time. But you sound different. Has something happened?"

Ric thought about whether to tell her everything that had happened, then decided not to. "Yeah, I've got lots to tell you, but that's not why I called, those things can keep until later. I just wanted you to know how much I've been missing you."

"Oh ... I guess I've missed you too, but I've been feeling really mixed up about everything. I know you're going through so much, but I'm just not sure I can handle it at the moment. I think I need some more space."

Okay, here goes!

"That's okay Cassie, you have to look after yourself too. I know I've been so focused on my own problems, and I've just dumped it all on you. I'll see if Mark can stay with me for another week or two."

"Aren't you going to tell me all the things you've discovered?" asked Cassie.

Ric responded with a quiet chuckle. "Sure I will, I'll bore you to tears with all my discoveries when we get some quiet time together. But today, I just want you to know I'm going to try to be different from now on."

Ric hadn't even mentioned the letter from his mum. That could wait. He *could* change, and then, Cassie *might* give him another chance.

They agreed she would call him in a few days' time, and he left it at that.

Straight away, Cassie phoned Lou. "I just talked to Ric, but it was really weird! He didn't talk about himself at all, he kept going on about how much he missed me. And Luke's just invited me to spend the weekend with him on Straddie."

"Are you going?"

"I was, but now I'm not so sure."

As Ric put the phone in his pocket, he noticed two shadows on the sand. The little girl and her father were standing next to him. "Are you going to be okay mate?" asked the father. "You done your ACL?"

"Yeah, how did you know?" said Ric.

"I've got the same scars, from a footy injury. Can I give you a hand?"

He pulled Ric to his feet. The little girl offered him her hand too, pretending to pull him up. Ric thanked them as they walked with him back to the path. He limped badly for the first few steps but eventually regained his usual stuffed-knee gait and made it back to his apartment.

"Hey Mark, I'm sorry about what I said before. You've been a good mate; you didn't deserve that."

"Yeah, that's okay. I was being arrogant. So how did things go with Cassie?"

"I think she was planning to break up with me."

Mark frowned.

"I did what you said. I put myself in her shoes. I had to keep urging myself to do it, but it worked. She's gone away to think about everything. She said she'll call me in the next few days. But she's not coming back to Cairns. So, I'm going to need you to stay another week or two."

"Sorry mate, I can only stay until next weekend. After that, I have to get back to Brisbane. I'm on call next week."

"Okay, maybe that'll be long enough, but I guess it all depends on what Uncle Wilbur wants to tell me."

Chapter 36

More Than He Ever Wanted to Know

North Queensland, September 1997

Ric arrived at the hospital to find Wilbur snoring in the Coronary Care Ward. The old man opened his eyes, reached for Ric's hand and grasped it firmly. "How you been?"

"I've been okay, Uncle Wilbur. We've been out bush, seen some interesting country and heard lots of wonderful stories. Hey, some of those stories were about your people."

"Yeah, that's good. I'd love to hear those stories, but first of all, I need to have a yarn with you. Where's that niece of mine, the one who calls herself Nadine these days?"

"Ah, I don't think she's coming up today. She's a bit wary of me. But she is setting up a meeting with some of the old ladies … um … Elders I meant to say."

Wilbur smiled. "What, them old girls? They'll love having a good-looking fella like you all to themselves. They'll spin you lots of yarns. Still, you may learn a few things. But they won't tell you what Nadine should be telling you, because they don' know about this thing."

Uncle Wilbur paused for a moment to catch his breath. "You sure she's not coming up today?"

"I don't think so, Uncle. I may have upset her."

"It's not anything you've done Ric, it's just who you are. I really wanted her to talk to you about this stuff when you were both here last time. But then my heart played up again. Now maybe I'm gonna have to tell you myself. Pull up a chair and make yourself comfortable. You might have noticed; I sometimes beat around the bush with my stories."

Ric smiled and settled back in the chair. He was beginning to enjoy old people's stories. Wilbur's style was even more circuitous than Bill's. Firstly, Ric had to know what a tomboy Nadine had been as a young girl, but she was also a real good looker, and she started to get mixed up with a bunch of older boys.

Her family could see what was happening, so they decided to move off the reserve and into town. Then when she finished school, she went away to university down in Townsville. She used to come home to Cairns on holidays, but she'd always go back to the reserve to see her aunties and her grannies.

"One time, she met a young white fella who was working out there. It looked pretty serious for a while, but she broke it off. The next thing we knew, she'd taken off to Sydney and joined up with that radical lot."

"Right," said Ric.

Wilbur went quiet. Ric sensed that the old man was peering with his one good eye, straight through Ric's eyes and into his mind.

"Naddie told me it was you who really saved my life. She said she almost froze up, but even with your bung knee, you got down and kept my heart pumping until the ambulance came. I think it was meant to be, Ric."

"How do you mean, Uncle? I've done CPR lots of times. When you're a doctor, it's like second nature."

"That may be so, but I think you can probably do other stuff too, things you don't learn in no medical school."

Ric frowned and glanced at Wilbur, to find the old man looking intently at him again. His skin started to prickle, that same feeling he'd noticed a lot recently.

"Do you ever have strange things come into your head, from out of nowhere?"

The goose bumps spread all over Ric's body. His mind swirled. Shapes entered his mind, this time all jumbled together. He spoke slowly. "Yeah, sort of. Sometimes my mind gets – distracted, I suppose. But how did you know I was seeing things?"

"It will take a while to explain all this. You sure you got plenty of time?"

Ric nodded, trying to remain calm. His jerking knee betrayed him.

"When I was younger, I got really angry. I used to go out and work on cattle stations, just as hard as the white station hands, but I only got about a quarter of their pay, and even that went into a bank account controlled by the local buliman … that old cop never let me have much of my money."

"It was a long while before it dawned on me why we were being treated this way. I got all fired up and tried to change everything. The manager of the reserve threatened to send me to Palm Island, where they used to send all the so-called 'troublemakers' in those days. I started drinking heavily. That's when those scenes started coming to me."

Ric's knee stopped jerking. "*You* started seeing things, Uncle Wilbur?"

Wilbur chuckled. "I thought that might get your attention. Yeah, I saw things all right. I gave up the booze because I reckoned it might have been the grog talking. I've never touched it since, but those scenes kept on coming."

"What did you do?"

"I told the Elders what was happening. They helped me understand and they taught me about our culture. Up till then, I'd never wanted to know. They also explained there used to be some other fellas in our Mob who had this same ability."

Ric shifted in his chair, wondering how this story could be of any relevance to him. He kept trying to interrupt, but Wilbur stayed him with an extended palm and a stern look.

"I want to tell you something else as well. It's about what happened after Nadine broke it off with that young white fella. I heard her and Nancy talking – Nancy was her mother. They had some terrible arguments. I didn't know what they wuz arguing about, but I did hear her tell her mother she was gutless for not taking on the system."

Ric frowned, trying to grasp where this story was going.

"I was disgusted with Nadine for saying that to her mother. But then I saw in my mind, what happened to her mother. That helped me understand why Nadine is the way she is."

"What happened, Uncle?"

"That's something Nadine will have to tell you Ric, it wouldn't be right for me to say. But after that, I cut her a lot of slack. When she came to see me after my heart attack, I told her about what I'd seen when she was a young woman."

Ric squirmed. His gut churned, the fear rising in his brain. He willed the seeing not to begin again. He didn't want to know what had happened to Nadine's mum. His face went pale for a moment until he recovered a little, and Wilbur continued.

"After I told Nadine I'd seen all this so long ago, she got 'especially furious with me for not telling her back then. It was only because she thought I was gonna die that she backed off. But you see Ric, I've never felt that Nancy would want me to know."

"So that's what you wanted her to tell me, Uncle, whatever it was that happened to her mum? But if she'd bottled it up and been angry about it all her life, why would she want to share all that stuff with me?

"Well, she doesn't actually *want* to share anything with you, but that's the problem. When I was in that ICU, I saw you, sort of at a crossroads, needing to make a big choice in your life. And I saw Nadine there with you too. I know, deep in my heart, Nadine could tell you many things that would help you make sense of everything."

Wilbur closed his eyes. He did look exhausted from the long speech. He was an old man, recovering from a life-threatening incident, and trying his best to help the situation. He had every right to be exhausted.

Ric remained sitting at his bedside, not at all surprised when Wilbur raised one eyelid and gave him a wry smile.

Chapter 37

Ric Has Second Thoughts

North Queensland, September 1997

Back at Palm Cove, Ric didn't sleep well. The scenes he'd tried to suppress had surfaced again in his dreams. He lay awake trying to recall the details. He failed, although he had no difficulty remembering the fear.

Later in the morning, Mark ferried him over to see Nadine, then took off to the library to do more research.

Nadine met Ric at the door of her office. "Gees, you look like shit! Have you been on the grog again? Are you sure you're up to meeting the Elders this morning?"

As she led him down the corridor, Ric gritted his teeth. "Yeah, thanks Nadine. I had nothing at all to drink last night. I spent the afternoon with Uncle Wilbur, then I went to bed early."

Nadine stopped so suddenly that Ric almost ran into her. As she whirled around to face him, her face contorted. "What did he tell you?"

"Ah, we talked about what's been happening to me. He seemed to sense what I've been going through. He's experienced similar things."

"What sort of things?"

"Could I have a bit of time with you after the meeting with the Elders? It's a bit too complicated to tell you now."

"Hmm," said Nadine, turning to move on.

"But some of the things he told me, were about you."

Nadine whirled around again, the blood coursing into her face.

"Uncle Wilbur said he understood why you feel the way you do, why you get so — passionate about things. But there were some other things he wouldn't tell me; he said it was up to you to tell me yourself."

"I bet he didn't use the word 'passionate'. There are lots of other words that old bugger uses to describe me, most of them not very complimentary."

Nadine said no more until she ushered him into the meeting room. There, she was formal and respectful when she introduced the Elders.

They in turn tried to maintain their dignity at first, welcoming him to Country and asking about Albie and the other boys. It wasn't long before one cracked a joke, which started them all giggling like teenagers.

Annie was the oldest, a large woman with wispy white hair hanging loosely above her shoulders. She wore an ancient pair of spectacles which she constantly pushed back onto the bridge of her nose. Though she laughed often, she watched Ric closely.

"Where you from, Ric?" asked Annie.

"Ah, I was born up here in Cairns, um, Aunty … Can I call you all 'Aunty'?" asked Ric, looking embarrassed. This brought on more peals of laughter.

"We call *her* Aunty, but you can call me Pearl," said the slim woman with the high cheekbones, the one who wore her dark hair in a tight ponytail.

She turned to a stocky woman with yellow tinges in her brown hair. "You can call this one Ginny. We the young ones," she said, drawing herself high in the chair to strike a pose.

Ric was embarrassed, not knowing how to respond, until Ginny smacked his thigh, laughing again. Ric managed a tentative smile.

"Who your Mob?" asked Annie, again looking intently at Ric.

"Aunty, I'm ashamed to say I really don't know. I do know I was adopted at birth, which I didn't suspect until recently. I went to see my mum, the one who brought me up, and she told me that was true. She said my birth mum didn't want me to know her name, and then last week, she gave me a letter from her."

"What did the letter say?" asked Ginny.

"Ah, I haven't opened it yet. I've been pretty busy." All four women frowned. "I was hoping to open it with my girlfriend, but she took off to Brisbane and I'm not sure if she's ever coming back." Ric cleared his throat.

"Anyhow, my best mate came up to drive me around, and he took me out to his grandpa's cattle station. We went up to Deadend Ridge as well. Then since I've been back, I've spent a lot of time with Uncle Wilbur. Yeah, pretty busy. I've got the letter locked up safely in the glove box of the hire car."

Ginny looked over to Annie and Pearl. They seemed to be communicating something. After what seemed like hours, Annie spoke. "Naddie, bring us some tea and biscuits."

Ric prepared himself to hear a broadside from Nadine. She strode across the room and sent a questioning look towards Annie, which was followed by a response he was unable to read.

Nadine spoke quietly. "I'll bring the tea Aunty, but it looks like you're going to need lunch as well."

The tension eased from Ric's body as he began to feel comfortable with the Elders. They were treating him as if they'd known him forever. He had no idea why he'd earned their acceptance.

"Have you got one of those fancy new phones with you?" asked Ginny.

"Oh yes, sure, I'll turn it off," said Ric, fumbling in his backpack.

"First of all, why don't you call your mate and see if he'll come and join us. We could be here quite a while."

Ric looked around at the others. They smiled their encouragement. He phoned Mark, explaining the situation. Mark agreed to come in. "Oh, another thing Mark. Could you get that letter out of the glove box for me?"

The Elders' faces relaxed in unison.

"That old rascal Wilbur, eh? His heart must be getting better. He's got our Nadine here, all riled up," said Pearl.

When Mark came in, he handed the envelope to Ric, who held it for a while, then dropped it on the coffee table, causing Nadine to frown.

Nadine's face was stony. "So your birth mum has written you a letter, saying she never wanted you to know who she was. Are you going to respect her wishes, Ric?"

"I think so. But I haven't read the letter yet. It was opened by my mum when I was little."

"Why haven't you read it?" asked Nadine.

Pearl spoke up. "Nadine, Ric's been trying to work things out. He's spent a lot of time with your Uncle Wilbur."

Nadine screwed up her face. "I know, Aunty. Uncle Wilbur mentioned that on the phone just now. He's told Ric things he had no right to tell him. But he also said Ric now knows for sure he was adopted. Were you ever going to share that piece of information with me, Ric?"

"I was, when I met with you after this meeting."

"Right," said Nadine, pouring tea for everyone, and saying no more.

Annie talked about what happened to children in the old days. She also told them about how the people used to live, and about the old clan gatherings. Neither Ric nor Mark was surprised when she told them what had happened at Deadend Ridge.

"Oh, you must have known my people at the station," said Mark.

"We did," said the Elders, without adding any more detail.

"It wasn't always a good place for our Mob, Mark," said Nadine.

Annie reached over and patted her knee. "Leave it for now, Naddie."

Nadine walked out of the room, leaving the Elders to engage in small talk. She returned carrying a huge tray loaded with sandwiches and fruit. Ric and Mark ate frugally, each unsettled by the morning's events. The Elders had no such reluctance, wolfing down the sandwiches but eating the fruit only after encouragement from Nadine.

"You told your mate to bring the letter in, Ric. Are you thinking of opening it now?" asked Annie.

"Well, I have to open it sometime," said Ric, reaching for the envelope and carefully removing the old letter. He smiled wryly when he saw that it was written on Cairns City Hospital letterhead.

"Ric!" said Nadine, almost screaming at him.

He looked up to see Nadine's face contorted. His mind raced through conjectures. *Had she written the letter? Was she about to be exposed?* Ric continued to stare at Nadine, his hand frozen on the old letter paper.

"Listen to me, Ric," said Nadine. The tone of her voice had changed. It was no longer shrill, it was soft, almost motherly. "I think you should wait until you can read it with Cassie."

"I'm not sure whether Cassie ever wants to see me again."

"Ric, you've probably worked out that I can be a real bitch at times. This is one time I'm not being a bitch. I only met your girlfriend once. It wasn't the best of circumstances, I know. But I saw that she was a strong, caring young woman.'

"Umm, yeah she usually is."

"I'm not surprised you two have run into difficulties. I don't think you realise what sort of woman you have there. If you let her go, you could regret it for the rest of your life."

The Elders exchanged looks.

"Maybe Nadine's right. Maybe you should wait until you see your girlfriend. If you show her some respect by saving this letter to read with her, she'll know how important she is to you," said Ginny, to encouraging nods from Annie and Pearl, and a look of relief from Nadine.

Ric folded the letter, carefully inserted it back into the envelope and handed it to Mark. "You look after it, mate. I think I'll fly back to Brisbane with you this weekend."

Each of the Elders had stories to tell and advice to give, all of which helped Ric to broaden his understanding of how so many Aboriginal children were adopted or fostered to white families in earlier days.

Once they were sure Ric understood, Annie said, "Well, now it's time for my nanny nap." The others promptly stood and gathered their belongings.

"Come and see us again when you're back in Cairns, Ric," said Ginny.

"Ah, I'm not sure if I'm coming back, Aunty."

"You'll be back," said Annie.

Chapter 38

Nadine Softens

North Queensland, September 1997

Nadine packed the remaining food into carry bags for the Elders to take home. After they'd gone, she said to Ric, "Well let's have that meeting now. Would you like your mate to stay?"

"It's okay," said Mark. "I've found some old books in the library. They're about the early settlers in Grandpa's country."

"It wasn't always your grandpa's land," said Nadine. "It was Aboriginal land. We believe it always will be. Our people and our ancestors belong to that Country."

Mark frowned and shook his head.

Ric intervened. "Mate, I'm going to see Uncle Wilbur again later this week. Why don't you come and see him with me? We could talk about all these things."

After Mark had gone, Ric said, "Nadine, I do think you're being a bit hard on Mark, but never mind, that will keep till later. I want to ask you something. Was there another reason why you didn't want me to read my letter here and now?"

"What? You didn't believe what I said. You think I was just faking my concern for you? That I don't have any idea about relationships? I wasn't always a stroppy old bitch."

Ric remained silent.

"You know Uncle Wilbur thinks you may be one of us?"

"Yes, I think my face reminds him of someone."

"It's more than that. As I said, he has … insights … about people and events. He's picked up something in you." Nadine suddenly seemed to realise another possibility. "Do you see things like he does?"

"Ah, I don't think so. Well, maybe I do. Lately I have been seeing things, sometimes in dreams, sometimes when I'm wide awake."

Ric watched as a startled expression spread over Nadine's face. He was puzzled.

"Does that happen to you, too?"

"No Ric, it's not that. I've got enough problems with the things I find out the regular way. But something's just occurred to me. Do you already know some of my secrets?"

Ric frowned, again unsure what to say. This time, the tingling spread from his back right down his legs. He didn't have time to work out how to answer that question.

"I *was* pregnant once Ric, my family doesn't know, but Uncle Wilbur does."

Ric took a deep breath and told himself to think quickly.

"Was that when you were in Sydney?"

"Right, so you *do* know these things?"

Ric laughed. "I only know you went away to Sydney unexpectedly. And I didn't see that in my mind. It was your sister Nora who told me."

"Nora? What does *she* know? Did she know I was pregnant?" asked Nadine, her voice rising.

"Nora never told me you were pregnant."

"But you *knew* I was pregnant?"

"No, I didn't actually *know* you were pregnant. But when you were so wary, even antagonistic, with me, I started to imagine things. At that time, I was desperate to find my real mother. But now I have a letter from her."

Nadine's face remained expressionless.

"You must be very good at poker," said Ric.

When all he got was a scowl from Nadine, he decided to press on.

"I started to wonder if you were trying to push me away, because you'd realised you were my mother. But then I worked out I would have been born during the time you were in Sydney."

"What? I thought you were older than that!" blurted out Nadine. "I thought you would have been born before I went off to Sydney."

Nadine looked rattled. Ric tried to keep his feelings in check. "So, did you have the baby adopted?"

Nadine flushed. "I did have the baby adopted. I never told my family. But did you really think I was your mother?"

"The possibility did occur to me at that time."

"And how did you feel about that?"

"Ah, I didn't know what to feel. I wondered why you were so angry with the world, well mostly with white people, and particularly with me. But most of all, I wondered if you would accept me."

"Right," said Nadine. "Thanks for being honest with me. There *are* some things I'd like to tell you. Like how it feels to adopt out your baby, and the turmoil of emotions you go through, not just at the time, but for the rest of your life."

Tears welled in Nadine's eyes and dripped down her cheek. Ric sat quietly, listening, and trying to empathise, but struggling to comprehend her swings of behaviour.

Nadine finally composed herself.

"You know Ric, my mind was so stuffed up at that time, I never identified the baby as Aboriginal. Now when I work with our Link Up people, I meet all these Aboriginal kids who've been taken away from their mums and brought up by white people. And they're desperate to find their Aboriginal families."

Ric stayed quiet.

"But my baby wasn't taken away, I *gave* him away!"

"Yeah, I think I understand, but you were probably very young at the time."

"My baby may never even *know* his mum was Aboriginal," said Nadine, who now seemed desperate to blurt things out. "I've spent my whole life feeling guilty and ashamed. Maybe all this shit I put out, is a shield to stop anyone getting too close. And then you turned up."

Ric had tears building in his eyes. Nadine laughed.

"I bet you didn't expect us to be like this."

"That's for sure."

"Anyhow, I don't want to say any more right now. Maybe I will, later on. Maybe not."

"Nadine, I want you to know that Wilbur didn't tell me any of what you've just told me, but he did tell me one thing. He said he'd seen you and your mother in his mind. He said you were arguing, and he knew what you were arguing about. He didn't say any more, but I thought you should know he told me that much."

Nadine's face went pale. She swayed on the chair. Ric caught her shoulders before she fell. When she settled, he apologised for upsetting her.

Nadine touched his hand.

"It's okay Ric. Thanks for telling me. There are some things I've kept bottled up for so long. I don't know if I'll ever be ready to talk about them."

Ric walked out to the front office and arranged for a staff member to drive her home.

When Ric called Mark, he told him in strictest confidence that Nadine had adopted out a baby. "I know you're unhappy with how she's treated you, but I sense there's been a lot of pain in her life."

Ric decided to phone Cassie. To his relief, she picked up this time. "I'm coming home this weekend. Mark has to get back to work, so I'm travelling with him. But first of all, we have another family gathering, and this one's at a waterhole I love, so it might be a bit more relaxed."

"That's good," said Cassie. "In fact, that's really good. You're sounding a lot better. Is it because your knee has improved?"

"Yeah, my knee has improved a little, I can walk without the stick now. But it's not so much because of my knee, it's my head that's better. Anyhow Cassie, I just want to say, there are lots of things we need to talk about when I see you again."

Chapter 39

A Family Full of Surprises

North Queensland, September 1997

When they arrived at Crystal Cascades, Ric's uncle Steven was the first to greet them. He pulled Ric over to meet a fit-looking man in his late forties.

Ric studied the man's features carefully before finally breaking into a smile. "Uncle Harry! It's great to see you."

"And look at you Ric, you're even bigger than me now! And you're a professional footballer too."

"I was, until I tore my ACL. Are you the reason why the family put on another gathering?"

Steven butted in. "Actually Ric, Harry wasn't the reason for the gathering, *you* were. When we heard you'd discovered you were adopted, we all wanted you to know you're still very much part of the family, and we all still love you, mate. Then when Harry heard that Sis was organising this, he made a special effort to fly over from Perth to join us."

On cue, Cecilia and Ted came over. "So how do you feel Ric, now your suspicions are confirmed?" asked Ted.

"Don't mind him, he's always putting his foot in it," said Cecilia, giving Ted a withering look.

Ric's initial irritation faded as he looked around the room and realised Ted had verbalised the question the whole family would have wanted to ask.

"It's a fair question Aunty Sis so I'll answer it the best way I can. At first, I was pretty angry with Mum and Dad for not telling me, but I did understand they were trying to protect me. I've talked to a lot of people since, and I've realised how little I knew about why a mother might give her child up for adoption."

Ric noticed that some of his aunts were tearing up, one in particular. He continued.

"By the way, are Mum and Dad coming tonight?"

Cecilia replied. "I'm sorry Ric. Your father just called saying Margaret's not feeling well." She lowered her voice. "She's had a difficult time in the last few weeks. She wanted me to tell you she accepts they should have told you earlier, and she understands why you were angry, but she just couldn't face us all today."

A hush fell over the gathering.

"I'll go over there and give her a call," said Ric.

The conversations remained subdued until he returned.

"I've had a good talk with Mum. She's okay now, she might even join us later."

Ric sensed that his relatives were exhaling the breath they had been holding for a very long time.

When his parents arrived, he made a point of hugging them and ensuring they tagged along as he spoke to everyone in the room.

Later, when he said his farewells, he mentioned he was heading to Brisbane that weekend, but he wouldn't leave it so long before he returned.

At breakfast the next day, Mark and Ric discussed the gathering, and all the snippets of information he'd gathered during his visit to north Queensland. After a feeble attempt to make sense of it all, they agreed that time may help to put everything into perspective. Ric was beginning to feel settled until Aunt Cecilia called.

"Ric, how are you this morning?"

"I'm good Aunty Sis. Hey thanks for organising yesterday. It was great to get everything out in the open. Mum and Dad seemed pretty relaxed by the end of it."

"Yes, it was good you took the initiative there, Ric. Ah … can I come over to see you this morning?"

"Sure," said Ric, after a moment's hesitation. "Is Mum all right today?"

"Yes, Margaret's fine, it's not about her. It's just something I need to discuss with you."

"Well Aunty Sis, Mark and I are sitting here at the beach, having a yarn. Would you like to join us?"

"Umm, can I speak with you privately?"

"Oh … Okay. I'll see you soon."

Ric turned to Mark. "Aunty Sis wants to talk privately. I wonder what that's about?"

"No idea, mate. Hey listen, I'll nick off anyway. I want to catch up with that psychiatrist I met at Ron's place, before we head back to Brisbane."

Ric's aunt Cecilia arrived with a serious look on her face.

"Is everything alright?" asked Ric.

"That depends on how you look at things."

Cecilia flopped into a chair and took a deep breath.

"Did you ever think it strange that I didn't move out until you were eleven?"

Ric thought for a while, trying to recall his childhood. "I didn't think it was strange, I thought it was wonderful! Whenever mum and dad were busy, I had you to play with. I do think you spoiled me though."

Cecilia smiled. "Maybe I did spoil you a bit. Do you think that's made it harder for you to work things out with Cassie?"

"I don't think it's your fault, Aunty Sis. I think I just got a big head when I succeeded so well with both the footy and the medical career. But yeah, I've learnt a lot about myself in the last few weeks. I've worked out I need to try harder with Cassie. Hey, is that why you've come over, because you were worried about me and Cassie?"

"Well partly, Ric. And it's partly because I wanted to ask you in person, how you're feeling about being adopted."

"I think I'm okay about it now. And of course, I've got my birth mother's letter to read yet."

"Remember yesterday you said you've learnt how adopting mothers feel. That's a pretty big call for a young male to make. Ric, I know you've got a lot to deal with at the moment, but do you think you could cope with a bit more?"

Chapter 40

Aunt Cecilia

North Queensland, September 1997

Ric studied his aunt's face. "You mean you'd like to tell me why you lived so long at our place?"

"Yes. That, and maybe other things too."

The prickling sensations returned. "Have you always known I was adopted?"

"Yes, I worked it out and so did most of the family. But none of us ever raised it with Margaret. She was pretty uptight about the whole thing, so we decided to respect her wishes. We expected she would tell us sooner or later, but she never did."

"Right. So why did you stay on living at our place?"

"Yes, well that's a long story, and you may find it a bit unsettling."

"If it's something you want to tell me, I'm keen to hear it, Aunty Sis."

Cecilia began with a confession. "When I was fifteen, I was a bit of a rebel, and I ran away from home. The police tracked me down and brought me back, but I kept running away again. One time, I hitched a ride down to Brisbane with a truckie."

"Hey Aunty Sis, you took a big risk there."

"Yes, I know. I was so lucky he was a decent bloke. He treated me like his own daughter and told me I could stay with his family until I sorted things out."

"Did you let anyone know where you were?"

"After a couple of days, I decided I'd keep in touch with someone in the family, so they wouldn't send the police after me again. Your Mum was the person I decided to call. And I only told Margaret where I was, on the condition she didn't tell our mother."

"Wow, was Mum any help to you?"

"She was okay, I didn't tell her much. I managed to get a job as a waitress, then I fell in with the wrong crowd and moved into a share house. I started drinking and partying and before long, I was doing drugs. I never did any shooting up, but I did smoke bongs, and I took all the party drugs I could get my hands on."

"I'm finding it hard to think of you as a wild teenager. To me, you were always my sweet aunty."

"Yeah well, I was pretty wild alright. I met some musicians who'd come down from Cairns. Even though I wasn't yet sixteen, I started travelling with them, and we eventually turned up back in Cairns. I'd fallen for one of the guys and I was living with him by then."

"In Cairns? At fifteen years old, you were living with someone in your own hometown, and your family didn't know?"

"Yes. You'd be surprised how easy it is to lie low in your own city. But with musos, you often work all night and sleep all day. I kept up my weekly phone call to Margaret, but I let her think I was still living with the family in Brisbane. Eventually, the band broke up. My boyfriend and I picked up some work here and there, and then we moved into our own place."

"But you still didn't see your family?"

"I really wanted to see my mother, but by then we were into the drugs big time. We started fighting, kept breaking up and then getting back together again. My boyfriend finally decided to stop using, and he picked up a job as a courier. I kept on using, so he told me he'd leave for good if I didn't get myself clean."

"Wow, so that was what made you give the drugs away?"

"No, I told him to bugger off, thinking he'd miss me and be back again soon. But I never saw him again. He did send me a message via one of his mates, who said he was still hoping I'd give up the drugs. Then his mate said, 'he told me to tell you he already knows' ... that was a really curious thing to say, eh?"

"What did he already know?' asked Ric.

"His mate said he had no idea, and then he walked off. Anyway, I put it out of my mind. I wasn't going back to my family as a homeless druggie, so I booked into rehab, and went through the horrors for a while. When I got clean, I was desperate to reconnect with my family, but there were a few other things I had to do first."

Cecilia stood and paced around the room, then suddenly excused herself and went to the bathroom.

"Aunty Sis," said Ric when she returned, "you've shared a lot about your personal life with me today. I do find it a bit disturbing but most of all, I'm concerned for you. Why are you telling me all this? Would you like me to try to find someone who can help you?"

"No Ric, I just wanted you to know, so you didn't always have me on a pedestal. And … I'm okay these days, well most of the time."

"Was it Mum who invited you to come and stay with us?"

"At first, Margaret was disgusted, outraged I'd been deceiving her. She basically read me the riot act. She said I could stay at your place until I sorted myself out."

"Okay, so that explains why you first came to live with us, but it doesn't explain why you stayed so long."

"Yes, I know. But after I got on top of things, I realised Margaret was doing it tough with you as her new baby, struggling to get enough sleep. I offered to help her, and it turned out to be good for both of us. Then of course, our mum got breast cancer and died when you were a few months old."

"Yeah, I never knew her."

"No. Margaret went to pieces after Mum died. John asked me to stay on to help her. Months turned into years, and I ended up being your part-time live-in aunty."

Ric knew Cecilia had told her story with love and warmth in her eyes, but there was something else. He wondered if she resented spending so many years looking after him when she was so young herself.

Cecilia seemed anxious to continue her story. "By the time you were getting ready for high school, Margaret was fine, so I decided it was time for me to spread my wings again."

"You must have been heading towards your late twenties by then, around the same age I am now."

"Yes, I was. I moved into a share flat, scored a job in an accounting firm, and met Ted."

Ric grimaced.

"Yeah, I know, he's a bit full on, but he really is a kind, lovely man underneath. And he's good with the kids."

Ric's face relaxed. "So things have finally worked out for you, Aunty Sis?"

"Yeah, they have … I'm content now."

Ric detected the slight uncertainty in her response. He tried hard to stay quiet in case there was more she wanted to say. Cecilia said no more, waiting for Ric to speak.

"Aunty Sis, I've been thinking and behaving like a child longer than most people my age. When you're studying Medicine, you feel like a school kid for six long years at uni, then you're suddenly confronted with life and death, and everything changes."

"Yes, it must be difficult when suddenly, people's lives depend on you."

"That's true. But until recently, I've never reflected on my childhood enough to realise you'd been through all these hassles. I'm really sorry I never understood what was happening to you."

Cecilia smiled as tears dripped down her face. "Ric, you were only little, and I wouldn't have expected you to know. But now you're all grown up and finding out about your own history, I thought I'd share these things with you."

"I'm really glad you did, Aunty Sis. Oh by the way, we're flying back to Brisbane on the weekend. Would you like to come over for lunch again before we go? You could meet up with Mark if he hasn't got himself glued to the library desk."

"I would Ric. Well, maybe. Let's just see how the week goes."

As his aunt drove away, something gnawed at Ric's brain. He was trying to process all she'd said, and why she had such a need to share it all with him. Then he remembered. Just before he'd asked her why she was telling him, she'd said there were other things she had to do first. He couldn't recall her telling him what those things were.

Chapter 41

You Can Get Too Much Information

North Queensland, September 1997

Ric was still pondering Cecilia's conversation when Nadine called. "Where're you staying Ric? I'm coming over."

"Hey Nadine, you don't need to do that. I'll ask Uncle Wilbur not to tell me any more of your business, so you won't have to worry about that happening again."

"Ric, that old bugger has got himself into a tizz. There is no way you could stop him saying what he wants to say. He thinks he knows everything, but there are some pieces in the puzzle even *he* doesn't know. I need to talk to you first. You got any cold beer?"

"Er, yep, I've got some light beers in the fridge."

"That'll have to do then," said Nadine, abruptly hanging up.

Ric wandered around the apartment trying to clear his brain. *Why does Nadine want to see me again? Bloody hell, everyone wants to tell me things these days.*

Soon, there was a rap on the door.

"You whiteys are always locking yourselves in, when you're not locking us out," said Nadine, with an evil smile. "You sure you don't have any full-strength beer?"

As Nadine appeared to be back to her old abrasive self, Ric responded in kind. "That serious, eh? No sorry Nadine, light beer is all I've got. Anyhow, you're driving."

"You've got a big couch; I reckon I could doss here."

Ric frowned as he watched her scout around the room like a broody hen, deciding where to roost.

Nadine's voice softened. "You remember I told you I adopted out my baby because I'd got pregnant to the wrong man. Well, I have to admit he wasn't actually a bad man. He took all the shit I gave him, and he kept coming back for more. The oldies thought he'd be good for me too. I just walked out on him and took off to Sydney even before I knew I was pregnant."

"And now you're going to tell me why?"

"I think you already know."

"Because he was white?"

"Correct. Up until that time, I hadn't even noticed what colour he was … well, maybe I had. Lots of guys used to flirt with me in those days. With the white guys, I used to lead them on. They thought us black girls were an easy lay."

Ric screwed up his face.

Nadine nodded slowly.

"Oh yeah. I used to love seeing the shock in their eyes when a black girl dumped them. But this white guy was different. He cared about me, and about what I wanted to do with my life. I'd never come across a guy like that."

"So why did you dump him again?"

Nadine laughed. "Well young Ric, you're about as subtle as me today."

"Sorry."

"The reason I dumped him was because he was white."

"But you just said he was different to the other white guys."

"He was. But I was just so angry and disgusted with how white people treated us."

"And you've been like that ever since? Hating all white people for what they've done to your people?"

"Pretty much. Yes."

"I'm starting to understand why you might feel that way. I've become aware of things I've never noticed before. Like no one I know has ever invited an Aboriginal person into their home, and the only Aboriginal people I knew up till now were the guys in my footy team."

"You're getting there, Ric. Our Mob has already noticed you're more accepting than most white people. Your mate Mark, he tries to understand, but it's all head-stuff for him."

"He's a really decent bloke."

"Hmm, maybe. I think he'll get there sooner or later, but he needs to get off his intellectual perch and get to know our people, if he really wants to understand."

"Yeah, okay. But I'm thinking you didn't come here to give me a lesson on racism. I suspect you came here to tell me why you began to hate white people. It's something personal, right?"

" Yeah, you're right, but you need to understand the politics first. And there's something I need to know about you. I need to know about your ... gift."

"My gift?"

"Don't bullshit me, Ric! I know you have the gift. Uncle Wilbur virtually said as much. You just know things. You see things."

Ric realised Nadine was watching him closely. He wasn't sure whether he was looking alarmed, or guilty or embarrassed. But he knew his face had given him away.

"Of course you do," said Nadine. "First Uncle Wilbur, then my young cousin, now you."

"I'm not sure if I have any special gift, Nadine. In fact, some people think I'm losing my mind, seeing things that aren't there. I know Mark is concerned I may have a mental illness, that's probably why he's keeping an eye on me."

"I'm not interested in what Mark thinks. What I want to know is, have I been in any of these scenes you've been seeing?" Nadine looked directly into his eyes. "You don't have to answer, it's clear on your face. And was my mum Nancy there too?"

Ric squirmed. "A couple of times recently, I started to see a younger version of you with an older woman. You seemed to be arguing. For some reason, I did assume she was your mother. Then I started to feel, more than see, what you were talking about."

Nadine gasped.

"I knew it would be wrong for me to continue. I concentrated really hard to put it out of my mind. But it just keeps coming back, day and night."

Nadine exhaled.

"Thanks, Ric. You showed respect to me and my mum by pushing those things away. But you won't be able to suppress them forever, not unless you go on medication. Uncle Wilbur did that once. It worked for a while, but he said he felt like a zombie. I don't want you to do that, at least not for me."

"You want me to let that scene play out in my head?"

"No Ric. I want to tell you about it myself."

Ric opened another beer, grimacing as he handed one to Nadine. "I can see why you asked if I had anything stronger."

"Yeah," said Nadine proceeding to tell her mother's story.

Chapter 42

Nadine's Story About Her Mother

North Queensland, September 1997

"My mother, Nancy, grew up on a cattle station. Her family was treated well for those times. They had food and shelter, and some of them earned a small wage. As my mother grew older, she became friendly with one of the station owner's boys, the oldest one."

"When he was a teenager, he was sent off to boarding school down in Charters Towers. Mum's family and the boy's family all assumed that would break them up and they would go their separate ways, which would be best for all concerned."

"Mum was realistic. She knew he'd inherit the station, and she'd never be accepted as the station owner's wife. She tried to make a life for herself. She got friendly with one of the nurses at the clinic, where she'd often volunteer to help with the babies. The nurse was impressed with her work and arranged to get her into a hospital to do nurse aide training."

"Each year when the boy came home on holidays, his father would take him away to stock camps for weeks at a time. He and Nancy would see each other when they could. They'd kiss and hold hands, but Nancy realised the boy was being kept away from her. She was even more convinced when the station manager offered to pay her fares, so she could go to the hospital for an interview."

"Anyway, she was accepted into training and was due to commence the following month. She was about sixteen at the time, and the boy was the same, and about to go back for his last year at the college. When he found out Nancy was going into town to train as a nurse aide, he was upset."

"He told her when he finished college, he wanted her to leave the station and come to the city with him. He was obviously a love-struck teenager with stars in his eyes. You would understand why if you saw a picture of her at that age. She was a real stunner. But as I said, Nancy was a realist. She really cared about the boy. She knew they'd be happy for a while, but his family would never accept her."

"Nancy was stronger than that. She left the station and went to stay with her aunt in the nearby town, planning to lay low until she started at the hospital. Her aunt asked Nancy to help with her cleaning job. Aunty used to clean the school and the clinic at night and the pub during the day."

"The boy talked to her cousins who told him where she was. He arranged an overnight stay at the hotel in the town, aiming to surprise her while she was at work. He went in on the Friday night before he headed back to college."

Nadine looked out the window. Ric could see she was swallowing hard and holding back tears. She shook her head violently and dropped her face into her hands. When she lifted her head, she was staring straight at him but when she spoke again, her voice was flat.

"Some men from the neighbouring station were in town that day. They'd seen Nancy cleaning at the pub in the morning. They found her at the school that night while her aunt was working at the clinic. They offered her a bottle of sherry, but she refused and told them to go back to the pub. She finished cleaning the school and was hurrying over to join her aunty at the clinic, when it happened."

Nadine swallowed hard.

"One of them grabbed her and put his hand over her mouth. She struggled and fought and tried to scream. There were four of them. They all held her down, hitting her face and punching her."

Nadine looked away, trying to control herself.

"They tore off her clothes and all four of those bastards raped her, one after the other … She fought hard, but they just hit her more."

Ric rose to comfort Nadine.

"Let me finish," she said with a snarl.

Ric tried to control his disgust. Explicit scenes of violence flashed across his mind. He pushed them away, trying to remain focused on what Nadine was saying, even though he didn't want to hear any more.

"After what seemed like hours, Nancy began to lose consciousness from all the blows to her head. She looked to the side and saw the legs of another man approaching from the direction of the pub. She looked up through the blood and tears and saw that this man was her boyfriend from the station. She managed to get her mouth free and call out his name."

"What did he do? How could he fight off four men?" asked Ric, his face now drained of blood, and his voice cracking.

"They were gutless bastards. They just pulled on their clothes and ran off. But you know what's the saddest thing of all, Ric?"

"No."

"Her so-called boyfriend looked at her, vomited into the bushes, then walked away. Her aunty found her hours later, unconscious and bleeding. They called in the Flying Doctor on a night rescue flight. She spent many weeks in Cairns City Hospital. Twice she tried to throw herself out the window. Twice they brought her back. She took months to recover physically. I don't think she's ever recovered mentally."

Ric sat transfixed on the couch, looking out towards the deep blue ocean.

"Did they convict those bastards and throw them into prison?"

"What do *you* think, Ric?" Not waiting for an answer, Nadine continued. "The four men must have cleaned themselves up and gone back to their station. They had their stories all sorted and their alibis watertight by the time the police interviewed them next day. The case went to court, but the defence had it thrown out because there was no corroborating evidence."

"Surely the boyfriend testified?" asked Ric.

"Nancy never told the police she saw him there, so he was never called as a witness. She didn't think it would be worth telling the court she'd seen him that night. It was all white people on the jury anyhow. She knew they wouldn't believe her, so what was the point? Anyhow, she never wanted to see him again."

"Did he go on to become the station manager?"

"No. He didn't finish college. He left the station that weekend and later on, he joined the army. The word is that he was injured overseas and then spent time in Perth, dealing with PTSD. Later on, he took his own life."

"Right. And what happened to Nancy after she got out of hospital?"

"She went back to the station for a while, that was the only home she had. Eventually most of our family moved into town. That was better for her, given what had happened, and how she was struggling mentally. Of course, she was also pregnant."

"Oh. With you?"

Nadine gave a curt nod and stared at the wall.

"After our Mob left, there were only a few Aboriginal people left on the station. When the manager heard his son had died, he roped in his next oldest son, the one who'd gone down south to study accounting. Apparently, he was a decent bloke."

"This next oldest son on that station, was his name Bill?"

"Yeah, I'm pretty sure he would be Mark's grandfather."

Nadine had not even started on her second beer. She looked at the bottle then at her watch, frowned and said, "Hey, Mark will be here soon, won't he?"

Ric nodded.

"I think I've lost my taste for drinking tonight. I'll head home before he gets here."

"Should I share all this with Mark?"

"What do you think?"

"I don't think you'd want me to do that, at least not yet."

"Maybe not ever. Let's see how he goes, after he's yarned with Uncle Wilbur."

Ric walked Nadine to her car. "I'll be seeing your uncle tomorrow."

"Ah yeah, could you come to my office first? I want to see you before you go to the hospital. I need to prepare you for something," said Nadine as she drove off.

Ric struggled to believe that such a crime could go unpunished. He found it even harder to accept that Nadine's mother and her people had to accept that the system didn't treat them with justice. He knew if it had been him, he would have wanted to wreak revenge.

Are these kinds of things still happening? Why aren't all Aboriginal people angry, like she is?

It was a member of Mark's family who had walked away from Nadine's badly injured mother. He couldn't face Mark. Other thoughts entered his contorted mind.

What if she is my birth mother?

He hobbled out and walked along the beach. Slowly his thoughts took shape. He shouldn't tell Mark. He also understood that, rationally, Mark couldn't be held to blame for what had happened. Yet still, he now understood the antagonism Nadine felt towards Mark.

Ric's mind was still flitting between converging streams of uncertainties as he walked through the door and saw Mark sitting on the lounge, drinking one of his beers. With an effort, he said, "Sorry mate, I just needed to get out for a while."

"You okay?" asked Mark.

"Yeah, I'm okay now. It was pretty intense with Nadine."

"Want to share?"

"No, not really, it was confidential. What have you been up to?"

"I've been reading some books in the library, and then I went to the newspaper office and scrolled through their microfiche records. I've discovered some interesting things about what happened in the back country when settlers came. And some of it refers directly to our family property."

"No shit," said Ric, momentarily forgetting he had to treat Nadine's conversation as confidential.

"Huh? What have you found out?" asked Mark.

"Ah, things were not so good for Aboriginal people in those days."

"Yes, so I've read," said Mark, "even though those reports were written by white people, there's a lot of evidence showing how badly the settlers behaved during the clashes in those days. It's only recently that researchers have been uncovering it."

Ric was about to express his nascent feelings when Mark said, "There are some newspaper reports of a court case in the town near our station. They said a young Aboriginal woman claimed she was sexually assaulted by four men, but they weren't convicted as there was no corroborating evidence. There was also a small piece a few months later, about a mass migration of Aboriginal families out of that area."

"Did the paper say the two incidents were related?"

"No, not exactly. But there was some speculation in the Letters to the Editor section."

"Maybe your grandfather's people would know about that incident?" said Ric, as nonchalantly as he could manage.

"Yes, I'll call him tomorrow and ask him what he knows. It's strange he didn't mention it, when he told us all the Aboriginal people had moved off the station," said Mark.

"Yeah. Anyhow mate, I'm heading off to bed. I've got to go and see Nadine tomorrow and then I've got to get back to Uncle Wilbur. He's been asking to see me again."

"It sounds like that old man is becoming fond of you, Ric. You remember Nadine suggested I get to know him as well. Do you think I could come too?"

"Yeah for sure, if he agrees."

"Thanks. Hey, maybe he knows something about that incident. He would have been alive then, from what you say."

Ric wondered how Mark might respond if he knew what Nadine had told him.

Chapter 43

Nadine Has More Surprises

North Queensland, September 1997

Next morning, Ric woke with his brain in overdrive.

Why didn't I return to Brisbane as soon as I got my mother's letter? And what if Nadine is the woman who wrote it? But really? Could I ever relate to her as my mother?

Ric sighed as he navigated his way through the paint-chipped corridors to Nadine's office, clutching two flat whites and a box of pastries.

"You don't need to butter me up, Ric. All you have to do is shut up and listen."

Ric took a deep breath, pressed his lips together and nodded.

"Okay, so Uncle Wilbur somehow knows I was pregnant, and he must have worked out I gave up my baby for adoption during the time I was living in Sydney. I tried to get him to tell me how he knew, but he never would. But he did promise he wouldn't tell anyone else without my permission."

"Well, he didn't tell me, but it was clear he knew."

"Fair enough. But he kept saying I should tell you everything, so you can understand what happened to you. I got really angry and asked, 'Why should I tell this young Migaloo fella, when I haven't even told my own mother?' He just smiled and told me I should."

"Look Nadine, I really don't need you to tell me anything more."

"Ric, I've become fond of you, but you do have some very irritating habits. If you keep interrupting, you'll only make it harder for me, okay? You remember we talked about how I got pregnant during that period I was living in Sydney?"

"Yes."

"I didn't have the baby in Sydney, I had my baby in Cairns. And I gave the baby up for adoption right here in Cairns."

Ric's jaw dropped. He was speechless, but only for a moment.

"How could you have a baby and gave it up for adoption here in Cairns, without your family knowing?"

"Just settle, petal. Stay with me a bit longer."

"I'd travelled up to the Tableland with a friend from Sydney. Her mother was sick, and she didn't want to drive all that way by herself, so I offered to come with her. We agreed as soon as she'd settled in and organised things with her mum, she'd drive me down to Townsville and I'd hop on a Greyhound bus back to Sydney."

"But that didn't happen?"

"No, my baby began to come a few weeks early. My friend took me to the local hospital. They said it wouldn't be safe to have the baby there, so they transferred me to Cairns."

"Gees, that must have freaked you out."

"It did. But thankfully it was a Friday night and there was a bad storm, followed by drenching rain all weekend, so there weren't many visitors at the hospital. And I'd already been off work hanging around my flat in Sydney for a couple of months before that, so my skin colour was even paler than usual. Nobody asked if I was Aboriginal, so I didn't have to tell them."

"Didn't they suspect something? They would have wanted to know what antenatal care you'd had, and who your next-of-kin was, wouldn't they?"

"I told them I was from Sydney, up here visiting a friend. They phoned my doctor and confirmed I'd had my antenatal care in Sydney. I filled in the adoption papers soon after my baby was born. I managed to discharge myself from hospital by the Sunday night and then my friend took me to Townsville, and I headed back to Sydney."

"Surely the hospital authorities would have wanted to follow up to see if you were okay?"

"Yes, I had a couple of phone calls after I'd gone back to Sydney. They asked me to go to my doctor for follow up, which I did."

"That's incredible."

"It was amazingly simple to get away with. I couldn't believe my luck that there weren't any other Murri patients in the maternity ward, especially as there were several other babies born that weekend."

"And you're telling me all this because?"

"When I looked at the forms you filled in at our agency, I noticed the date when you were born … That was the weekend I had my baby."

Even though Ric knew it was coming, it hit him hard. Images flooded into his mind. He found himself reeling, and he had no idea how to respond. His eyelids fluttered just before he blacked out. When he became conscious, a voice was speaking tenderly to him. As he began to focus, he realised with a start, it was Nadine's voice.

"Ric, I know all this is very disturbing for you. It's disturbing for me too. I've been wondering how I would cope if we found out you were my son. Strangely enough, I've been shocked to discover I may be okay with that."

Ric was lost for words.

Nadine spoke again. "But Ric, no matter how I feel about you as a person, I can't convince myself that you *are* my son."

"Huh? Why do you say that?"

"Maybe it's a Murri thing. But it's hard to accept so many coincidences …"

"Hang on a minute," said Ric, his brain finally clicking into gear. "Did you know your baby could have been adopted out in Cairns, as they regarded you as a Sydney woman?"

"They told me it was likely that the baby would be adopted in Brisbane, because there were a lot more parents wanting to adopt down there. Anyhow, I couldn't ask them *not* to adopt the baby in Cairns because the only good reason I could give, would be that my family was here."

"And then they would have insisted on involving your family?"

"Yes, then the whole Aboriginal adoption process would have been brought in."

"But you're a proud Aboriginal woman. And you're very close to your family."

"Yes, but the family would have pressured me to keep the baby. Of course, I know now how selfish I was … I really didn't think about my baby at all, did I?"

"Hell Nadine, you're being a bit hard on yourself. You were only a young woman, and you were making all these difficult decisions without any support from your family."

As Ric tried to compute everything Nadine had said, many questions came to his mind.

"Did you ever think of the baby you'd given up? Did you remember his birthday and wonder how he was?"

"No not much, Ric … Only every birthday for the last twenty-six years and most days in between."

Ric could see that Nadine's eyes were flashing, but he could tell her anger was quickly dissolving into raw emotion. He decided to try to distract her with the first curious question that came to him. "So you've known for weeks that I was born on the same weekend you had your baby?"

"Yes."

"And Uncle Wilbur knows too?"

"I think he does. He asked me whether I had any thoughts that you were my son. I told him outright 'no way' but he may not have believed me, because he started asking me to tell him where I actually had my baby."

"Did you tell him?"

"No bloody way. I told him he had no right to interrogate me. I told him he couldn't know the emotions a woman in my situation would feel. I gave it to him. I said, 'This is women's business,' so he backed off. But I always wonder if that cagey old bugger already knows something before he asks a question. Anyhow all I can say is, to the best of my knowledge, he doesn't know I had the baby here in Cairns."

"So why else would he want to see us together?"

"Well for starters, he doesn't know I've spoken to you twice in the last twenty-four hours. I don't know exactly what he wants, but I'm pretty sure he's going to encourage you to search further."

"I hadn't planned to search any further. Remember, you were the one who challenged me to honour my birth mother's wish. Have you changed your mind about that?"

"I don't know. Maybe you will need to know some day. But anyhow you haven't actually read your mum's letter yet, have you?"

"No, I haven't. Hey, wait a minute. Did you write a letter to your baby?"

Nadine paused. She seemed to be steadying herself before answering. "We all did, Ric. The head nurse on the ward knew how bad the adopting mothers were feeling, and she encouraged us all to write a note to our child."

"Well, I could send you a copy of the letter after I've read it with Cassie. Then you'd know if it was yours because you'd recognise the handwriting."

"I may not want to read it Ric, I'm not sure how I'd cope. But anyhow, the nurse said she wouldn't pass on the letter unless it was typed, and unless there was no identifiable information in it. She said this to all the adopting mothers. I've only got vague memories of what I wrote."

Ric decided not to press the matter.

Chapter 44

Wilbur and Ric

North Queensland, October 1997

When Ric arrived at the hospital, he was still reeling from everything Nadine had shared.

Wilbur greeted him, jolting him out of his reverie. "G'day brother. You've been talking to Nadine."

"I have indeed, Uncle Wilbur," said Ric, no longer surprised by anything Wilbur knew. He decided to take a lead from the old man and get straight to the point. "She told me she had a baby, and she gave it up for adoption during the time she was living in Sydney."

"And what else?"

"She said I would have been born about the same time."

"About the same time, eh?"

"Yes," said Ric, now a little wary, wondering what else the old man knew.

"I bin growlin' that one for a long time now. She's such a hardhead. I wanted her to tell you that, because I knew you'd find out sooner or later. I'm glad she told you herself. Did she tell you where she had the baby?"

"Ah, she told me a lot of things, Uncle. Some of them were confidential."

"That's okay. So you know she had her baby in Cairns, and it was the same weekend that you were born?"

He does know. But why hasn't he told Nadine he knows?

Ric realised there would be no point lying to Uncle Wilbur, but he also felt a growing loyalty to Nadine. He hadn't replied, but his lips had pursed. He needn't have worried about what to say.

"Don't worry, I'll explain to Nadine I already knew, and that you didn't tell me."

"How *did* you know, Uncle?"

"Maybe that's something I should tell Nadine first, eh?"

"Yeah, of course."

"Now, there's something I have to ask you. Have you been thinking Nadine's your birth mother?"

Gees, he's not beating around the bush today.

"It seems possible, Uncle."

"And how do you feel about that?"

"I've grown to have a lot of respect for her, and I feel for her, especially after what happened to her mother." Ric tried to recall whether Wilbur knew that history. He began to fear he may have broken a confidence.

"Yeah, it is a sad story Ric, enough to make you bitter and twisted for the rest of your life. Nadine has been that way for a long time. But she's softened as she's got to know you. Maybe at first, she thought she must have been your birth mother, now she's not so sure."

Ric realised he had no idea whether Nadine had told Wilbur these things, or whether Wilbur just knew.

"Now Ric, you haven't finished telling me how you *feel* about the possibility of Nadine being your mother."

This time, Ric thought carefully before he spoke.

"On one hand, I would be honoured and proud to have someone like her as my mum, although, and I'm not sure if all adopted kids feel this way or not, but I'm not really *feeling* like I'm her son, at least not yet. And I know this could be a dumb question, but if Nadine is my mother, does that make me Aboriginal?"

"That's not a dumb question Ric. And there's no simple answer. But is it important for you to know whether Nadine is your mum?"

"I'm not sure about that either. When I came up here, all I really wanted to do was to find out for certain I was adopted, and to ask my parents why they hadn't told me. I only contacted your family because Albie and the boys wanted me to meet you all. They said that I might be a Murri, but I think they were just having a bit of fun with me."

"Or maybe they were giving you a hint."

"Yes, maybe they were. But now I know I was adopted; I'm just looking forward to reading my mum's letter. I don't think I need to know who my birth mother is. And I used to wonder why my mother gave me away. Now I understand that when a woman gives up her baby, it isn't that she doesn't love her baby, it's just that she can't keep it."

"And you really don't want to know?"

"Of course, in one way I would love to know, but I've figured out that really, I would prefer not to know, unless my birth mother *wants* me to know."

Wilbur seemed pleased with that response. "Can you live with that?"

"I think so, Uncle. I thought about applying to the department for contact with my mum. I may still do that, because even then, my mum would still have the right to choose if she wanted contact, but I haven't done that yet. Maybe I'm putting it off."

Wilbur seemed to be assessing what Ric had said, before he said any more. It seemed to Ric that he was now changing tack.

"Ric, you remember when we talked about seeing things. I know you have that sense and I know you've pushed it away, but you won't always be able to push it away. I tried, but it was no good. I could help you work out how to handle that ability of yours. Maybe if you allowed some of those things to come into your mind, you could learn to manage the other ones."

Ric interrupted, asking the question that was uppermost in his mind. "Uncle, do you think I may be seeing things that happened to my mum?"

"I'd be very surprised if you didn't."

"Will you teach me how to manage this thing, Uncle?"

"I will, but it's gonna take a long, long time. And I won't begin today. Because I want to finish off that story I started to tell you last time we spoke. And your friend Mark has left a message that he'd like to visit me today, while you're here."

"Right," said Ric, wondering if he would ever get to the point of knowing where conversations were going.

"You remember when I told you about working on the stations, and how I got wild about how we were being treated, then I hit the booze really bad?"

"Yes Uncle, I remember."

"And how I told you that when I started seeing things, the Elders helped me understand how to handle all that?"

"Yes, that's why I'm hoping you'll be able to teach me."

"Well, you're going to have to be patient Ric, because first I need to tell you a little bit more about the station where I worked, and the ones who had that ability in the times before I was born."

"You're going to tell me the story of the station out there near Deadend Ridge."

Wilbur smiled.

"Come out to the verandah, it's a bit more private out there. You better grab a comfortable chair. This story could take a while."

Ric moved the chairs together, grabbing a third one when he noticed Mark at the reception desk.

"G'day young Mark. Come and join us," said Wilbur. "Your family is part of this story too."

"Thanks Uncle Wilbur. I've been reading about our station. I have a lot of questions for you. When I phoned my grandpa, he said he knew you."

"That would be Bill, the next oldest brother, eh?"

Mark gave a half nod.

"Yeah, I was mates with his older brother, before he took off. But I did sorta know your grandpa Bill, he was a few years younger than me."

"Do you know why the other brother went away? Grandpa was a bit vague about it. The curious thing is, according to the old newspaper reports, his brother left soon after a crime was reported in the nearby town. I asked Grandpa whether his brother was involved, but he didn't answer."

Wilbur watched Mark's face as he spoke. It seemed to Ric that Wilbur was reading their minds. Well perhaps not their minds, maybe he was reading their hearts.

"Uncle Wilbur, do you know anything about who committed that crime? I know no one was convicted. Was my grandpa's brother involved?"

"Mark, your grandpa's brother is gone now. You probably heard he was a very troubled fella, and that he took his own life."

Mark nodded.

"He came back to the station that night and he left the next day. As far as I know, he never actually told anyone he was involved in the crime. It was one of our Mob who was assaulted. That crime had a big effect on all of us. And it had a big impact on your grandpa's family as well. None of us will ever really know the truth."

"But what about you, Uncle Wilbur? I understand that you see things, you know things. Surely with such a horrific event, you would have seen it. Is the victim still alive? Can I talk with her?"

Uncle Wilbur's head snapped back, as if he had been punched. He was in the middle of a long intake of breath when Ric spoke.

"I'm sorry Uncle. Leave this to me. I think I'm beginning to understand what Nadine has been trying to tell me about certain white people," said Ric through clenched teeth.

He turned to Mark. "Mate, you're way out of line. Uncle Wilbur is a respected Elder. He's not one of your patients, who you have a duty to quiz so you can get to the bottom of their mental illness. When you speak to an Elder like you just did, you show no respect. And why would a woman who's suffered such an atrocity want to talk to you, a descendent of the brother of the man who abandoned her. I think you should leave now."

Ric's voice had become so loud the ward nurse came out to intervene.

Mark looked stunned.

Uncle Wilbur went quiet for a while. "Listen up you two boys, you've both got a lot to learn."

"Mark, you can't learn everything about people's culture and history from books. You have to get to know people, to know how they feel."

"And Ric, good friends are very hard to find. Mark has stuck by you in the hard times. He's learning some worrying things about his own family. You have some special gifts, but you have so much to learn. And you'll need to learn how to control your temper."

By now, both young men were hanging their heads. The nurse had been observing the interaction. She smiled when she heard two quiet voices say, "Sorry, Uncle."

Wilbur began to tell his story, as if no questions had been asked, as if no angry words had been spoken. He spoke with gentle warmth, varied at times from controlled anger to unbridled mirth, sharing the stories of his people and his family.

Neither of the lads interrupted.

Chapter 45

Meanwhile, back at the Hospital in Brisbane

Brisbane, October 1997

Unbeknown to Ric, his absence from the hospital in Brisbane had brought two of his senior colleagues closer.

Matthew and Phil continued their meetings at the club. It was now a weekly ritual, to the annoyance of Matthew's partner Bec, but to the relief of Phil's long-suffering wife.

They had each taken on senior responsibilities early in their careers. They acknowledged that while their youth may have been characterised by risk-taking, their middle age had become staid. Even Friday night drinks were now relished as a novel experience.

When the alcohol hit their brains and their tongues loosened, they compared young Ric's impulsive behaviour with their own approach to life.

After they'd ruminated over Ric's decision to go to Cairns, Matthew raised the issue which had been bothering him for weeks.

"Phil, when we had our first meeting here at the club, you talked about a stuff-up when you were younger. You said something like 'You just have to go through the pain and the shame, hoping your credibility will be restored some day.' What was that all about?"

"I wondered if you'd remember those words, Matthew. The memory of that incident is driving me insane at the moment."

"Why now?"

"You'll work that out when I tell you what happened."

"Okay, I'm intrigued."

"You're not meant to be intrigued, Matthew. Perhaps tonight you're meant to be my counsellor, maybe even my confessor."

"Hang on a moment while I adjust my dog collar."

Phil managed a smile.

"As you know, in the seventies we were still working ten or twelve hour shifts each day, and then we'd be on call every second night and weekend. When we were off duty, we partied hard, got drunk and did crazy things. But usually, we managed to sober up enough to provide reasonable medical care."

Matthew settled back into the folds of the leather lounge.

"Of course, we'd been cloistered like monks during the long years of study. When we finally got a chance to socialise, we were somewhat *enthusiastic* in our romantic endeavours. Most often of course, we'd be socialising with other hospital staff."

Matthew flashed a curious smile and a raised eyebrow.

"Calm yourself Matthew. I could never have lived up to your philandering reputation. Mine were dalliances which rarely developed into intimacy, but I did have a lot of fun trying. Unfortunately, on one occasion I was having too much fun. It was bloody irresponsible, I know."

Phil's face was now grim. He swallowed, hesitated, then resumed the story.

"One week there, I'd already worked sixty hours by the Saturday morning, and then they asked me to stay on to work the whole weekend. There was this bloody big storm event, all the roads were flooded, and none of the weekend staff could get to work."

"That was a bit unfair when you were already stuffed. How did you cope?"

"I think we all became a bit manic. Of course, the storm caused lots of casualties, and we soon filled all the available beds. We were under so much pressure, it felt like cabin fever. The only way we could keep going was by lightening up, saying silly things, playing stupid games."

Phil's story now became more erratic.

"I was infatuated with one of the nurses, although I couldn't work out whether she was leading me on or pushing me away. I was doing my Obstetrics and Gynaecology term, but that weekend I was backing up for ED."

Phil paused and took a slug of whisky.

"The nurse and I started teasing each other, doing stupid things like hiding the stethoscopes or locking one or other in the pan room, but then it got a little out of hand. It was sheer coincidence, but three mothers were giving their babies up for adoption that weekend. And two of the babies looked so alike we could only tell them apart by their name tags, so the nurses placed the two babies' cots on opposite sides of the nursery."

"Oh no, don't tell me. You swapped them around?"

"I did more than that. When she was on a tea break, I swapped them around, cut off the name tags and carefully hid them on a shelf next to the cot they were in. I hovered around the corridor waiting for her to discover the missing name tags, at which point I'd planned to come in and go 'da da,' and she'd be furious."

"Hell Phil, that was risky."

"Yeah, in retrospect, it wasn't just risky, it may have been illegal."

"Well, what happened? Let me guess. When she couldn't locate the name tags, she reported the problem to management, and you had to fess up?"

"If only she'd done that. I would have been reprimanded, which would have been fair enough."

Phil lowered his head.

"Are you going to tell me what *did* happen?"

"She discovered the name tags were missing and immediately realised it must have been me playing tricks on her. That would have been fine except there'd been a Code Blue in the medical ward, and I'd had to race downstairs to assist in the resuscitation."

"But you came back and showed her where you'd hidden the name tags."

"I did, but it was no use. She'd only discovered the name tags were missing after she'd taken the two babies to the bathroom to wash them. And she couldn't be certain which side of the room which baby had come from."

"Bloody hell," said Matthew. "Then you both had to put in your Incident Reports?"

"Then we *should* have submitted Incident Reports."

"But you didn't?"

"No."

"Why not?"

"We were both shit-scared, Matt. We panicked. We put replacement name tags on the babies before anyone discovered them missing. We reassured each other we'd work it out and we'd replace them again if necessary."

"And did you ever work it out?"

"Not really. We stared at the babies over and over, and went back to see the mothers, hoping for a clue in their features but it was hopeless. When the babies had their next bath, we discovered one of them had a small *cafe au lait* spot on the left side of his lower back."

"So that would have identified the baby?" said Matthew.

"Sadly not. Neither of us had recorded the spot before, which itself was a bit negligent. The whole thing was a wake-up call, it really knocked me around. I've been obsessively diligent ever since. The thing I'm most ashamed of, is that I never had the guts to own up and face the consequences."

"What about the nurse?"

"She hadn't done anything wrong up until the point where she failed to submit an Incident Report. She didn't put in a report as she knew by doing so, I would be exposed and of course disciplined, maybe even suspended."

"She kept your secret?"

"Yes, she did. And we're still together."

"Ah, I see. And you retrieved the original cut name tags, and destroyed them?"

"I intended to do just that. But when I went back to look for them on the shelves, they were gone."

"Did you ever find them?"

"No, I think the cleaner must have put them in the rubbish."

"Right," said Matthew. "Well, it's highly likely you did no harm as the babies were being adopted anyway. And I suppose there'd be nothing gained by disclosing now."

"It gets worse, my friend."

"Worse? How could it get any worse?"

"That was the weekend Ric was born … he was born in Cairns, and I suspect he's discovered he was adopted."

Matthew groaned.

"Nowadays he can apply to the department to make contact with his birth mother and if he does that and she agrees to meet him, there's a fifty per cent chance that woman won't actually be his mother."

" Oh!" said Matthew.

The two doctors sipped their whisky in morose silence for what seemed like an eternity.

Later in the evening when they'd emptied the crystal decanter, Phil roused himself. "Matt, now I've shared this with you, I'd like your advice on what I should do next. But I reckon we've both had too many whiskies tonight. Could you spare me some time next week to sit down and think it out logically? Young Ric is coming to see me soon."

"Yeah, for sure Phil," said Matthew, his voice slurred. "Just promise me you won't go around telling anyone else before we talk again."

"I give you that promise."

Matthew awoke the next morning with a pounding head and a foul taste in his mouth. Bec had set up bedding on the couch, telling him she didn't need another Friday night snorefest. He was unsteady as he staggered to the toilet and then he scalded his hand making coffee.

He managed to say a raspy 'good morning' when Bec emerged from the bedroom.

She responded with a tirade. "If you're going to make a habit of getting pissed at the club every Friday night, why don't you book yourself a room and stay there?"

Matthew held his head, gritted his teeth and asked, "Can we talk about this later? I need to get some coffee into me, and then get to work."

"Yeah, that'd be right. Work always comes first for you!"

"Okay, okay, I'm really sorry. It's Saturday, so I should be able to get away early. Maybe we could have lunch at the Yacht Club? And then afterwards, we could go for a stroll down by the bay and have a talk."

"No Matthew, I have a better idea. I'll go down to Sandgate and stay with my sister. You can work things out for yourself."

Chapter 46

What Was Uncle Wilbur Trying to Tell Him?

Cairns, October 1997

Back at the hospital in Cairns, Uncle Wilbur continued his story.

"When them white fellas first came, they killed many of our people and left the rest of us starving. And a lot of our people got sick from the new diseases the white men brought with them. The ones that survived all this, tried to find work on the cattle stations if the white fellas would allow them to stay."

"Grandpa said in the old days, there were lots of your people living on his station," said Mark.

Ric grimaced, but Wilbur's face showed no offence.

"Mark, our Mob was always happy to work with your grandpa's grandfather and your grandpa's father, and they would have been happy to work with your grandpa as well. They were different from a lot of other white people. But when that terrible thing happened, our family couldn't stay there any longer."

"Did they blame my family for the assault?"

"We never thought your grandpa's brother was the one who did it, though we were pretty sure he knew who did. But he wouldn't stand up for that girl against those other white men, and he didn't go to the police. He just walked away, and we never saw him again. Your grandpa Bill had to come back to run the station."

"But didn't my grandpa treat people properly when he took over?"

"Bill was a decent sort of bloke, and he promised he would do his best to protect everyone who stayed on."

Mark and Ric exchanged glances, each shifting uncomfortably in their chairs.

"But 'ere, I'm getting ahead of myself. I wanted to tell you about Bill's grandfather, 'is name was Warwick. He got on well with one of our Mob , a fella called Jupilunka. I wanna tell you his story too."

Mark and Ric listened intently. They found the story to be almost identical to the one Bill had told, about Deadend Ridge. It was obvious that Bill's grandfather must have got most of the story from Jupilunka.

"Jupilunka had become head stockman on the property, but he was also our main law man as well. The Elders trusted him with all the old stories. He became a healer, and he used his skills well. Sometimes he'd encourage people, sometimes he'd frighten them into following the old laws."

"Ju-pi-lun-ka," said Ric, trying hard-to-get his tongue around the name.

"That's right. Jupilunka was my grandfather. He taught my father all those laws and customs, and my father passed them on to me. It was my duty to pass them on to one of my sons, but I didn't have any sons. I did have a nephew and I tried to teach him, but he died young."

The two listeners began to murmur their appreciation for the story and their sorrow for his loss, but Wilbur would have none of it.

"You white boys don't know how to stay quiet, eh? Youse would never've been able to stay still in the long grass, downwind from the 'roos. Hey, you'd have empty bellies every night around the cooking fires!"

"Uncle, was there something more you wanted to tell us?" asked Ric.

"Yair, plenty more. Jupilunka had an extra skill. He could see things and he would know things, long before anyone ever told him those things. At first, the Elders thought he was strange, going all 'womba' like we say. Others thought the devil had got control of him. But then they realised it was a special ability he had."

Mark interrupted. "Uncle Wilbur, I think my great-grandfather called him Jimmy, I don't think my family ever used his proper name."

"Jimmy was not such a bad name," said Uncle Wilbur. "Often them whitefellas would give our families smart-arse names so they could laugh at us. Names like Moonlight or Ketchup or Mainland or Brumby. There are hundreds of them names, and the families are still stuck with them today."

"Uncle, weren't you going to tell us more about your nephew?" asked Ric.

"I *was* going to tell you about 'im, but it seems we have another visitor, and it looks like she's got something she wants to say."

Nadine didn't mince her words.

"Uncle Wilbur, I thought I could trust *you* of all people, to keep your promise! Now you're sharing my story with this other white fella too."

Wilbur gazed at Nadine's flushed face and waited for her to stop speaking. He held her eyes and with an almost imperceptible movement of his lips, indicated that she should calm herself and sit in the chair which Ric had vacated for her.

"Naddie, I bin telling them the story of Jupilunka. They'd already heard about 'im from Mark's grandfather Bill. The white people knew him as Jimmy. You know what Nadine, I think this young Mark fella 'ere, was just about to say his grandfather had told him the exact same story."

"That'd be right, Uncle. It's what we call 'cultural appropriation.' These white fellas stole everything else, now they're even stealing our stories!" said Nadine, her voice rising.

"You finished yet girl?" asked Uncle Wilbur in the harshest tone any of them had ever heard him use. "Just stay quiet for a bit, Naddie. You're nearly as bad as these young white fellas, interrupting an old man when he's teaching them things."

Nadine's face smouldered. She folded her arms but stopped lashing out.

"Jupilunka and Warwick learnt to trust each other and to respect each other's ways. It looks like Warwick has passed on that respect through the generations to Bill, and Bill is now teaching Mark."

"He's a bloody slow learner then!" said Nadine.

"That's enough, Naddie. These white fellas get most of their learning from books. They're slow at picking up things from just listening and watching. You should know that from the work you do, and from them white fellas you used to hang around with when you were younger."

Nadine flinched, reddening slightly.

Wilbur softened. "I was getting to the part about how Jupilunka learnt to control those things that kept coming into his mind."

"I think I'll go and make some tea," said Nadine.

"In the early days, Jupilunka got into a lot of trouble. People thought he'd use his ability to cause them harm, but he never did. Over time, the Elders got him to talk about the things he saw. They asked him whether he could think of any reason why he would 'see' those things."

"Yeah, that would have been helpful," said Ric. "If only I knew where those thoughts came from, they wouldn't freak me out as much."

"Well, those same Elders noticed Jupilunka was very clever at watching people's faces. And he was good at seeing the way that person held their body. And he would listen to the way their voice changed. He could work out many things this way."

Ric found his head nodding as Wilbur explained.

"But he worked out he had to become smarter, which meant sometimes telling people what he knew, and sometimes not telling them, or at least not telling them until they were ready."

By now, Nadine had rejoined them. She passed around the tea and the hospital grade biscuits. "You'll need to dunk these in your tea, Uncle. If you chew on them, you'll break all the teeth you've got left."

The old man smiled. "Now Nadine, you've been listening to the last part of the story. It's time for me to ask you something."

"I think I know what you're going to ask, Uncle. You're going to ask me two things. First, do I agree Ric may have that ability. And secondly, do I think he is my son."

Mark gasped.

Uncle Wilbur laughed. "Ay lookout, maybe you can read my mind."

Nadine scowled.

"Just gammin, Naddie." She still didn't look mollified. Wilbur spoke again, this time more gently. "But are you gonna answer your own questions?"

"Yes Uncle, I think it is quite possible Ric has that ability, but no, I don't think he is my son."

Wilbur frowned and raised his eyebrows. "And Ric, you've been pushing away those things you saw, about Nadine and her mother."

Mark's eyes widened. Nadine flashed an angry glance at her uncle.

Ric was the one to speak. "Nadine has shared a lot of things with me, Uncle Wilbur. That scene hasn't been coming back anymore. I think it's because Aunty has already told me what happened."

Uncle Wilbur smiled his quiet smile.

Mark was now frowning and leaning forward on his chair.

Ric grasped his forearm and squeezed tightly, but Wilbur now spoke directly to Mark.

"Ay, I can see there's many things you want to ask about. Some things you may never know. But I *can* tell you a few little things that may help you settle down. I *know* your grandpa's brother didn't commit that crime, but he did know who the guilty ones were. I *know* he spent the rest of his life disgusted with himself for not telling the police."

"How do you know those things, Uncle?" asked Mark.

"Yeah, how do you know?" asked Nadine, her voice almost strangled.

"Him and me had been mates for a long time. I went and found him the next morning. He was out in the scrub vomiting and mumbling to himself. I thought he must have had a belly full of grog, but he told me he'd drunk nothing. He wouldn't say much, he just kept shaking, and he looked terrified."

"I kept asking him to tell me what happened but all he'd say was 'I'm weak as piss! I'm gonna have to deal with myself.' I tried saying, 'Tell me about it. What have you done?' but he just said, 'It's not what I've done, it's what I haven't done.' When he disappeared, I thought he must have topped himself. But it wasn't until much later he did that."

Nadine had listened to this with gritted teeth and flashing eyes. Ric found the courage to put his arm around her shoulders and squeeze gently. To his surprise, she didn't resist.

Mark looked at Ric, frowning again.

Ric turned to him. "Mate, I think we should leave Nadine with Uncle Wilbur for a while. Come with me to the canteen and I'll buy you a coffee."

As he walked from the room, Ric saw Nadine motion with her lips towards Mark, and slowly nod. He looked from Nadine to Wilbur. The old man confirmed that yes, he could tell Mark about what happened to Nancy.

Chapter 47

Is Wilbur Rambling Again?

Cairns, October 1997

Next morning, Ric escaped to the beach as the sun rose over a quiet ocean. He sank down on the sand at the very spot Cassie had seen the 'log' many weeks earlier. For once he felt no panic as the images rolled through his mind, like an old newsreel. Each time they came, he seemed to grasp some new understanding. He found he could let most of them just float around. But not the last one.

In this one, he was a newborn baby being held by a woman. Her face, indistinct at first, was beginning to clear from the red haze that obscured her. Each time this scene recurred; it took a massive effort to shut it down.

He found a shell and used it to scrawl names in the sand. He ran through all the people he'd met, all the relationships, all the thoughts they'd shared. Slowly he began to understand how important all these people had become to him. As he made his way back to the apartment, he made a decision.

"Mark, I've got an idea. Let's book the function room for Friday night. I want to invite my whole family over to meet all the other people I've met on this trip."

"You sure that's a good idea?"

"Not sure at all mate, but I want to do it anyway. It could be an interesting evening," said Ric, with growing enthusiasm.

"Yep, it could be interesting all right," said Mark. "Your folks are going to have a ball with Nadine … and if you are looking for interesting, why not include my grandpa? He wants to connect up with the people who used to work on his property."

"Yeah. That could be … interesting as you say. I suppose he and Uncle Wilbur could yarn about old times on the station. Of course, if Wilbur's not well enough, your grandpa could meet some of the other people." Ric stopped mid-sentence, realising Bill knew nothing at all of Nadine's feelings about what happened to her mother.

"You okay mate? You look like you've just seen a ghost."

"Hmm, maybe I have. Listen Mark, I'm sure Uncle Wilbur would be very happy to meet your grandpa, but he may prefer to do that one-on-one, rather than at a party. Hey, I could ask him when I see him this afternoon."

I could also ask him how Nadine would feel about meeting Bill.

"Yeah, I need to check with Uncle Wilbur first. I'm not sure how Aboriginal families will feel about meeting up with Bill. Could you hold off inviting your grandpa?"

"That was half a century ago, Ric. Do you really think it will still be a problem for these people? Surely they've moved on by now."

Ric grimaced. "It could well be a problem, mate. Remember when you told me we should try to work out how other people would feel, before we put our big foot in it?"

"Yeah, okay. I'll wait to hear what Uncle Wilbur says."

Ric invited his parents to lunch. After they settled in, he broached the subject of the party. He mentioned that some of the guests would be from the hospital, and some would be from local Aboriginal families.

"Well Ric, leave the family to us," said Margaret.

John looked at his watch. "Okay Margaret, we better get going. Ric has to visit that old man he helped resuscitate. Just out of interest Ric, do you follow up all of your patients so well?"

Ric scowled. "You know what Dad; Uncle Wilbur has never been my patient. He is a great old man who needed some help at the time. He's also a man of wisdom who's already helped me a lot. I hope you'll be able to treat him with respect."

Margaret pulled her husband away. "I look forward to meeting him."

Ric smiled to himself as they walked out.

Hmm, he's about to get an earful!

Ric phoned through the invitations. Ron agreed to bring Sophia, Aunty Nora said she'd bring the grandkids, Nadine surprised him by not only accepting with good grace, but also asking if she could bring the Elders too.

Ric headed off to the hospital. He found Uncle Wilbur sitting on a bench under a strangler fig tree, waiting for Nadine. There was no evidence of the original strangled tree, but long aerial fig roots hung from the sky and, lower down, the trunk spread and formed into wooden curtains growing out from the base.

"G'day Uncle Wilbur. You're looking much better. There's something I need your advice on. It's about Nadine."

"Ay lookout! You changed your mind about finding your mother?"

"No Uncle. I'm still okay about leaving that alone. I have to admit though, I've been seeing a woman holding me as a tiny baby, probably just after I was born. I've managed to block it out of my mind so far."

"That's good."

"I'm holding a party, inviting all the new people I've met, to come and meet my family. I hope you can come too, but there's one big problem. Mark wants to invite his grandpa, and I'm not sure if Nadine would cope with that. What do you reckon?"

"Strewth, d'ya think you could slow down a bit? I'm a bit wary about coming to a party – the last party I went to didn't end too well. Though I suppose I did meet you, eh? Yeah, I *would* like to meet up with old Bill, but as for him and Nadine, I'm not so sure. Let me talk to her first."

"What are you doing out here, you silly old coot," said Nadine striding towards them. "Oh, g'day Ric, I didn't notice you there."

"Hi Nadine, I was just inviting Uncle Wilbur to my party. He's not sure he'll come. Maybe you could persuade him?"

Nadine looked doubtful. "I'll try. Oh, and Nora says you can stay with her when you're discharged today."

Ric smiled as he watched Wilbur walking gingerly across the lawn, leaning on his niece's arm.

As Mark drove him to Nora's place, Ric said "Well mate, Uncle Wilbur is thinking about it, but it looks like he doesn't want to meet your grandpa at the party."

"Oh, that's a shame. When I rang grandpa, he was very enthusiastic about meeting Wilbur. He's coming down Friday."

As soon as Ric arrived at Nora's place, Wilbur pulled Ric aside and shook his head. "I'll be right to meet up with Bill by myself, but I'll need to keep him out of Nadine's way. She's still edgy about that family."

"That's okay, Uncle. Bill will be down in Cairns on Friday, so he could come over to meet you here."

Ric settled down under the mango trees with Wilbur, drinking tea and talking about the things that kept appearing in his brain. Wilbur had other stories he wanted to tell.

"You 'member I told you about that nephew of mine, the one who died too young?"

"Yes Uncle, you mentioned him a few times."

"Fair enough. Did I tell you much about him?"

"Not that I remember."

"Right. Settle back then," said Wilbur. "He was a wild young boy, his name was Jamayl. He was a good worker, but he was also a bit of a dreamer. He'd listen to my stories when he was a young tyke, then he'd go around in a sort of trance, singing and talking to himself."

"Well, I might have the trance thing going, but I haven't done much singing," said Ric.

"Yair, he used to sing alright. When he was a teenager, his cousins taught him how to play guitar. After that, he never did much schoolwork, and he never played much sport either. He'd make up his own songs, and he'd spend hours in his room or under the trees, just singing and playing an old busted up guitar."

"He sounds totally different to me."

"Not so different when he started seeing things."

"Oh."

"I offered to teach him how to handle what he was seeing, but he got angry. One day he just cleared out, and we didn't see him for a few years."

"Still, he came back?"

"Yes, and he had a girlfriend in tow. He told me he was dead keen on her, but they'd been having lots of fights. And he told me he could now stop seeing things whenever he wanted."

"Wow, how did he do that?" asked Ric.

"He said he would take a little pill. He called it a 'downer'. He had 'uppers' and 'downers' and all sorts of pills in between. I thought he must have been a junkie, so I tried growlin' him like I used to do when he was younger."

"Did that do any good?"

"No, he walked away again, and I didn't hear from him for a couple of months. When he came back, he told me he was 'clean' but he'd started seeing things again. So, I worked with him a lot more, and we were starting to get somewhere. He'd tell me what he saw, and we'd talk about what it meant, and try to work out where the thoughts might have come from."

Ric nodded, trying to work out how he could learn to do that.

"One day, he told me he was seeing something new. This time, he wouldn't tell me what it was. He was in a terrible state, saying over and over, 'Uncle, you've got to help me, there's going to be another one.' I did my best to calm him down and get him to talk about it, but he was having none of it. He just took off. Next thing I heard; he was dead."

Ric waited for Uncle Wilbur to resume. Wilbur had no intention of resuming. He sat perfectly still, staring into the distance.

"Uncle, did you want me to hear that story, so I'd know how important it is, to talk about what I'm seeing, and to get some help?"

Wilbur nodded. "Yes Ric, I did want you to understand those things. That was one of the reasons I told you the story. And it took me a long time to work out what he meant when he said there would be another one ..."

Ric interrupted. "Uncle Wilbur, how should I handle the scene where I see myself as a baby, being held by a woman who might be my mother?"

Wilbur hesitated before responding. They spoke for a long time about what the scene could mean. Wilbur reminded him there would probably be other people in the room with a newborn baby, possibly other relatives, or maybe a nurse or a doctor.

Eventually, Wilbur drew it all together for Ric. However, his conclusion came after another long period of silence. Was Wilbur drifting off? Or was there something else he wanted to tell him?

"Ric, you've decided you don't want to know who your mother is. You're respecting her wishes. But this is a decision your mind has made. Maybe your heart doesn't agree."

"I understand what you're saying, Uncle. I still feel it would be cheating on my mother, to find out that way."

"It would be. I think maybe those things could have a deeper meaning for you. Maybe they're telling you your mother has changed her mind. And she might be waiting to see if you're ready to know."

Ric could hold his other question no longer. "Uncle Wilbur, do you know who my mum is?"

Wilbur paused, his eyes glazing and his breathing steadying.

"I know many things Ric. I know things you don't know, and I know things your mother may not know. But it wouldn't be right for me to tell you these things. You're gonna have to be patient. If it's meant to be, it will be."

Ric looked up, intending to ask more questions. Wilbur waved the questions away.

"Oh, another thing Ric. I think Bill and me will have lots to catch up on, just the two of us."

Chapter 48

An Effort to Reconcile

Cairns, October 1997

On his way home, Ric's mind replayed the conversation. Once again, he found himself admiring the wisdom of the frail old man. He still had the nagging feeling that he'd missed something. *It's like those floaters in my vision. When I look towards them, they scamper away.*

Mark didn't argue too much about not inviting his grandpa, when he heard Wilbur would spend Friday afternoon with him.

As the party got under way that evening, Ric's parents arrived first, followed by Aunty Nora and her two grandchildren, plus a couple of cheeky cousins who'd invited themselves. Ric was busy introducing them all, so Mark undertook the role of greeting the next guests.

One arrived with a bottle of wine and proffered her cheek as she gave Mark a brief hug. It was Nadine, which made him flustered, and caused Nadine to burst into laughter. "What, you don't hug black women, Mark?" she asked, causing him to blush even more and stutter out a denial. "You do, oh well that's good, come here then," she said giving him an even bigger hug this time.

Ric came over beaming at Nadine, and availing himself of a hug as well, mainly to save Mark from further embarrassment. Margaret wanted to meet Nadine. They seemed to hit it off immediately, so Ric dragged Mark away, asking him to organise the drinks for everyone, a request for which Mark was grateful.

Ric went over to rescue his father who was talking to Aunty Nora and the kids. To his surprise, he found John involved in animated conversation, not only with Nora but also with the Elders, all three of whom had just arrived. "Dad, do you know these folks?" asked Ric.

"Yes I do. Nora here, comes to the parent-teacher night with her grandchildren. She's virtually a full-time carer for these little rascals," said John tickling them, and causing them to shriek. "And Annie is the

Elder we consult whenever we have issues with kids' truanting. I don't know what we'd do without her."

Ric had the decency to feel guilty, admitting to himself he'd assumed his dad knew no Aboriginal people.

Nora drew Ric aside. "Is that your Mum over there yarning with Nadine?"

"Yeah, they seem to be getting on fine," said Ric.

"Hey, we didn't realise Mr C was your father. My big sis has often clashed with him. In fact, he's asked us to keep her away from the school. That's why we introduced Aunty Annie," said Nora.

"Right, well let's hope they don't clash tonight," said Ric. He noticed that his mother was pointing out John, and saw Nadine look away.

"Don't worry Ric, I'll go over and meet your mum, and keep Nadine occupied for a while," said Nora.

Margaret took on the role of introducing Steven, Cecilia and Ted when they arrived. Ted and Steven soon excused themselves and gravitated towards Mark. Cecilia stayed with Nora and Margaret, while Nadine came over to join Ric serving drinks.

"Well Ric, now I know where you got your pig-headedness. I've clashed with that father of yours on more than one occasion."

"So where did you get *your* pig-headedness, Nadine?" said Ric, who then wished he could eat his words, remembering the way she was conceived. He hung his head. "Oh shit, I'm sorry Nadine. That was thoughtless."

"It's okay Ric, thanks for apologising. I think you know exactly where I got my obnoxious characteristics, eh?"

"Yeah."

"Anyways Ric, I'll be courteous to your father if I have to speak with him. Otherwise, I'll just keep out of his way. Your mum is nice. I'll go back and join them and have a yarn with your aunt."

"Great, thanks Nadine. Cecilia was always my favourite aunty. She helped to bring me up. We haven't had much of a chance to talk since I've been back."

"Well, it would be good to get to know her then. Uncle Wilbur couldn't make it?"

"No, he invited Mark's grandpa over for a yarn this afternoon, and Nora tells me they're still deep in conversation about the old days on the station."

Nadine winced then checked herself. "Yeah, I think Uncle did know Bill, before that … incident happened."

Ric took her elbow and manoeuvred her back to the others.

"I think Ric may have found another aunty," said Margaret to Cecilia.

"Two new aunties," said Ric, putting his arms around Nadine and Nora and pulling them together. "And this is my all-time favourite aunty," he said, indicating Cecilia.

As the evening progressed, Ron and Sophia spent a lot of time talking with the Elders about various Aboriginal families and asking how the children were progressing.

Ron found a chair and sat with eyes cast downwards, slowly shaking his head.

Ginny spoke. "Hey, Dr Ron, is it time for your nanny nap?"

He looked up and saw she was looking at him with a cheeky smile on her face.

"It's so good to see people getting on well here tonight," said Ron. "When I first started working in north Queensland, things were very different between your people and white people, eh Annie?"

Annie nodded.

"What I've never been able to understand, is how you've all tolerated so much, without becoming angry and bitter. When I saw the way your people were treated, I wanted to lash out at people. Some of your Old People settled me down, but I still can't understand how you can be so forgiving, after all that's happened."

"It's pretty complicated, Dr Ron. Maybe what you see is not really what we feel. You may have to be black to really understand," said Annie.

"Some of us used to rebel against the system," said Pearl. "We've come a long way since then. After a lot of fights, we eventually got some of the things we needed. We got medical services, legal services, housing services, child care services, all run by our own people …"

Ginny joined in. "But most of our people are still poor, and there are lots of social problems. And none of us earns very much even if we do manage to get a job."

"I know," said Ron.

"Maybe we could talk again one day," said Annie with a rueful smile.

Ron detached himself from the group and gravitated towards Ric. He spoke firmly, adamant that Ric should come and work in north Queensland. "It's obvious you would be well accepted by the Aboriginal community."

On the other side of the room, Mark drew Sophia aside and asked her how she would assess a patient who was having visions. Sophia removed her psychiatry hat and talked to him about the Romany people in Eastern Europe, and the skills and abilities of the wise ones. Mark had a confused look on his face. When Ric and Ron joined them, they soon lapsed into small talk.

Ric surveyed the gathering. As he grabbed himself a light beer, he worked the room, checking if everyone was comfortable. Then he gave a short speech thanking everyone for making him welcome. As the party began to break up, Ric noticed Nadine and Cecilia still conversing in the corner, until Ted motioned it was time to leave.

Nadine seemed reluctant to go, so Ric asked if she would like to join him and Mark on their balcony for another drink.

"I don't think I should have another drink. Maybe you could make me a cuppa? It's got to be better than that muck I gave you at our office."

"You and Ric settle down and have a chat. I'll make the tea, Aunty Nadine," said Mark. "Hey, I just saw you grimace. Don't I get to call you Aunty Nadine now that you've given me a big hug?"

Nadine managed a chuckle. "You're getting cheeky now, boy," she said as he walked to the kitchen.

"He's all right, Nadine. Just needs to think things out first. It was the same when he was learning how to play football."

When Mark was out of earshot, Nadine spoke quietly to Ric. "I met your aunt Cecilia a long time ago."

"Is that what you were talking about?" asked Ric, only mildly surprised, thinking after all, Cairns was not a big town.

"No, she didn't seem to remember me, and I couldn't remember where it was that we met. But I asked her what you were like as a little boy."

"I think I was spoiled."

"No doubt about that. Anyhow, your aunt kept asking me more and more about myself. We've arranged to have lunch together."

"That could be interesting," said Ric.

Chapter 49

Ric Returns to Brisbane

Brisbane, October 1997

Cassie gave Ric a perfunctory hug when she met him at the airport. Although Ric wasn't sure how to interpret that greeting, he'd already decided to continue the new approach which seemed to work during the phone call.

"I have so much to tell you Cassie, but you go first. What have you been up to?"

Cassie shot him a piercing glance. Ric held his breath. Cassie seemed to be vacillating about how she would reply.

"Well, I've been seeing a fair bit of Luke. He's a really great guy and I thought I might be getting the hots for him. I even thought about spending more time with him on Straddie. Then I realised he's so up himself ..."

"Phhoarr!" said Ric. "Hang on a minute. Luke, the surfer dude. Why did you ... why did you say he's so up himself?"

"He told me he knew I was getting keen, so he decided to treat me like a kid sister who needed to sort herself out. He kept making *excuses* for you! I felt so embarrassed about how I'd behaved, when all he was thinking about was defending you."

"Ah," said Ric. "What happened again?"

"Well, we never actually *did* anything, but I had gone a bit gooey-eyed over him. I'm glad you went out of contact for a while, because it gave me time to think. Of course, he was right. I was jealous you were spending so much time finding out about your adoption which, I know, was pretty damn selfish of me. Anyhow, I met him for lunch yesterday and told him I was moving on."

Ric shook his head. "I've gotta meet this guy."

"NO!" said Cassie, flushing bright red.

"I thought you told me once, he'd teach me how to surf," said Ric, now enjoying himself.

"Okay, I deserved that. Maybe one day, I'll introduce you. Not until you've told me all your stories."

"Well, I don't have anything nearly as exciting as a secret affair with a hot surfer dude ... Ow!" said Ric, rubbing his shoulder. "Where did you learn to punch like that?"

"You were saying?" said Cassie.

Ric abandoned his teasing. He told her the whole story. Except what he'd been seeing. He did disclose Nadine's confidences, as she had given him permission to do so. Then finally, he came to what was uppermost in his mind.

"Cassie, my birth mum wrote me a letter. I'd like you to read it to me. Would you do that?"

Cassie thought for a few moments. "Okay, I'll read it to you, if that's what you want."

"I do."

As soon as they arrived at Cassie's apartment, Ric carefully unfolded the old letter and sat on the couch with his eyes closed, as Cassie read it to him.

Dear Little One,

I know it's silly of me to begin with 'Dear Little One', because if you ever get to read this letter, you won't be little anymore! I expect you'll grow into quite a big boy, or maybe you won't even get to read it until you're a fully grown man.

I would love to be watching over your shoulder as you read my words. In fact, I would prefer to be telling you all these things myself, and to be there to love you, and feed you and tuck you in each night, and watch you grow up.

Sadly, that will never happen, because I can't keep you.

Giving you up is the hardest thing I've ever had to do.

But I can't give you all the love and care you need. In fact, I can't give you anything really, just this little letter. I do hope you receive it one day.

I want you to know I will always keep you in my heart, as long as I live.

I don't want you to ever find me, or even know my name. It would be just too hard for both of us.

I've asked the doctors to find a very special mummy for you, someone who can care for you properly, because I can't.

I hope one day you will understand.
With love from
Your first Mummy.

"Bloody hell Ric!" said Cassie, with tears streaming down her face. "Reading that letter to you was the hardest thing *I've* ever done. I can't even *imagine* how your mother must have felt when she was writing it."

Ric found himself unable to speak. He put his arm around Cassie. They sat together on the couch reading the letter, over and over.

"You know what Cass? I already know everything I need to know. There's absolutely no need for me to search for more. Unless my mother comes looking for me, I'm going to leave things as they are."

"You sure about this?"

"Yep, I'm sure. And even though I know Aunty Nadine had her baby that weekend in Cairns, there were two other women adopting out their babies at the same time. And she kept saying she didn't feel I was her son. So if she, or whoever was my mum, doesn't want me to know, I'm happy to leave it at that."

"Babe, I totally understand why you feel that way. But wouldn't you like your birth mum to know you'd found out about the adoption, and you've read her letter, and that you'd love to meet her if she'd changed her mind about meeting you?"

"What, you mean fill in the forms and give her the option of meeting me or not?"

"Yes, that's exactly what I mean. She would have been distressed when she wrote the letter, she may have been very young, and she may have changed her mind since then."

"That's true Cassie. But if she'd changed her mind, wouldn't she have tried to find me?"

"Well, she might think you still don't know you're adopted, and she might think it wouldn't be fair for you to find out that way."

"Hmm, I hadn't thought of that. And I'm assuming my mother isn't Nadine. Anyhow Cass, I don't want to think about it anymore today. I've got to work out what to do about footy, and what to do about my career in medicine. Most of all, I want to get to know you again."

"Good. I think I could enjoy that," said Cassie snuggling in.

Chapter 50

Ric Meets His Mentors

Brisbane, October 1997

Ric and Cassie spent most of the weekend at home and they finally agreed they should move in together. And there was passion to rekindle. By Sunday evening, they grudgingly conceded that Ric might need to think about his career.

"I'd better get some advice before I see Phil. I don't want him pushing me into agreeing to come back permanently."

"Isn't Matthew the Director of Training?"

"He is, but I've heard on the grapevine he and Phil have become a lot closer lately. They've even been going out drinking together on Friday nights."

"Isn't there anyone else who could be a sort of mentor? What about the woman you spoke with after you escaped into the forest?"

"Yeah, good call, that's Claire. I'll see if I can get an appointment with her tomorrow."

Cassie smiled. Ric noticed.

"What's so funny?"

"Well, when I met her at your going away party, I happened to notice how gorgeous she was. And she did have dinner with you alone one night."

"Okay, now you're teasing me. Seriously, she must be at least ten years older than me."

"So you've done the calculations?"

Ric was over the emotional intelligence approach. He picked her up and spun her around.

"Why Ric, I think I saw you blush!"

"It's the exertion Cassie, you must have been in a good paddock while I've been away."

This time, Cassie's punch almost unbalanced him. He lifted his hands in mock surrender. "I'll be good, I'll be totally professional.

Could you help me work out what approach I should use? For the career discussion I mean," said Ric in a low growl.

Claire seemed delighted to see him, even more so when he told her he was thinking of coming back early, at least for the duration of his rehabilitation. "And after that?" she asked.

"Yeah, a lot of things have changed for me over the last month or two. Have you got any spare time today?"

"If you'd like to grab a bit of lunch for us both, we could eat together here in my office, and we can discuss whatever you like."

Ric returned with salmon bagels and two flat whites.

"Aw, you are sweet," said Claire. "So how did you go with finding out whether you were adopted?"

"Oh, you haven't heard. Yes, my parents confirmed I was adopted. And they gave me a letter from my birth mum. Cassie and I read it on the weekend."

Claire gripped his forearm. "That sounds incredible. How do you feel about everything now?"

"I feel okay. My birth mum didn't want me to know who she was, so I'll have to respect that. And so many other things have happened, my head is clearer now."

Claire nodded, sipping her coffee.

Ric told her about the events of the last few weeks. He omitted the confidential bits about Nadine and her mother. He did tell her he'd met someone who adopted out her baby the weekend he was born, although she was certain she was not his mum.

"And she's an Aboriginal woman, right?"

"Yes, she is. She and her family think I might have some Aboriginal blood."

"Interesting. It must all be fairly emotional for you."

"Yes. It's been a bit disturbing over the last couple of months, meeting all of those people, white and black, and hearing their stories."

"That's understandable, Ric. Have you been experiencing any more thoughts of harming yourself?"

"None at all, Claire."

"And what about those things you were seeing?"

"Well, I still see things from time to time, but old Uncle Wilbur has been helping me. He's so good, I don't need that counsellor anymore."

"Right … So, you're thinking you might come back to work sooner?"

"Yes. I thought I would offer to work part-time during the rehab period. Would that be possible?"

"It may be, yes. I think you should start by brushing up on your skills, and then come to a few clinical meetings before you return. I could check with Matthew about this, and one of us could brief Phil before you meet with him."

"Sounds like a plan, Claire. I'll be meeting with Phil on Wednesday."

When Claire and Matthew met with Phil, he listened to the proposal, clarified a few matters in relation to Ric's mobility, then indicated he was open to accepting Ric back at the hospital.

"Matthew tells me there are rumours Ric's been trying to find out if he was adopted. I wonder if that was why he was so distracted," said Phil.

Claire kept her face blank. "Phil, I haven't heard those rumours. As you would expect, Ric has discussed some matters with me in confidence. All I can say is that he is much more settled now. Perhaps he'll disclose more when he sees you tomorrow, perhaps not."

Phil looked from Claire to Matthew. "Quite so. Okay Matthew, is there anything else we need to discuss with Claire?"

"No, I think that was all. Claire, did you have anything else?"

"No."

When Claire and Matthew pushed their chairs back to leave, Phil spoke again. "Oh Matt, could you spare me a few more minutes? There's another matter I'd like to discuss with you."

"I think it's time for some straight talking," said Matthew after Claire had left, and before Phil had a chance to say another word. "Firstly, I think we need to be careful about respecting Ric's confidentiality. Secondly, I'm confident that at this time, Ric isn't intending to pursue things further. That relieves some of the pressure on you …"

"Thanks, that's good Matt. But I suspect there's a third thing you wanted to say?"

"Yes, there is. In my view, you have no need to disclose anything to Ric at this point. Depending on how he thinks in the future, it may be kinder never to disclose to him, unless he desperately wants to know."

"Yes, I see what you're saying. Hmm. That's not all you wanted to say though, is it?"

"No, it is not. Now you've shared the details of the incident with me, I feel compromised if I don't give you my honest advice, even though I know it may have major ramifications for you and for your wife."

"Matthew, can we discuss this calmly on Friday night?"

Matthew didn't respond. He inhaled deeply and bent his head forward, clenching his jaws.

"Matt, I suspect I've come to the same conclusion as you. I want you to know I've already decided to report the incident and accept the consequences, which of course may be considerable. I just need to plot out how and when to do that," said Phil, with a wistful smile.

Claire was waiting in Matthew's office when he returned. "What was that all about?"

"How do you mean?" asked Matthew.

"Why was Phil so interested in Ric's personal life? It's not like him to even know the names of his junior staff."

"Well, it was probably because Ric had made a couple of serious mistakes, which were out of character for him. He knew Ric had sought counselling, and then he heard the rumours. Oh, and of course, he had known Ric's parents as a teenager. Ric's mum was Phil's teacher in Townsville."

"Right. It really is a small world. Anything else?"

"Claire, you've been firm in not breaching Ric's confidences."

"Yes."

"Can I just say there are some things *I* need to keep confidential?"

Claire threw Matthew a challenging glance. "Okay, I accept that. But these confidential matters, are they likely to impede Ric's return to part-time work?"

"No, they won't impede his return."

"Right. I'll give him a call and let him know," said Claire.

Ric encountered no resistance when he pitched his proposal to Phil. The director indicated the hospital would be pleased to have him back. "We need to bring you back slowly, though. I'll ask Matthew to design a program to ease you back in. Maybe one day, you'll make a decision to stay in medical practice, and give up footy altogether?"

"I am starting to think about my future. This injury has given me lots of time to think," said Ric, hesitating for a moment. "Oh, by the way, you were right about my mum. She wasn't pregnant at the time you saw her. She confirmed I was adopted, and she said how sorry she was that she hadn't told me."

Phil looked unsettled for a moment. "Are you okay about all that?"

"Yes, I was angry for a while, but I've learnt to understand things better lately. Oh, and my mum gave me a letter that my birth mother had written to me."

Phil hesitated again. After a few seconds he said, "Did you find that helpful?"

Ric remembered this was Phil, whose emotional intelligence level was almost down in his boots. "Yes, it was good to know she didn't want to give me up, and that she was really sorry she had no other choice," said Ric, trying to stay matter-of-fact, thinking Phil would have no interest in the emotional impact the letter had on him.

Phil seemed to confirm this when he regarded him blankly. "Well, that seems to be a good outcome then. Why don't you make an appointment with the Director of Training, and we'll organise a transition to work program for you."

As soon as Ric left the room, Phil called Matthew. "I've advised Ric to see you about his return to the workplace. He told me he found out he was adopted, and he had a letter from his birth mum. He seems settled but do you think Claire would tell you if she heard him say he was going to try to find her?"

"She might, Phil. How would that change your plans?"

"Well, in that case, I would like to be the one to tell him about the possible switch. As you know, I've decided to report the matter to the authorities anyhow. I know that I could be suspended, or maybe even deregistered. Even so, I'm not going to delay reporting it any longer."

Chapter 51

Matthew and His Favourite Story

Brisbane, October 1997

Matthew organised a series of meetings with Ric to develop the training he needed. One day, they met in the hospital café to map out the remainder of Ric's upskilling. Ric had become more comfortable with his Director of Training, so he shared Ron's career advice and mentioned how comfortable he'd felt with the Aboriginal families he'd met in north Queensland. Finally, he shared the story of his adoption.

Matthew appeared relieved when Ric said he wouldn't make any further efforts to find his birth mother. Ric waited to hear Matthew's thoughts, but he was surprised when Matthew diverted the conversation away from his adoption.

"Yes, I think you would love working in FNQ, I know I did. I very nearly settled up there."

"Interesting. Why didn't you?"

"Well, things just didn't quite work out for me. And of course, I had to come down here for my specialty training."

"But surely you could have returned once you finished your training?"

"Yes, but that never happened. I know you must see me as a stuffy old physician. I wasn't always like this. In fact, I had a few flings in the north, and I did some really crazy things. Yeah … there was one woman up there who I still think of to this day. You got time to hear my favourite north Queensland story?"

Ric hesitated, wondering whether he should politely excuse himself before his Director of Training disclosed something which he might regret. He wasn't sure what to do. Perhaps Matthew's story would be helpful in understanding the lure of the north which was now dominating Ric's thinking. He nodded and settled back in his chair. It soon became obvious Matthew's story was deeply personal.

"I was working on a remote community up north. A young woman came out to visit her family there. I'd recently bought a boat, and I'd persuaded her to come fishing with me one night after work. Her name was Joyce, and this night we headed out towards one of the nearby islands. She suggested I cut the motor and not anchor the boat, just let it drift with the tides and the currents.

Her eyes scanned the silky grey surface of the ocean as the swell rolled through the channel. A half-moon was up and there were only a few wispy clouds, otherwise the sky was awash with stars. She had this big red plastic reel clamped between her thighs, and she kept sliding her fingers up and down the thick green line, feeling for nibbles.

She yelled, *Got ya!* She reeled in, pulling with alternating hands along the line. I watched as her muscles strained and the line tightened over her fingers causing her face to tense. I started to move towards her, then she gave me a none-too-subtle shake of her head. *I can handle this,* she said, as she hauled the fish closer to my tinny."

You could see the scales shimmering under the surface as the fish flipped from side to side, trying to disgorge the hook. Her face was a mask of concentration. She had her tight curls tied back. Her ponytail flicked from side to side as she pulled the fish closer, letting the heavy line fall unwound to the bottom of the boat.

She called, *Help me!* as she was pulled to the side of the boat. I stumbled over the fishing tackle and grabbed for the line which was now cutting her fingers. *Not the line you idiot, grab hold of me!*

I was of course, happy to oblige. I folded my arms around her waist and held her tight.

I can't hold it. I should have worn those bloody gloves, she said.

Hey Joycie, I know it was a good size fish, but it didn't look that big, I said.

I'm not fighting a fish anymore, you stupid Migaloo. A big shark's got hold of it!

I said *Oh, bugger. How about I grab a knife and cut the line?*

No bloody fear you won't! Sharks are good eating, feed the whole family.

What do you want me to do?

She said, *Do you reckon you could hold this line with those soft flabby hands of yours while I get the gloves on?*

Reluctantly I let go of her waist. I cursed the heavy line as it cut into my fingers. I tried moving it slowly from side to side as Joycie had done, hoping the damn shark didn't get off. It didn't, so I began to feel pretty smug.

Wow! So you managed to land the shark? asked Ric.

Nah, she didn't trust me to do that. She had the gloves on, so she took the line and started playing the shark. I didn't have time to feel sorry for myself.

She said, *Hey dreamer, what'd you do with that big gaff hook?* I grabbed the hook and started to move towards Joycie.

She shouted again. *Gees Matthew, do you want us both in the water with an angry shark? Stay where you are, get the other pair of gloves on, and slide the gaff over to me. When I get the gaff hook in, I'll hand the line over to you.*

Although it was a cool night, I broke out in a sweat. I couldn't believe the weight of that shark. And she'd been hauling it in without any obvious effort. *Lean back,* she called as she swung the shark into the boat. It thrashed around between the aluminium seats, lunging at Joycie. She was trying to control it with the gaff hook. *Do ya' think you could grab that tomahawk and bash this thing on the head?*

After my first tentative hit, the shark turned on me. As Joycie growled and pulled it away with the gaff, I thought, *bugger this!* I gave the shark a thwack with the back of the axe, narrowly missing Joyce's arm as the axe rebounded. The shark shuddered and gradually stopped moving. Blood oozed into the sea water sloshing around my feet.

Joyce sat there looking at me. *Gees Matthew, you're sweating so much, you'd think it was you who'd pulled in the bloody shark.* I looked at the shark, trying to regain composure. I reckoned that thing was nearly four feet long. *Are you sure it's dead?*

She said, *I'll make sure of that,* as she lifted the shark and cut its throat, letting the blood drain into the bucket. Trouble is, I don't think it'll fit into your little fishing bucket.

I was grateful that over the next couple of hours, all the fish we caught did actually fit into my bucket. As the night wore on, Joycie decided we'd caught enough. She took the shark and most of the reef fish, leaving a couple for me. When I dropped her home, the kids and the old folks gathered around. I found myself thinking. *Well, that was an interesting night. I wonder if she'll ever come fishing with me again?*

A few days later, after I'd convinced myself that was the end of it, I rounded a corner and found Joyce chatting to some children. *Hey, how did the family enjoy the fish?*

Yeah, good thanks. We loved the shark the best, eh kids? One of the younger girls piped up. *Yep, that's for sure. Hey Joycie, is this fella your boyfriend now?*

No shush bubba, no chance. He might have a new boat, but he doesn't have a clue how to fish.

The girl thought about this, then nodded. *Oh, fair enough,* she said as if of course, there was no way this fella could be Joyce's boyfriend if he didn't have a clue how to fish.

Before I had time to think about this, Joycie said, *come on kids, I better get you off to school. I gotta go and catch that plane.*

Where are you heading? I asked.

I'm going back to town. I was only here on a one-month placement, gotta' finish my degree.

I thought this was your home?

Yeah, I was born here, and this will always be home, but I have to get on with my life now. I won't be back until the end of term.

Can I give you a call next time I'm over there?

She called over her shoulder *Yeah, I s'pose so, See ya,* as she wandered off with the children.

I did call her whenever I got over to town. She even went out with me for a few months, and I was getting pretty keen, but I was never sure whether she felt the same about me. Then I got rostered up to the Torres Strait. When I came back, I couldn't find her. Her friends said she'd gone down south to study. I tried to call, but I never managed to see her again."

"Hey Dr Matthew," said Ric. "That wasn't just a fishing story, was it?"

"No Ric, it wasn't. I've never really forgotten that woman. I guess as time has gone on, to my mind, she has become the ideal woman. She was feisty, confident and gorgeous. It's been hard for me to think of any other woman in the same way."

"Is that a message for me, too?"

"It may be, Ric. I noticed Cassie out and about while you were in north Queensland. Are you two still together?"

"Yes, all good thanks doc. I lost my way a bit there, and Cassie was having second thoughts. Anyhow, we're back together now and we're working things out."

"Good to hear, Ric. Well, you've sorted out your love life and your adoption, and now you're sorting out your medical career. All you have to do now is work out what to do about the footy."

"Yeah," said Ric.

Actually, I'm not certain I've sorted out any of those things.

Chapter 52

Phil

Brisbane, October 1997

Matthew drove slowly to the club that Friday night, talking to himself as he went.

"Why did I tell that fishing story to young Ric, when I'd intended to share it with Phil? I wanted to ask his advice on whether I should contact Joycie after so many years."

He arrived at the club to find his friend ensconced in his favourite armchair. Phil pointed to the crystal whisky decanter.

"It's a twenty-year old malt from the Isle of Skye."

"I can smell the peat from here," said Matthew. "How's your week been?"

"I've had better. But I have made some progress, if you could call it that."

Matthew's lips tingled as the aromas of the whisky percolated through his senses. He raised his glass and asked, "So what sort of progress have you made?"

"Well, my friend, I've phoned the medical indemnity people. One of their young lawyers is preparing a response. Their initial advice is that I'll probably have to disclose to the CEO in Cairns and the CEO here at our hospital. It's likely the Health Department will need to inform the Department of Families people. They may have to inform the relevant ministers as well."

"Okay, so they'll keep it all low key."

"Yeah, right. Anyhow, if their initial advice is confirmed, I'll tender my resignation, effective immediately. Oh, and I'm thinking seriously about advising young Ric as well."

"Bloody hell, Phil. Are you on a death wish?"

"Possibly. I'm thinking maybe a change of career would be a good thing for me. I could return to university and study for a different profession. Of course, that's if I don't end up in prison."

"Phil, I think you need to stop right there. You've only received preliminary advice from a young lawyer. You don't have to resolve the whole thing tonight."

"It's been hanging over my head for so long, I need to sort it out."

"Why not go and have a word with the boss? Tell her what you've done. Offer your resignation if you must, but at least give her a chance to respond. She has access to very senior legal counsel."

"You mean postpone the inevitable?"

"It may not be inevitable. This mistake occurred almost thirty years ago. There's a fifty percent chance the baby went to the intended adopting family."

"Maybe so, maybe not. At the time we didn't report it, because in those days the child wouldn't be able to search for their birth mother. That's no longer the case with the change of legislation in the eighties. The child may now discover a 'mother' who is not actually his mother. That could traumatise the child all over again."

"Phil, there are a lot of 'maybes' there. I've never thought of you as gutless."

"What are you saying?"

"I'm saying that in the scheme of things, it would be easy to just make the big dramatic confession, tell Ric, tell everyone else, hang your head in shame, resign and go hide out in another profession. What were you thinking? Archaeology?"

"Why would that be so gutless?"

"Because there is another option. You could 'fess up, face up and carry on. You'd cop criticism, and you'd have to eat humble pie for a while. You could still come out of it with your career intact. And you could continue working here. Heaven knows, it may be good for our staff to know that even you can stuff up sometimes. Hang on a minute. Is this the reason why you've been so lenient on young Ric?"

"It could have blurred my judgement."

"Right, Phil. I suspect at this moment in your life, I'm your closest confidant. And if that's the case, I'm not going to let you throw your whole life away, just because you're ashamed of something you did in your mid-twenties. Tomorrow morning, you're going to discuss it with our CEO, and I'm coming with you."

"Is that so?"

"Yes. And you can offer your resignation if you like, but then you're going to take her advice on what to do next."

"Am I now?"

"Yes. And you're going to finish this wonderful whisky, then we're both going home early."

Phil lapsed into thought.

During the evening, Matthew distracted him with stories of his own mistakes and misdemeanours. He finished with his old fishing story.

"Don't be coy, Matt. From what I heard, she wasn't the only young woman you seduced," said Phil, his tongue loosened by the whisky.

"No, you're right. There were others I regret too. And because most of the girls were on the pill, I didn't always use protection. I caught a few …"

"Right Matthew, I think that's quite enough detail."

Next morning, Matthew hustled Phil into the CEO's office.

The CEO treated his offer of resignation with due respect. After a few moments thought, she said, "Phil, I'm confident you won't have to resign. I'll seek advice from our legal people and get back to you as soon as I can. Leave it with me until then."

"I still think I should resign. I won't be able to maintain my dignity nor expect loyalty from my staff, when word gets out and they realise what I've done."

"Phil, I don't want you to resign but it is of course your prerogative. In either case, you will have to report the matter to the Medical Board. Unless they insist on making it public, I think it's highly likely all of the other authorities will want to keep the information in-house."

"That sounds very much like a cover up to me."

"Sometimes it's important *not* to disclose things, especially if disclosure could possibly cause more harm than good. You know that from your own experience."

Matthew grasped his shoulder.

"Come on Phil, we've both got work to do."

"I will disclose to Ric, if he starts searching for his mother again," said Phil as they walked back to his office.

Chapter 53

Cecilia and Nadine

Cairns, October 1997

Late one balmy morning in Cairns, Cecilia and Nadine met at a nondescript café in downtown Grafton Street.

"When I was talking to you at Ric's party," said Cecilia after ordering her coffee, "I had a feeling I'd met you before. I've been trying to work out where it was. It came to me in the shower this morning."

Nadine smiled.

"You knew! Is that why you arranged for us to meet?"

"Yes, I knew I'd met you before, but I couldn't remember where it was either, until the day after the party."

Cecilia lowered her voice. "We met in the maternity ward, didn't we? We both gave our babies up for adoption, and I remember there was a third woman too. When Ric was growing up, I used to think about you both all the time, because he was born on the same weekend that we had our babies. I've always known – one of you has to be Ric's mother."

Nadine's smile morphed into a frown. "You and I had both been living in Sydney, so they would have allowed your baby to be adopted up here, just like mine. Why couldn't it be you who is Ric's mother?"

"The doctors knew I had moved permanently to Cairns by the time my baby was born. They were adamant that meant my baby couldn't go to adoptive parents in Cairns, so they arranged for him to be adopted somewhere else. One of you two must be his mum."

"Do you remember anything at all about the other woman?'

"Not really," said Cecilia. "All I remember is she was softly spoken."

"Yes, and I remember you told us you'd been doing drugs, and your family didn't know. And I seem to remember you'd got yourself clean, and didn't you tell me that your boyfriend had died?"

"You have a good memory, Nadine. I remember a few things about you too. You told us about your life in Sydney and about your baby coming a bit early after you'd come up to the Atherton Tableland. I think you were helping a friend with her sick mum."

"I wonder why we remember so much about each other, yet we remember nothing much about the other woman?"

"I think we were both a bit younger than her, and we thought our babies looked so much alike, they could have been twins. Hey, remember how the nurses wouldn't let us cuddle them? They told us it wasn't hospital policy as it would only make it harder for us to part with them."

"You're absolutely right, we spent a lot of time together that weekend, just the two of us. It's a pity we didn't keep in touch, not only with each other, but with the other woman too. It's likely she is Ric's birth mother."

"Well, she could be his mother, and so could you. Why won't you even consider that possibility?"

"I have considered it. I've even spoken to Ric about it. And bloody Uncle Wilbur!"

"Hold on a minute. You've spoken to Ric. What did you say to him?" asked Cecilia.

"I told him I had a baby on the same weekend he was born, and I admitted I had the baby in Cairns. I told him I didn't think he was my son, and I should know. I told him other women were adopting out their babies and one of them must have been his mother."

"Bloody hell! How did he take all that?"

"He seemed to accept it. Your sister had given him the letter. You remember we all wrote a letter to our babies?"

"Oh yeah! I'd forgotten that. Margaret never mentioned she had a letter from his birth mum ... no, of course she didn't. She never even acknowledged that he was adopted." Cecilia screwed up her eyes. "Gees, it's so hard to think. Has Ric read the letter yet?"

"No, he hasn't. He decided to take it back to Brisbane so he could read it with Cassie. He asked me whether I'd like to see a copy of it afterwards, and I said no. Apparently your sister had read it, and she told him that his birth mother didn't want him to ever know her name."

"Hey, we all decided to put that in our letter, we all felt the same way, didn't we," said Cecilia, her voice trailing off. After a few seconds, she spoke again. "You mentioned Uncle Wilbur. Is that the old man Ric told us about?"

"That's the one. They've become very close, since Ric helped me save his life, but it's more than that. Wilbur's trying to help him with the things he's seeing."

Cecilia looked startled.

"Seeing?"

"Oh shit, sorry. Ric hasn't mentioned any of this?"

"I'm not sure what you're talking about. I don't think so," said Cecilia, her voice quivering. "Hey, this is all a bit sudden Nadine, are you going to tell me about what he's seeing?"

"I don't think it's up to me to tell you. I didn't mean to blurt it out like that. Hey, hang on a minute, there was something else I blurted out. I told Ric that you and I had met before."

"Right," said Cecilia, clenching her teeth and rubbing her temples. "Did you tell him the circumstances?"

"No, I told him it would be up to you to tell him if you chose to."

"I've already told him enough, Nadine. Just last week, I told him about running away and getting into drugs and stuff. But he's always thought of me as his sweet aunty. I almost told him I'd had a baby, but I couldn't do it. I was the one who used to cuddle him and nurture him. My sister couldn't do those things because she was having mental health issues at the time."

"He's an adult now. Wouldn't it be better to tell him?"

"Not after I saw his reaction to the little bit I did tell him. He tried to say the right things, but he looked so shocked. I think he's still struggling to come to grips with it all."

"Yeah, he has got a lot to deal with," said Nadine. "It sounds as though you have too?"

"Hmm. I haven't told my husband about the pregnancy or the adoption, if that's what you mean. I also haven't told him about the other partners I had at that time. God, it's hard to think!"

Nadine squeezed her arm.

"Okay, so Ric knows you had a baby on the weekend he was born, and he knows there were two other women. You've told him you're certainly not his mother. And you've told him you've met me before. Don't you think he might guess something?" asked Cecilia.

"He may not put two and two together. For one thing, the two conversations were a week apart, and for another, Ric knows I meet a lot of people in the course of my work. But … yeah, he may have made the link. And of course, he may have … had other thoughts about it." Nadine hesitated.

"You were going to say, *He may have seen things in his mind,* weren't you?"

"Why do you say that?"

"Because my old boyfriend used to say things like that. He'd say, *I can see things,* or *I just know things, Sissie,* then he'd stop."

"Wait a minute. He called you Sissie?" asked Nadine.

"What? Yeah, my family used to call me that when I was little. I told him once, and he decided he liked that name better than Cecilia."

Nadine was the one who now had shivers running up her spine. Her whole body began to shake.

"Nadine, are you okay?"

"Ah, to tell you the truth, I don't feel so well. I have to go and see that old man, Wilbur. The way I'm feeling, I don't think it would be safe for me to drive. Could you take me?"

"Of course, is Wilbur a healer?"

"Sort of."

"I'd like to meet him."

"Sure, if you drive me to him, I'll introduce you."

Nora was mixing dough when Nadine arrived. "Old fella wants damper and golden syrup for his morning tea. He said he might be getting visitors. Oh, I see you *have* brought company," said Nora.

"Actually, she brought me. I asked her to drive because I'm not feeling too good. You remember Ric's aunt Cecilia? Could you keep her busy for a few minutes while I go and see Uncle Wilbur?"

"Yeah, orright, go on then, he's out there," said Nora, pursing her lips out towards the back verandah. Turning towards the front door, she said, "Morning Cecilia. Come on in and pull up a chair, I was just making damper. Nadine's gone to get Uncle Wilbur."

When Nadine finally came into the kitchen with Wilbur on her arm, Nora noticed her face had relaxed.

"Cecilia, this is Uncle Wilbur. Uncle, this is Ric's true aunty, Cecilia. He sometimes calls her 'Aunty Sissie,' when he talks about her," said Nadine with a knowing look.

"Good to meet you, bub," said Wilbur. "Ric told me about his aunty Cecilia. He never told me they called you 'Sissie', though. Yeah, our

Mob often call our women by that name. I remember some of them women," said Wilbur, gazing into the distance.

"Uncle Wilbur sees things that most of us can't see," said Nadine.

Cecilia squeezed Wilbur's scarred forearm. His muscles were as tight as ropes even though the skin sagged loosely over them. "Uncle Wilbur, can I ask you something?"

"Of course you can, bub. Ask whatever you like, so long as you're ready to hear the answer."

Cecilia's face was fair. In her late forties, she still had a blush in her cheeks. As they watched, her face gradually drained of blood, becoming deathly white. She spoke in a whisper. "Uncle Wilbur, have you seen my face before?"

Wilbur looked down. "I have, Sissie. I saw your face a couple of times, but it was a long time ago. One of those times was with Nadine."

Cecilia and Nora both gasped.

Nadine locked eyes with Cecilia and then shook her head, looking at Nora.

"What?" asked Nora.

No one answered the question. Cecilia spoke again.

"Uncle Wilbur, I won't ask any more today. Can I come back to see you some other time, maybe with Ric?"

"You would always be welcome Sissy, so would Ric."

Cecilia and Nadine walked to the car. "I think we better swap drivers on the way back, you're the one who doesn't look so good now," said Nadine. "I'm glad you picked up not to say any more in front of Nora."

"Yes, I'm staggered to realise how much your Uncle Wilbur knows."

"He is amazing. But there is one question that I've always shied off asking him. I suspect it's one of the questions you've avoided today."

"So, you haven't asked him if Ric is your son?"

"That's the question all right. And no, I haven't. I don't think it would be fair to Ric for me to ask."

"Hmm, I'm a bit shaken by all of this. When you didn't want me to say any more in front of Nora, was that because she doesn't know about your pregnancy?"

"No one in my family knows, except for Uncle Wilbur. And as I said, I've recently told Ric."

"Who definitely isn't in your family?" asked Cecilia with a challenging smile.

"I really don't think so. And what about you? Are you now reconsidering whether you should tell him about your pregnancy?"

"Do you think he would keep it confidential?"

"Yes, I think he would."

"Okay, I'll give it some thought."

"Good plan. Meanwhile, I'll catch up with Ric when I go to Brisbane next week for a conference."

Chapter 54

Things Become a Lot More Complicated

Brisbane, October 1997

"Hey Cassie, would you mind if we had a house guest for a couple of days?" asked Ric when he returned from a day of upskilling at the hospital in Brisbane.

"No worries, babe. Is it someone from Cairns?"

"Yep, it's Nadine. She's down for an agency conference, but their budget's always tight."

"Sure, it sounds like you two have sorted out your differences. And it will give me a chance to get to know her better."

Nadine arrived the next day. Ric was late getting away from the hospital, so Cassie drove out to the airport to pick her up.

"How's he going?" asked Nadine, as she hopped into the front seat of the hatchback.

"Ric? Yeah, he seems more settled since he went to Cairns. He's changed a lot, Nadine."

"How do you mean?"

"He's acting more responsibly. And he's much more aware of other peoples' feelings. It's like he's grown up since he's spent that time in north Queensland."

"Does he tell you everything?" asked Nadine.

Cassie hesitated. "I think so. He shared your story with me. He did have your permission, didn't he?"

"Yes, he did."

"It was amazing to hear you adopted your baby out on the same weekend he was born, and yet you're not his mother. He said by strange coincidence, there were other women adopting their babies out that weekend too."

"There were two others. And I've been speaking with one of them."

Cassie turned to glance at Nadine, swerving the car onto the gravel shoulder of the road. "Shit, sorry about that," she said, righting the vehicle. "Are you going to tell him?"

"I don't have her permission, so I'm going to try to manoeuvre him into talking with her."

"Yeah, I don't know how he'll feel about that. Oh, and I've been meaning to say how horrified I was when I heard your mum's story. I can understand why you struggled to continue with that boyfriend, in fact with any white boyfriend, after what your mum disclosed."

"Yes, but I will admit I've often regretted dumping that guy. It wasn't fair what I did to him, although it was probably best for all concerned. I've been pretty angry most of my life."

"Ric said you're not as angry anymore."

"Yeah, he keeps saying we've all had a good influence on him. You know, he's had a good influence on me too. He's even tried to block out those thoughts where he keeps seeing me and my mum. It means he's learnt a lot about respect."

"He's seeing you and your mum? I didn't know he was still seeing things," said Cassie, holding the wheel tighter this time.

"Oh God, sorry Cassie. I've gotta' learn to keep my big mouth shut."

"I think maybe you and I have a lot to chat about, Nadine," said Cassie, as she pulled into their driveway.

As Nadine unpacked her bags, Cassie spoke quietly to Ric. "Nadine and I had a good talk on the way in. She told me you're still seeing things and you see her and her mother, and you're pushing it away. Why didn't you tell me all this?"

"I'm managing those things, Cass. Lately, those scenes aren't coming as often. Uncle Wilbur has been helping me. Actually, I'm thinking I need to see him again, before I go back to work. Do you reckon you could come to Cairns with me again sometime soon?"

"Maybe Ric, but you're not getting out of it that easily. Why haven't you been telling me?"

"Ah, I was just glad to be back with you again, and you seemed so happy to see me too. I didn't want anything to spoil it all."

"Hmm. We need to talk more about this, maybe tomorrow. Oh, another thing, Nadine says she's met someone in Cairns she'd like you to meet. Yeah, maybe I will come with you. Anyhow, you need to have a quiet talk with her tonight."

Ric popped the cork on a bottle of sparkling wine and tried his best to keep Nadine and Cassie chatting together, hoping Cassie would forgive him for hiding his secrets from her. He tried not to think about what Nadine hadn't yet told him.

He found out at breakfast the next day.

"Gees Ric, can you make me some strong coffee?"

"Feeling a bit dusty, Aunty?

"That bubbly went straight to my head."

"Was there something you wanted to tell me?"

"There was. Maybe Cassie should join us."

"That sounds ominous."

"Not really. It's just that she and I started talking about this on the way in from the airport yesterday. And you share everything with her anyway."

"Not enough apparently," said Ric heading to the bedroom to rouse Cassie. "I haven't told her much about what I'm seeing. She's really not impressed."

"Oh yeah, sorry about that. I blurted it out without thinking. Are you still seeing things?"

"Occasionally," said Ric, putting his arm around Cassie as she joined them. "I'm going to tell Cassie all about it today."

"Yeah, well I've got to spend all day at the conference, so you'll have plenty of time for that. Now Ric, there's something I need to tell you. You remember I told you there were three of us putting our babies up for adoption at the same time?"

"Yes, I remember. I found it hard to believe three women could be simultaneously giving up their babies on the same weekend, mainly because by then many single mums were keeping their babies."

"You think I lied to you?"

"I wondered whether you were trying to protect me."

"Ric, I never told you a lie. There *were* two other women. I've spoken with one of them recently. She asked me to tell you she wants to talk to you."

"What? No way. You know my mum didn't want me to find her. I can show you her letter if you like."

Nadine shook her head. "Ric, you will want to speak to this person."

"Why?"

"You already know her."

"Huh? Who is she?"

"I promised I wouldn't tell you. She wants to call you today. Can you give me a time when you could take the call? I think it would be good if Cassie was with you too."

Ric stood up and paced around the room, muttering to himself. He sat on the couch and held his head, then closed his eyes and groaned, saying 'No, No.'

Cassie sat and hugged him, until his eyes opened.

"Seeing things again?" asked Nadine.

Ric's eyes were glazed, and he nodded slowly.

"I'm sorry Ric," said Nadine, "but I still think you need to talk to this woman."

Ric continued to argue. Eventually, he agreed on a time. If he was going to do it, he didn't want to spend all day wondering. He suggested mid-morning, after making sure Cassie would stay with him.

The phone rang much earlier than he expected. He recognised the voice. "Hi Aunty Sis. Hey, I'd love to talk to you, but can I call you back later? I'm expecting another call."

"Did Nadine set up the other call, Ric?"

"Yes, she did. Hang on a minute, how did you know? Oh God," said Ric, staggering to a chair. "Were you one of the other women?" he asked as his whole body began to tremble.

Cassie took the phone and explained what was happening. Cecilia suggested they put the call on speaker mode.

"Aunty Sis, why didn't you tell me, maybe not when I was little, maybe when we spoke last month? Were you my mother all along?" asked Ric, in what sounded to Cassie, more like hysteria than shock.

"Ric, why don't you listen to what your aunt has to say?" said Cassie, holding his hands.

By now, Ric was blubbering.

"I'm sorry Ric. All those years ago when I worked out Margaret had adopted a baby who was born on the same day as mine, I felt sick. I panicked. I arranged to meet a social worker from the department and told them what had happened. They looked into it and came back saying there was no way you could be my son. My son was adopted to a couple in Brisbane."

"Well, you could have told me and explained all that to me, at least now I'm older."

"Yes, I could have, and I almost did tell you when we spoke. Do you remember when I told you my story, I said I still didn't make contact with my family for a while, because there was something I had to do first?"

"Yes, I remembered that after you'd gone, and I've been meaning to ask you what it was."

"Well Ric, that was it. I had a huge belly and I wanted to give the baby up for adoption before I rejoined the family."

Cassie was still holding Ric's hands as he digested his aunt's story. Ric still hadn't said much, so Cassie broke the silence.

"Cecilia, I know you would have had a lot of joy playing with this one when he was a cute little toddler, but it must have been hard for you at times. You must have often thought about your own baby and how he was going."

"I did Cassie. In fact, I still think of him. It's been very hard keeping this secret for so long. When Nadine and I recognised each other, we just started babbling like teenagers."

"Aunty Sis, I wish I could give you a big hug right now. It will just have to wait until we come back to Cairns next week to see Uncle Wilbur."

"I'll really look forward to that hug, Ric. And maybe then, we could talk some more about the other woman, the one who must be your mother."

"It doesn't matter Aunty Sis. In her letter, my mum said she didn't want me to ever know her name, so I'm going to respect that wish."

"You never know Ric; she may have changed her mind."

"Yeah, I dunno, Aunty Sis. I'll think about it."

Chapter 55

A Surprise for Matthew

Brisbane, October 1997

Ric was still thinking about his aunt's words when Nadine arrived home.

"So Ric, did you take the phone call?"

"I did."

"Well, at least now you know. Are you feeling okay about it?"

"It was a shock at first, but then I remembered Aunty Sis had hinted at this, and I didn't follow it up. Yeah, amazing. Hey Nadine, I just remembered some other things I've been meaning to follow up, and one at least was related to you."

Nadine tensed.

"When I was talking to Uncle Wilbur, he mentioned something about when you grew up, you changed your name. What name did you go by when you were younger?"

"Oh, is that all? Yeah well, Nadine is my real name, but all the other kids thought it was a funny sort of name. So, I always answered to my middle name, which was the same name my grannie had, old Grannie Joycie."

"Ah, and you don't use that name anymore?"

"No. I reverted to 'Nadine' when I went to uni, and I've stuck with it ever since."

After dinner Ric tried to speak with as much nonchalance as he could muster. "Hey Cassie, I'm having a quiet drink with my mentors tomorrow afternoon. Why don't you come along and meet them, and maybe you too, Nadine?"

The two women agreed.

Ric spent that whole night tossing and turning in his sleep, thinking about his subterfuge. When he finally got up, he had made a decision.

"Morning Nadine," said Ric next morning. "There's something I should tell you."

Nadine looked wary.

"When you set me up to talk to Aunt Cecilia, you at least gave me a hint about what it was about."

"Yairr," said Nadine.

"I just can't do it, Nadine."

"Can't do what?"

"I can't give you a nasty shock with those mentors I arranged for you to meet. You already know one of them. Only last week, he was telling me stories about you. That's why I asked what name you used when you were younger."

Nadine's eyes became narrow slits. "That mentor who was telling stories about me, is he a doctor?"

"Yes."

"A doctor who knew me when I was still using my second name? Ric, you little shit! You were going to spring Dr Matthew on me without warning?"

"I had second thoughts overnight."

"That's a bloody good thing, Ric. I may have never forgiven you."

"I figured that, but Matthew talked about you so fondly. I'm sure he'd love to meet you."

"Well, I sure as hell wouldn't love to meet him. And don't you go telling him you've met Joycie either. He's probably a doddery old dreamer by now, and that's the last thing I need."

"He is old, about your age I would think," said Ric with a cunning smile. "He's actually a very astute physician and a very caring man, I think you'd still like him."

"Just because he got me pregnant, doesn't mean I was in love with him."

Ric couldn't disguise his surprise.

"Oh, so Sherlock didn't deduce that part of the story then?"

"No, and I'm not sure how Matthew would react to that bit of news."

"Well, he's not going to hear that bit of news, is he?" said Nadine poking Ric's chest with her finger.

"Did I just hear what I think I heard?" asked Cassie, stumbling from the bedroom.

"This boyfriend of yours was going to set me up to meet an old flame, without warning me."

"Ric, surely even *you* wouldn't do that?"

"It seemed like a good idea last night. I … er … had second thoughts this morning."

"I'm sorry Nadine, I had no idea that was why he was asking about your name."

Nadine was still shaking her head in disgust. "Bloody Matthew, I suppose he's married and has a tribe of kids by now."

"Not married, no kids, but he does have a long-term partner. Rumour is he's not happy with the relationship."

"Oh, so you thought I could help him split up with his partner, did you?"

"Umm, I really didn't think that far."

"You didn't think very far at all, did you Einstein. Gees Cassie, I thought this bumble head of yours had developed some sensitivity."

"Yeah, so did I."

"So what stories was he telling?" asked Nadine.

"Fishing stories."

"Fishing stories? Ha! Like when he almost overturned his dinghy and tossed us both into the water with an angry shark?"

"Yes, that was the story, although I think he described it a little differently."

Nadine took the opportunity to tell Cassie her version of the story.

"Are you sure you wouldn't like to meet him?" asked Ric, thinking Nadine had mellowed as she talked.

"Ric!" was the single word shouted by both women.

"Maybe not, then," said Ric, pouring himself more coffee.

Both women were still shaking their heads as they departed for work.

Next day, the more Ric thought about his former plan the less clever it seemed, which made it all the more perplexing when he received a call from Nadine just before knock-off time.

"Where are you having drinks?"

Ric gave her the details and decided to say no more.

Claire and Matthew arrived at the bar with Ric, followed soon afterwards by Cassie. The venue was upstairs from a café in West End, one of the few genuinely multicultural parts of this conservative city. The conversation moved from Ric's return to the hospital to the things he'd discovered about his family. After a few beers, Ric found himself regaling them with the stories told by Uncle Wilbur and old Bill.

By then, he'd concluded that Nadine was not joining them, so he encouraged Cassie to share the tale of the three women who had their babies in Cairns on the exact weekend he was born. Both Matthew and Claire listened intently to Cassie's story. Ric wound it up by saying his mother must be the third woman.

"Will you try to find her?" asked Matthew.

"No. I was given a letter from my birth mother. She said she didn't want me to know her name," said Ric, glancing towards the door. "Hey, look who's here! Matthew and Claire, this is Aunty Nadine."

"I thought you'd said your aunt's name was Cecilia," said Claire, looking confused.

Matthew looked even more confused. He stood, mouth agape, staring at Nadine. "I thought you were my old friend Joycie."

Nadine, Ric and Cassie burst out laughing.

"Perhaps I could explain," said Cassie. "As best I can understand it, Aboriginal people call their Elders 'Aunty' or 'Uncle' as a mark of respect."

"Ah, now I get it. Ric, have you discovered you have Aboriginal ancestry?" asked Claire.

"Well, not exactly, but I've taken to calling Nadine 'Aunty' and she has kindly accepted that from me, well most of the time," said Ric, with a questioning look to Nadine.

"Yeah, 'cept when you're being a hardhead," said Nadine.

"Okay. I'm still confused," said Claire, now looking at Nadine. "Did Matthew say you knew each other previously?"

Matthew interrupted.

"Ahh, I used to have a friend called Joycie – she had similar features except …"

"Yeah, thanks Matthew. Except that I look a lot older, is that what you're about to say?" said Nadine with an offended glance, which rapidly dissolved into a broad smile.

"No, ah, yes. Bloody hell, you *are* Joycie!" said Matthew standing up and hugging Nadine.

"Well Nadine, you must have been pretty special. Matthew here is usually the shy one. He's never given me a hug," said Claire.

Matthew coloured, causing all three women to burst out laughing.

"Sorry boss," said Ric. "I should have warned you. I didn't know at the time, but that fishing story was the clincher."

Cassie and Nadine burst out laughing again, prompting Nadine to tell Claire her version of the story, again embarrassing Matthew.

Claire by then, had figured it out. "Okay, so you two were an item in your younger days. Come on Ric and Cassie, I think we should adjourn downstairs to the café, and leave these two long-lost lovers to reminisce."

"You should definitely hug that one, next chance you get," said Nadine, as Claire walked away. "She's very cute."

Matthew sat on the bar stool, mouth agape and shaking his head.

"Or maybe not," Nadine said. "Ric tells me you're already in a relationship."

"Well young Ric may need to start showing respect to this particular elder, blurting out my secrets and setting me up like this!"

"Would you have wished he hadn't?" asked Nadine.

Matthew's face slowly creased into a smile.

Cassie and Ric had been home for hours before Nadine arrived in a taxi.

"So how was that?" asked Ric, earning a smack from Cassie.

"It was good, Ric," said Nadine. "And no, I didn't tell him I had a baby."

Cassie had a late start next morning, so she insisted on driving Nadine to the airport. "How did you feel about meeting Matthew again?"

"Yeah, thanks for checking up on me Cassie, I'm okay. It was a bit unsettling at first, but he's still such a lovely man, even though he's dopey. It was reassuring to know he's still a decent bloke."

"And will you keep in touch?"

"I'm not sure. Thankfully he didn't make a move on me, and I sure didn't give him any encouragement. Of course, there's no way I'm going to do that, while he's still with his partner."

"Say they split up; would you like to see him again?"

"Still not sure, Cassie. We both have responsible jobs, and we live so far apart."

"And?"

"Hey, it's not so easy to just follow your heart when you're my age. There was something else I noticed about Matthew. His mannerisms reminded me of someone, though I can't for the life of me, think who it is. Anyhow, don't go telling Ric any of this, or he'll try to set me up again."

"No, I won't. Ric's a bit of a romantic. Unfortunately, he isn't very subtle."

Nadine chuckled as she opened the door of the car.

Chapter 56

Ric's Resolve Unravels

Brisbane, October 1997

Before he returned to work, Ric decided there was one thing he could do, which might sort out his dilemma. He submitted the form requesting access to his birth mother.

Phil had arranged a meeting on Ric's first morning back. Ric wasn't surprised, expecting Phil to outline the parameters within which he would be employed, which was exactly what Phil did. Then he asked Ric to join him in the comfortable lounge chairs.

"There's something else, Ric. I don't normally pry into the private affairs of my staff. However, when you made those uncharacteristic errors, I asked Matthew whether there was anything of concern in your personal life. He didn't say much at the time, however he did inform me of some things last week, in order to reassure me that it would be safe to have you back."

"Fair enough," said Ric. "I guess he talked about how I'm coping with the news that I was adopted."

"Yes, he did."

"Well, as I mentioned last time I saw you, it was you who prompted me to search when you said my mum wasn't pregnant in the month before I was born. My mother reluctantly confirmed my suspicions. The fascinating thing is there were three women adopting out their babies that weekend in Cairns, and I've already met two of them. It seems the third woman is my mother."

Phil's eyes opened wide. It was a few seconds before he spoke.

"Interesting. And are you going to try to find her?"

"Well, my birth mum wrote me a letter saying she didn't want me to know her name. But my girlfriend and my aunt keep pestering me, saying she may have changed her mind. They suggested I should fill in the forms and tell my birth mum I would be happy to meet her, if she had indeed changed her mind."

"And?" asked Phil.

"I submitted the forms a few days ago."

"And how soon will you know?" said Phil, trying to swallow his gasp.

Phil's voice was cracking. Ric had no idea why Phil would be thrown by this conversation. He decided it would be best to just answer the question.

"They told me there's a protocol involved, and the earliest I would hear back would be in about four weeks' time. They said that mothers sometimes take months, or even years before they reply. Of course, in many cases, the mother has changed her name and not left a forwarding address, so they can't even contact her at all."

"Do you think you'll be unsettled while you're waiting for a reply?"

"To be honest, I don't expect I'll ever get a positive reply, so no, I don't think I'll be unsettled, I'll just put it out of my mind. Oh, and I haven't told anyone else I put in the forms, so could you please keep that confidential?"

"Of course. Why don't you want to tell anyone?"

"It's a bit complicated. My birth mother will most likely reject the application, because that's what she wrote in the letter. And the two women I already know, are both convinced I will never submit the forms. So, if either one of them receives an application, they may tell me about it, or ask my girlfriend if I've changed my mind."

"And that way, you will know in your own mind, if one of them actually is your mother, but you won't necessarily have to disclose to them that you know?"

"That's exactly what I've been thinking."

"And why wouldn't you want to disclose that to either of these women, Ric?"

"One of them is an incredible Aboriginal woman who has already suffered a lot. She has treated me like a nephew and taught me heaps about her community. If she doesn't want her son to know, I want to respect that. And if she does want to meet her son, I will seek advice from an Elder before talking to her."

"And the other one?"

"The other one is my mum's sister. She helped to bring me up for the first ten years of my life. She's my favourite aunt, and she loves me as her nephew. She went out of her way to ensure that her baby was not adopted in Cairns. So, if I am her baby, there must have been a terrible stuff-up, and she will be so shocked and upset."

"I see," said Phil. "If she told you she'd received the form and still didn't want to meet her son, that would be okay. Now what if she did want to meet her son? If you then withdrew the request, wouldn't that be a cruel thing to do?"

"Yes, I guess so … I haven't thought it through very well, have I?"

"Maybe not. But you have a lot of things on your mind. And have you decided about your football career yet?"

"I'm going to see my coach next weekend."

"Well young Ric, welcome back," said Phil, shaking his hand with vigour.

Phil's voice still sounded strained.

The hospital had arranged for Ric to commence as a supernumerary for the first two weeks, and then have four days off before returning to full-time work. He booked a flight to Cairns and asked Nadine to let Nora and Uncle Wilbur know he'd like to see them. He also booked an appointment with Ron.

Towards the end of his time as a supernumerary, Phil asked him to come to another meeting. Ric presumed he and Matthew were going to review his first two weeks, however there was no sign of Matthew.

Phil advised that Matthew and all the other consultants were pleased with his progress and were happy for him to resume full-time work.

"Great, thanks for the feedback," said Ric, preparing to leave.

"There is something else, Ric."

"Was there some other concern?"

"No Ric, you haven't done anything wrong … I did."

Ric frowned.

"You see, I'm in a very difficult situation. I may not be able to continue doing this job, or any medical job in the future. In fact, I may not be able to remain registered as a doctor."

"Dr Phil, that sounds very serious. Are you sure that you should be telling me this kind of thing? Shouldn't you be talking to Matthew or one of the other senior doctors?"

"I *have* discussed this matter with Matthew. But it concerns you, Ric."

"Chief, I want you to know you've always treated me fairly, perhaps even been too lenient on me."

"Thanks, I appreciate your feedback. But it does not relate to this current period of your life. It relates to the time when you were born. You mentioned you found it incredible to believe that three women gave up their babies in Cairns on that same weekend."

"Yes, I have found that hard to believe."

"You need to believe it. That is exactly what happened."

"Huh? How do you know?"

"I was on duty in the maternity ward that weekend."

"That's even more incredible! Did you meet the three women?"

"It was a long time ago but yes; I did meet the three women. I remember that weekend well."

"Are you serious? That means you must have met my mum! Why do you remember that weekend? Was it because it was such an unusual occurrence for three women to be adopting out their babies at the same time?"

"Yes, for that reason. And also, because the terrible weather caused me to stay on and work that weekend, when I was supposed to be off duty."

"I heard it was a wild weekend, weather-wise," said Ric, wondering what was coming next.

"There was a third reason I remembered that weekend. I made a serious error of judgement, and I committed an unforgivable misdemeanour. As you mentioned when we last spoke, there may have been a terrible stuff-up. Sadly, I may have been the one who caused it."

Ric didn't want to hear any more. Too many people had told him things he really hadn't wanted to know. He certainly didn't want to hear what Phil might say now.

"Right, well I'm pretty sure it was you who told me the most important thing is to learn from your mistakes, so you don't repeat them."

"I *have* learnt from my mistake Ric, and I certainly *haven't* repeated it, but now it may have repercussions."

"What, nearly thirty years later?"

"Yes Ric. Will you just settle down and allow me to finish the story, without further interruptions?"

Ric hesitated. What he most wanted to do at that moment was to walk out the door.

"Of course. Sorry," he said.

"It's just that you will need to concentrate hard this time, and I know you will be shocked and probably horrified."

Ric's mind began to see things again. There were women looking at babies, and he knew he was one of them. He gripped the arms of the chair, trying hard to concentrate on what Phil was saying.

"I was very young, younger than you are today. I was also much more frivolous than the man you see before you today. There was a nurse I was sweet on. We used to flirt and play tricks on each other. I set her up with what I thought was a brilliantly clever trick, then it all came unstuck."

"And it involved me?"

"That's the thing Ric, it may have involved you, I just can't be certain."

Phil blurted out the whole story of the baby swap, including all the details he'd told Matthew. "I am sorry Ric. I don't expect you to forgive me. I have notified the relevant authorities and I've tendered my resignation. The CEO hasn't accepted it yet. She's asked me to stay on while she seeks legal advice, however I expect to be stood down in the next few days."

Ric stared, open-mouthed and shaking his head.

"But Dr Phil, I really don't want to find my mother, so you don't have to do that. I only put the form in because people were nagging me. I don't expect to receive a reply."

"Nevertheless, you could locate the woman the department has recorded as your mother, and it could be the wrong woman. Or it could be the correct woman. You will never know for sure. Unfortunately, I can't think of any way you could ever work it out. I can at least pay the price for my stupidity."

"Bloody hell, Chief! We all make mistakes. Look, I'm not going to tell anyone what you've said, except Uncle Wilbur. Of course, I won't mention any names, and he keeps everything confidential anyhow. He may have some good advice for me. I strongly believe you shouldn't resign. I think you should reconsider."

"Thank you. You are a remarkable young man. I will think about what you've said. Of course, the matter may be taken out of my hands."

Ric nodded. "There was one more thing."

"Yes?"

"It's a pity you didn't record that *cafe au lait* spot you mentioned on the baby's left buttock, before you switched the babies."

Phil raised his eyebrows. Ric gave him a cheeky smile. He had already decided not to loosen his belt and expose the spot.

"Fair comment, Ric. That was further evidence of my incompetence," said Phil.

Ric stood and shook hands. "I'll let you know what response I get from the department."

"You're under no obligation to tell me, Ric. However, I would be very interested to know."

Chapter 57

Uncle Wilbur

Cairns, October 1997

As soon as they arrived in Cairns, Ric and Cassie drove out to Nora's place to see Uncle Wilbur.

"He's fading, Cassie," said Nora, as she watched Wilbur and Ric settle down on a tattered blanket under the old mango tree. "He's been pining for Ric to come back before he dies. I can't figure it out, maybe his mind's going. He keeps talking about his nephew, and saying Ric is the next one."

"That's sad, Aunty Nora. Are the doctors worried about him?"

"No, they said his heart is good now, and he's got plenty of years left in him. But them doctors don't know everything, Cassie. This old fella, he knows things. He knows his time is coming."

Cassie asked about the nephew Uncle Wilbur often mentioned.

Nora remembered her cousin as a gentle, good-looking young man who spent most of his teenage years making up stories and songs and playing with the younger children. He didn't hang out with other teenagers, but he did spend a lot of time with Uncle Wilbur. Then he went away down south and joined a band. Later he returned to Cairns; by then he was living with his girlfriend, so the family didn't see much of him.

"Did you ever meet his girlfriend?"

"No, they were heavily into music. And we thought they were on yarndi, and maybe even stronger stuff as well."

Cassie frowned.

"You know, weed. And other drugs too."

"Ah, is that why he died so young?"

"Maybe. Nobody in the family knew for sure. Of course, there were lots of rumours at the funeral. Uncle Wilbur probably knew but he never said."

Outside, under the mango tree, Ric was having a different conversation.

"Good thing yufella come," said Wilbur. "Not long now for me."

"Are you feeling crook, Uncle?"

"Not so much crook, ay. I just know my time's coming."

Ric had the sense to sit quietly, until Wilbur was ready to tell more.

"You been seeing many things these days, Ric?"

"I've been pushing them away, Uncle."

"What sort of things you been seeing?"

"Ah, I've tried not to look. I think most of them are about my mother, or about the women who believe they are not my mother," said Ric.

"So that would be Nadine and that lovely aunt of yours, eh?"

Ric was no longer surprised by what Wilbur knew.

"Are you really so certain neither of these ladies is your real mum?"

"Well, I'm almost certain," said Ric. He went on to explain all the reasons.

"I'm thinking maybe there's something you haven't told me."

What's he asking about now? It must be the baby swap. How the hell does he know about that?

"Uncle, I didn't tell you about the baby swap, because it doesn't matter to me if those two babies were swapped, as my real mother doesn't want me to know. I was going to leave it there."

"The knowledge will keep coming to you, Ric. Sometimes in what you see, sometimes in the stories from the Old People who may know who your mother is."

Ric looked startled. Wilbur continued.

"You're right though, finding out about your mother that way would be like cheating, eh?"

The old familiar prickling sensations ran up the back of Ric's neck. It suddenly occurred to him there was no need to keep his other secret from Wilbur. He confessed that he had submitted the form to the department.

Wilbur just looked at him, smiling his usual wan smile.

"How do you know all this stuff, Uncle?"

"It was one of those Old People I mentioned. They told me long ago."

"Well, who are these Old People, and how would they know about the swap? Uncle, I'm starting to feel trapped."

"Well Ric, life's gonna get even harder for you now. You'll soon have to choose whether you want to find out who your mother is."

"Yeah, I know."

"And you'll have to choose whether you want to know if you are Aboriginal."

"If I find out those other things, I may not have a choice about the last one."

"You always have choices, boy. Some choices are just more difficult than others."

"I'm not sure if I understand what you're saying."

"If you do find you have Aboriginal people in your family line, then you have to work out for yourself if you identify as Aboriginal. But it's not just your choice. The community will need to decide whether to accept you as Aboriginal."

Nora filled her big brown teapot many times that afternoon before the two men came in to join them.

Cassie accompanied Nora when she went to pick up the grandkids. When they arrived home, Ric greeted them, lifted one in each arm, and carried their wriggling forms out into the yard for Uncle Wilbur to tousle their hair.

"Hey kids, Cassie and I are buying takeaway tonight," said Ric.

"Deadly," said the kids in unison.

"What would you like?"

The children came up with many alternatives then Nora added some of her own. They decided to head down to the local food mall, where everyone could choose for themselves.

After filling their bellies, Ric and Cassie dropped them home and then drove to a lookout halfway up the range. As the sun dropped out of the western sky, Ric's eyes turned to the eastern horizon. Shadows lengthened and kookaburras cackled. The ocean changed from turquoise to dark green, then deep grey. Still Ric didn't speak. They wandered around the grassy picnic area saying little. Ric turned to face Cassie, moving closer and holding her hands.

"Would you consider moving up here one day? I've finally worked out what I want to do with my life."

Cassie's eyebrows rose slightly, but she offered a quiet smile.

"But first," continued Ric, "I need to see a few more people, and one of them is Aunty Sis."

Chapter 58

Families Entangled

Cairns, October 1997

When they arrived, Cecilia was relieved. "I'm so glad you've come early. Ted's out, so we'll at least have a few minutes to ourselves. I still haven't told him I had a baby, but he's figured out I must be hiding something. Oh Ric, I'm so sorry I didn't tell you before, I'd always intended to, I just kept putting it off."

"It's okay, Aunty Sis. Nothing you could ever do, or ever tell me, would stop me loving you, so please don't feel upset over me."

Cecilia burst into tears. Ric was devastated. He looked to Cassie for guidance.

She mouthed her words. "It's okay, that was lovely."

Cecilia recovered her composure and wiped her face just in time to hear car tyres crunching the gravel on the driveway.

Later, when they arrived at Ric's parents' place, Margaret took his arm and steered him out into the garden

"Ric, there's something I've been meaning to talk to you about."

Here we go again.

"Cecilia told me you've been seeing things."

I don't remember telling Aunty Sis about that.

"Ah well, yes sometimes I do see things. But don't worry about it, Mum. At first, I *did* think I was going troppo. Now I just work hard to put those things out of my mind."

"I understand you're seeking advice from Wilbur, the Aboriginal Elder?"

"Yeah, he's a wise old man and he's been very kind to me."

"Then there's something else I think you should know. Do you remember my father, your grandfather?"

"I remember Poppy, I used to love playing with him when I was little."

"Yes, you did. We always thought you looked a bit like him, with your darker skin and brown eyes, like a lot of our relatives from southern Italy. Anyhow, your poppy was one of those people who would know when a family member had become ill or had died, long before news arrived. Your great-grandfather apparently had that ability as well."

"Yeah well, although that's interesting, I won't have inherited anything from either of them as I was adopted."

"Hmm … Yes, that's true. But there's one other thing, and it's only recently come back to me. I'm a bit embarrassed to tell you this. Just before he died, your poppy once told me something in confidence."

Margaret's face flushed.

"I don't know why I'm telling you this. As you said, you were adopted."

"It's okay Mum, don't tell me if you don't want to."

Margaret took a deep breath.

"When my father, your poppy, was arranging his own father's funeral, one of Poppy's aunties told him that his father was her half-brother, not her brother. She said his father, that's my grandfather, was born before her mum and dad married."

"I suppose that wasn't unusual in those days, with no contraceptives."

"That's true, but this same aunty told Poppy that his father was not actually Italian, like her father. She claimed he was an Aboriginal man, who had cast some sort of spell over their mother so she would go with him, and then he'd got her pregnant."

"That sounds a bit far-fetched," said Ric, hoping his Mum couldn't see the goose bumps on his neck.

She could.

"I'm sorry Ric, I didn't mean to scare you. I'm sure he wasn't a witch doctor or anything like that, and anyhow, Poppy's aunty was apparently a bit of a drama queen. But now you have a lot of Aboriginal friends, I thought you'd be interested in the story."

"Mum, I don't think there ever were any 'witch doctors' who did that sort of thing in Australia! I am interested in what you said though, it's fascinating. Did Poppy's drama queen aunty tell him the name of the man who was supposedly his father?"

"Yes, she did, and Poppy did once tell me. But it was a long name, and I'm having trouble remembering it. Anyhow it probably doesn't matter because Poppy thought she might have made up the whole story, she was such an eccentric old woman."

"Surely Poppy would have checked his father's parent's names when he organised all the documents for the funeral directors?"

"Yes, but as you know, it was commonplace in those days, if a woman became pregnant to someone they hadn't intended, they would marry another man and put his name on the child's birth certificate."

Ric slumped onto a bench. The old gnawing feeling returned to his guts.

If only she could remember his name.

"Ric, are you alright?" said Margaret, coming quickly to his side.

After a few seconds, he nodded.

Ric and Cassie had decided on a quiet evening watching television until Mark called, saying his grandpa had been concocting something with Uncle Wilbur. Mark was flying to Cairns the next day. He invited Ric and Cassie to join him when he met Grandpa Bill and Uncle Wilbur. Ric agreed, no longer surprised by the momentum of events.

They collected Mark at the airport and drove straight to Uncle Wilbur's place. On the way, Mark filled them in on what he knew.

"Grandpa Bill told me how disgusted he felt when Wilbur confirmed his brother was somehow linked to that historic sexual assault. Then he said he was feeling old, and it was time for him to leave the property and move into town. He asked if I'd like to take over the property, saying a manager could work the farm for me."

"Wow, that's a generous offer," said Ric.

"Yes, it is, and totally unexpected and undeserved. The thing is, although I love the country out there, my life is in the city. Even though there must be other family members who would love to take over the station, he still seems hell-bent on getting me involved."

"Well, maybe you were the only one of the grandkids who ever showed any interest in the property. Remember how many school holidays we spent out there."

"Yeah, maybe."

On arrival at Uncle Wilbur's place, the two older men greeted the lads with firm handshakes. Their generation was not into hugging other men. Neither of them had any such reservations with Cassie.

Wilbur had the kettle boiling and the tin mugs ready. He'd lived so long in the bush that he never remembered to buy fresh milk. He was, however, a dab hand at stirring in the powdered milk without making lumps. He also had hot damper and treacle to share. Wilbur seemed to have appointed himself MC for the gathering.

"Old mate Bill here, me and him have been yarning about the old days. Turns out we've got lots in common, just different coloured skin, but that's only on the outside, ay? Seeing as how you wuz not that keen on taking over the property, he's worked out another arrangement."

Bill took over. "Yeah, Wilbur's shared a lot of his family stories with me. He also told me he's been helping Ric. It's good to have you all here today."

"Thanks Grandpa. I was flabbergasted when you made that offer, it was so generous. I just couldn't do justice to the property," said Mark.

"Yeah, fair enough son. I do want you to stay involved though, hopefully Ric here as well."

Now Mark and Ric were both frowning.

"You know I was never meant to get that property. It was meant to go to my brother and then down to his family. My brother always had big plans. He'd already chosen the woman he was going to marry. They had dreams of changing the way things were run out in the bush."

"I'm having trouble following you, Grandpa," said Mark. "Didn't your brother walk away from the station and never return? And didn't he die a few years later?"

"Correct on both counts Mark."

"So how can you make good on his plans and his dreams?"

"I've seen the expression on Ric's face just now. He knows what I'm going to do, and he also knows why, don't you Ric?"

Ric nodded.

"You see Mark, Wilbur has confirmed for me that the woman my brother was going to marry, was the woman who was assaulted. My brother was probably a witness to the crime."

Mark looked horrified. He opened his mouth to speak but Bill interrupted.

"My brother didn't do anything to help her, just walked away. He felt terribly guilty afterwards. He tried many times to make it up to her. Of course, she wouldn't have anything to do with him."

"I don't blame her," said Mark.

"Nor do I. Anyhow, he called me from Perth the day he took his own life. He asked me to look after her. The thing is Mark, I could never bloody find her. Maybe I didn't try hard enough. Or maybe she didn't want me to find her. Anyhow, the doctor tells me I've only got a few months to live now. I've got cancer in my liver, and it's already spread."

Mark's jaw dropped. He walked to Bill's side and wrapped his arm around the old man's shoulders.

"Git off with you!" said Bill. "If I had a horse this sick, I'd shoot him right now. I've had a good innings, too good, I suspect," said Bill miming the bent elbow.

"I want to fix things up before I go. I'm just so lucky I managed to catch up with Wilbur here, and that's thanks to you young fellas."

Cassie intervened. "Okay Bill, I think I've worked it out. You'd like the property to go back to the Aboriginal people, and you'd like Mark and Ric to make sure that happens. Is that what you're thinking?"

"You've got it bub," said Wilbur, re-entering the conversation.

"Right … So Ric, do you know who the woman is?" asked Mark.

Ric looked to Uncle Wilbur.

Wilbur nodded.

"Yes, I know."

"Why didn't you tell me?" asked Mark.

"Not my story to tell."

Bill butted in. "Wilbur hasn't told me her name either, Mark. Though he did say your friend here could come in handy smoothing the way."

Mark looked surprised.

So did Ric, who seriously doubted his ability to ever influence Nadine, let alone Nancy, whom he'd never even met.

Wilbur knew what was on his mind.

"Never mind, Ric. You'll have the skills when you need them, and I can put in my tuppence worth."

The two old men shook hands and then grasped the soft hands of the young ones. As far as they were concerned, the decision was made. Bill asked Mark to accompany him when he went to see the lawyer the next day.

"And Ric, there are a few Old People I've arranged for you to meet tomorrow," said Uncle Wilbur. "If you and Cassie could come out in the morning and pick me up, that'd be good."

Chapter 59

More Secrets

Cairns, October 1997

Cassie and Ric collected Uncle Wilbur soon after he'd finished breakfast. They were surprised when he directed them to the hospital, where Wilbur borrowed a walking frame and lead them to an office in the Administration Building.

There they were greeted by Ron, the paediatrician Ric had met previously, who explained that he'd been working with Wilbur for almost forty years. He also said they'd recently been discussing whether Ric should search for his mum.

"Well, I actually decided *not* to look for her, because she left me a note saying she didn't want to be found," said Ric. "But people keep telling me things, and it's very hard to know what to do."

"I think it's going to get a whole lot harder," said Ron.

"Why do you say that?"

"I had a phone call the other day. It was from a doctor who was one of the junior medical staff here at the hospital around the time you were born. He is now your Director of Medical Services. I understand he's already spoken to you."

Ric gave a wary nod.

Ron continued. "He's coming up to visit his old stomping ground. We're having him over for dinner tomorrow night. Would you and Cassie like to join us? And what about you, Wilbur?"

Ric hesitated then checked with Cassie before accepting the invitation. Wilbur was non-committal. After a few minutes, much to Ric's relief, the conversation lapsed into small talk.

Wilbur directed them to their next appointment, which turned out to be with Nadine and the three Elders. Nadine introduced them to Cassie. It didn't take long for Cassie to relax, as the Elders treated her like a long-lost family member.

"Ric, I didn't tell you when I first met you, you look so like my son, it's almost scary," said Annie.

"Why is that Aunty?"

"This old rogue here tells me it's not just that you look like my son. You've got the same abilities that he had."

"She asked me directly," said Wilbur. "I wasn't prepared to lie to her. She keeps thinking you're the son she lost."

"Jamayl," said Annie.

Wilbur explained the whole story to Cassie, including the things which troubled Jamayl's mind, however he didn't mention that Jamayl's girlfriend was a white girl. Ric knew Cassie was trying to comprehend what was happening, but he was in no state to enlighten her. He was still trying to understand the implications of Annie's statement.

Nadine spoke. "Ric, are you sure you don't want to work this out? There are so many things that just keep turning up."

Annie chimed in. "Yes. I for one, would love to know who your mum is. You could be one of our Mob, ay?"

Ric looked uncomfortable. "I do understand what you're both saying, but I want to respect my mum's wishes. Unless she gets in contact and says she'd like to meet me, I really don't want to go any further."

Annie had been looking troubled ever since she'd mentioned Jamayl's name. Now her face crumpled, and tears flowed.

"You two go on, I'll catch up with you later," said Wilbur. "I'll spend a bit of time here with these old girls."

As Nadine walked them to their car she said, "There's something I've been busting to tell you. I'm assuming you decided not to submit the forms to the department because your mother asked you not to find her?"

"I did make that decision …" said Ric, choosing his words with care as his gut began to squirm.

"Well, I'm so glad you confirmed that," said Nadine, stopping him from finishing the sentence.

"Why?" asked Ric, knowing exactly what was coming next, which gave him approximately ten seconds to work out how to respond.

"There has been another absolutely amazing coincidence. I received a form from the department yesterday, saying my son is trying contact me."

Ten seconds was not long enough. Ric remained stunned.

Once again, Cassie took over. She enveloped Nadine in a hug, saying, "How are you going to respond?"

Nadine took some time to reply.

"I always thought, if this ever happened, I would decline but lately I haven't been so sure. And of course, the 'Bringing Them Home' report has been in the media so much lately, I've even had to do TV interviews about it."

Ric explained. "You do know that report Cassie, it was the one about the Stolen Generations."

"Oh yeah," she said, although her face still showed confusion.

"It's alright Cassie, my baby wasn't stolen, it was different for me. I gave my baby away!" said Nadine, looking directly at Ric, her composure cracking.

"When I found out you were one of the babies born that weekend, it became even more personal. I'm thinking I owe it to my son to agree to meet him."

As Nadine's face flushed, Cassie comforted her again.

"It's going to be very emotional for you, Nadine. Do you have someone you can talk to, before you decide whether to meet your son?"

Nadine thought for a while. "Yes, I believe I do."

Each of them had different thoughts whirling in their minds. None of them could think of a sensitive way to verbalise those thoughts, so they reverted to small talk. The conversation soon petered out.

"Wow," said Cassie as they drove away. "These coincidences keep on coming. And Ric, if *she's* changed her mind, maybe *your* mother would change her mind too, if you applied."

"Maybe … I really don't know what I should do."

"Your mother must be the third woman. Why don't you put the form in to give her a chance to respond?"

Maybe I should stop keeping secrets from Cassie.

Ric stayed quiet, exasperated that his brain could barely respond to Cassie's logic especially when he tried to overlay the possibility of a baby swap together with the likelihood it was almost certainly his form. The other part of his reticence was fear. His mind kept throwing up a scene of a mother holding a newborn baby.

"Are you alright, babe?"

Ric put on a brave face, concentrating on blocking what he was seeing, and abandoning all attempts to reply to her question.

"You still don't want to investigate any further, do you?"

"No, I don't, although it's getting hard to avoid it."

Of course, given it was almost certainly my form, I could be Nadine's son. And if Nadine's and Cecilia's babies were swapped, I could be Cecilia's son. And if Nadine's and the third woman's babies were swapped, I could be the third woman's son. So basically, my mum could be any one of the three.

Ric became aware that Cassie was staring at him, waiting for him to continue.

"Are you going to share your thoughts?" asked Cassie.

"I don't think they're worth sharing. I'm feeling so troubled."

Damn it all, why did I put that bloody form in? I guess I assumed it would go to the third woman, and then I could put Nadine and Cecilia out of my mind. So much for that plan.

Chapter 60

More Confessions

Cairns, October 1997

Ric was now desperate to know what Phil was planning to do. He made an excuse to go for another walk along the beach, telling Cassie he had to clear his head. As soon as he was out of sight, he phoned the Brisbane City Hospital and asked to be put through to the Director of Medical Services.

"Dr Phil, thanks for taking my call. I hear you're coming up to Cairns tomorrow?"

"Yes Ric, I need some of that tropical sunshine."

Ric ignored the ploy.

"And you're having dinner with old Dr Ron. But my girlfriend and I will be there too."

"Yes, Dr Ron was one of my first mentors."

"Are you planning to tell him about the swap?"

"I've already told him. I'm waiting for the decision from the legal advisers. I thought I should give him a heads-up in case it all comes out in the media."

Bloody hell.

"And did you tell Ron anything else?"

"Well yes, I did. I explained the reason it was so urgent for me to move quickly was that you'd submitted the form."

"Right. I haven't told Cassie either of those things ... and one of the women I know has received a form."

"And has she agreed to meet her son?"

"She is thinking about meeting him."

"Well Ric, I think you should go ahead and tell your girlfriend. You can't have a meaningful relationship if you keep secrets from her. If you like, you could tell her that I didn't give you permission to share my confession about the swap until now."

Ric returned to the apartment. With a heavy heart, he told Cassie what Phil had said about the baby swap, but he didn't tell her he had submitted the form. Cassie accepted that he had only just been given permission to share Phil's story. She talked about the implications of the swap, but she wasn't prepared to leave it at that. She wanted to know what he'd been seeing.

"Sorry Cassie, I need to talk with Uncle Wilbur about that first."

And now I'm thinking that if Nadine has received the form, either she or the woman whose baby was swapped with hers, must be my mother.

That was another thing he didn't tell Cassie.

He escaped to the beach again and phoned Dr. Ron.

"Phil told me he'd spoken to you about the baby swap, and he'd also told you I'd put in a form, asking to find my mother."

"He did indeed. That was a big decision, Ric."

"Yes, it was, and now I'm regretting it. You see, I know the woman who received a form. She was one of the women who had a baby the weekend I was born, and she's considering whether to meet her son."

"And now you're having second thoughts."

"Yes. It will be awkward for me now. And it could be much worse for her. She's the one who's adamant I am not her son. And she doesn't know about the baby swap. If she hears about it, all hell could break loose."

"Ric, sometimes you have to be careful not to over-think these things. You may find that the outcome will be different from what you fear."

"You're sounding a bit like Uncle Wilbur."

"That could be because he's already spoken to me about all of this."

"What? Have you already told him about the baby swap?"

"He already knew."

"Because of his special ability?"

"Possibly. There is another reason too. I think he will understand if I share this with you."

Ric's legs wobbled. He slumped down on the sand, forcing himself to breathe slowly. The sky lit up with a sudden crack of lightning. Dark clouds gathered over the ocean.

Ron spoke again. "Uncle Wilbur was at the hospital the weekend of that bad storm. He'd caught a glimpse of his niece in the postnatal ward, which shocked him because he thought she was in Sydney. He knew how headstrong she was, so he came and talked to me before he approached her. Before he could go back and speak to her, she'd gone."

"Right, so he knew she had a baby. How did he know about the swap?"

"I asked him to look at the two babies because I was surprised how similar they looked. He kept looking at one of them, and he kept muttering words in the old language."

Ric knew what was coming next.

"It wasn't the baby with his niece's name on the tag."

"Right … Well, that makes everything even more confusing, Dr.Ron, could you at least ask Phil not to mention to Cassie that I've put in the form?"

"You will have to tell her these things one day, Ric."

"I know, I'm just not ready. There are some things I need to discuss first with Uncle Wilbur."

"Yes, I understand. I'll make sure Phil doesn't speak about those things in front of Cassie."

"Thanks."

The wind whipped up the waves as a storm closed in. Ric was still sitting on the beach with his head in his hands, water dripping off his hair, when Cassie found him. It took a lot of persuading for him to get up and go with her.

Over dinner the following evening, Ric remained adamant he didn't want to find out the identity of his mum. Cassie mentioned that Nadine had just received a form saying her son wanted to contact her, and she was considering meeting him.

"Did she indeed?" asked Phil, as if this were news to him.

An uncomfortable silence followed.

Sophia had been quiet throughout the dinner. She raised a chuckle when she said, "Oh, it's such a pity Wilbur isn't here. We invited him to join us tonight, but he suddenly had an excuse." Turning to Ron, she said, "Why did you have to tell him I was cooking vegetarian?"

Ron drew Phil out to the verandah with the offer of an aged port.

"I have some information that may help Ric eliminate one of the possibilities," said Phil.

"I thought you might."

"You did?"

"I have known something that could have indicated the babies were swapped, although I've never known how it happened until you called the other day."

"Hmm. You know how obsessional I was as a young doctor?" asked Phil.

"I don't think you've changed," said Ron with a smile.

"Well, I might have made a stupid, reckless, possibly illegal mistake, however …"

"Don't tell me. You recorded it in your diary."

"Yes. I clearly don't know whether we managed to reverse the swap or not. I do know the names of the two mothers whose baby's tags I swapped."

"So, given Nadine has received the form and it was almost certainly Ric's form, Nadine has to be one of the women and you know the name of the other one?"

"Yes. So that's my disclosure. And looking at your face, I suspect you already know their names as well."

Ron nodded.

"Now tell me, how did you know all this? And what else have you stored in that vice-like brain of yours?"

"That weekend, I found the name tags you hid on the shelf. I've kept them all this time. And what's more, I clearly remember the appearance of the third baby and his mum."

"And they were unmistakably Caucasian?"

"Yes," said Ron. "And by the way, she is a Cairns woman. I have cared for one of her other children over the years."

"Well, that means Ric's mum is either Nadine, whom he calls 'Aunty', or Cecilia, his actual aunty, who helped bring him up," said Phil.

"Yes, but I think Ric's still convinced his mum is likely to be the third woman, and I think he's desperately hoping that is the case."

Ron didn't mention the one tiny piece of information that Phil had omitted to record on the baby's record. Only one of the babies had a light brown mark on his left buttock.

Phil didn't mention the spot either. He hadn't recorded it because he hadn't found it until after the baby swap. He sat shaking his head and emptying his glass. "So, you think I should await the decision of the Medical Board, before I throw in the towel?"

"Yes, you should."

"Maybe I'll just enjoy some more of your port. Oh, by the way, one of my medical staff called to say he's visiting Cairns this weekend. I'm not sure what it's about. He says I have to meet him for drinks on Sunday afternoon. He remembers you fondly. He said he cried on your shoulder once, about a lost love."

"Ah, that would be Matthew," said Ron with a wry smile.

"Yes, how do you remember all our names? No matter. I think he's reliving his misspent youth. He was gabbling on about meeting up with an old flame, telling me he still thinks of her, and going on and on about the time he took her out fishing. I suspect he had a reputation with the ladies in those days."

"Hmm, I seem to remember he mentioned that fishing story when he came to talk to me about his relationship breakdown."

"Do you know the woman?"

"I've never met her, although I suspect I know who she is."

"Are you going to tell me?"

"Perhaps not tonight. When you see Matthew, tell him I'd be happy to see him again."

Chapter 61

Does It Ever End?

Cairns, October 1997

Next morning, Ric and Cassie were preparing to visit Uncle Wilbur when the phone rang.

"Ric, you little bastard!"

"Good morning, Nadine."

"Don't you go 'good morning' to me!"

Ric held the phone away from his ear. Cassie took it from him.

"Hi Nadine, are you alright?"

"I *was* alright until I got an unexpected phone call this morning. Why did I ever agree to meet that man?"

Ric converted the phone to speaker mode. "I assume you mean Matthew?"

"Of course, I mean Matthew. He just called from the airport. Says he's coming to see me now. Have you told him anything about my pregnancy?"

"No, I haven't told him, Nadine. Surely, you'd like to tell him yourself?"

Cassie shook her head and covered her ears.

"No way! If I ever did that, I'd never get him out of my life! I was about to tell him I was busy when he hung up. He sounded so bloody cheerful too."

"Well, he's not going to stay cheerful for very long," said Ric, after Nadine terminated the conversation. "I think we should move out of phone range this weekend. Maybe we could ask Uncle Wilbur if he'd like to join us on a trip out bush."

"Yeah, that's a damn good idea."

Wilbur didn't take much convincing. He had a swag packed and a battered Akubra on his head when they arrived next morning.

"It will be good to pay my respects to Country," said Wilbur. "And it will give my eardrums a rest too."

"You'd like us to stay quiet today?"

"No, youse will be fine, it's that niece of mine. She just gave me an earful about you interfering in her life. For once, I haven't got the faintest clue what she's on about."

"Ah, maybe we know," said Cassie. "Ric set up a meeting with an old flame of hers."

"What? Ay, I must be losing touch. I never knew she had any old flames. Except that one she had before she went to Sydney."

Ric raised his eyebrows and smiled.

"Oh, I see," said Wilbur. "No wonder she's ready to tear you apart."

It was a long and bumpy ride for the frail old man. Despite many hours in the back seat of the 4WD, Wilbur didn't complain. Instead, he talked about all the things Ric had been seeing, even though he knew Cassie was hanging on every word. He spoke of the writhing forms in the waters of Backstairs Passage, the fleeing people Ric had seen while walking on Palm Cove beach, and the scenes showing other people.

Each time, Wilbur coaxed Ric to consider where these thoughts came from, and what they could possibly mean.

"I've been trying to do that, Uncle. I read some more about Kangaroo Island as well. You remember how I'd worked out those writhing shapes were probably people drowning in the passage?"

Wilbur grunted.

"And because there aren't many Aboriginal people living on the island these days, my first thoughts were that the European sealers had forced the people into the water and drowned them?"

"You had told me that, but I wasn't so sure," said Wilbur. "I met some old fellas who came up here for a dance festival, and I asked them about this Kangaroo Island. They told me an old Aboriginal story about when the waters rose and cut off the island."

"That's exactly right Uncle. The anthropologists say the Aboriginal people used to be able to walk from the island to the mainland. A lot of people were caught on the island when the sea levels rose about ten thousand years ago. Some may have tried to swim across the passage when the waters rose."

Wilbur looked towards the hills, then turned to Cassie. "Bub, do you know anything about the things he's been seeing lately?"

Cassie looked startled. "Umm, he hasn't mentioned anything to me, Uncle Wilbur."

"But you do know, eh?"

Cassie turned to Ric. "I think I do know. You often thrash around in your sleep. Sometimes you call out 'Mum, don't come to me this way,' always those same words."

Ric pulled the big Toyota off the track and parked under a tree. "I didn't want you to know about those scenes, I thought you'd insist on knowing who the woman was."

"Ric, you don't need to keep secrets from your woman here. She's the one who can help you when I'm gone."

"You're right, Uncle. I do always try to shield her. Hey, hang on a minute, didn't the doctors say your heart was going strong?"

"I know them doctors are good with all that medical stuff, true as God. But they don't know what's in a man's spirit. It's gonna be time for me to join the old ones soon. You reckon you can drive this truck over to that funny looking rock over there? My gammy legs won't carry me that far."

"Is that rock special?" asked Cassie.

"It is to me and my people. Listen bub, would it be okay if Ric walked around the rock with me for a bit? I want to have a yarn with him about something."

"Yes, of course Uncle Wilbur."

They walked around the rock in silence. Wilbur's eyes were open, but his gaze was far away. This time, Ric was able to maintain his silence until Wilbur spoke.

"Ron tells me Nadine has got a form, and you haven't told either her or Cassie that you were the one who put it in."

"No, I haven't."

"I reckon you gotta' learn to trust Cassie, and I reckon you should 'fess up to Nadine too. She's told me about the form and she's thinking she might say yes."

"I screwed up on this one, Uncle. I keep thinking I don't want to find out who my mum is. Maybe deep down, I really *do* want to know."

"We all have to make choices in life. Sometimes, the choices aren't easy."

They walked in silence back to the vehicle.

"Why don't you two take a drive over to those hills. You could walk along the creek. There's a waterhole there, good for a dip. It's a very special place, that one. Come back and pick me up at lunchtime. I've got some culture stuff to do here before I talk with Bill."

As Ric maneuvered the 4WD up the rough bush track, his phone suddenly pinged. "Must be the elevation here, seems I have a signal," said Ric, handing the clunky phone to Cassie.

It was Nadine, saying Matthew was as thick as a brick. When she talked to him on the phone, she'd dropped him a few hints about the pregnancy, but he'd missed them all. Now she didn't feel so bad about not telling him. When she put on her cranky-black-woman-who-needs-no-whitefella act, he eventually got the message and went sightseeing.

"I was stupid for even thinking they might hit it off again, wasn't I?"

"Maybe she's just playing hard-to-get," said Cassie. "And maybe the most important thing for her at the moment, is considering whether or not to meet her son."

Back in Cairns Matthew had met Nadine in her local café. He gushed out that Ric had met an Aboriginal woman who'd had a baby in Cairns on the weekend he was born, and that she was adamant she was not his mum.

"Really?" said Nadine, employing her best poker face.

"Yes," said Matthew, "it gets even more interesting. I've heard on the medical grapevine there were other mothers giving up their babies that weekend and listen to this. There may have been a mix up during which the babies' name tags were swapped."

Nadine continued with her poker face.

"That's a bit hard to believe, hospitals are usually scrupulous about name tags."

"I have it on good authority there may have been a mishap with the tags. I'm not sure if Ric knows yet, but it could make it very difficult for him to find his mother. Of course, I must ask you to keep that confidential."

"Yes ... I won't mention it to Ric or even to Cassie," said Nadine.

As she walked away from the café, Nadine found herself muttering. "I promised not to tell Ric or Cassie. I didn't promise not to tell one of the other women."

She sent a message to Cecilia "We have to meet again, urgently!"

Chapter 62

Ric Goes Down

Cairns, October 1997

After Ric and Cassie had stripped off and enjoyed a swim in the waterhole, Cassie found a bed of mossy ferns to lie on while she dried off. Ric's mind was in turmoil, but it settled quickly when he looked over at Cassie. He couldn't resist her blatant invitation to join in some languid lovemaking.

When they returned to the 4WD, Uncle Wilbur was thoughtful. "You fellas took your time … Our people say that waterhole is the one where the Creation Spirits live."

Ric decided to ignore the inference. "How did you go with the culture stuff, Uncle?"

"It was good to reach out to the Old People, their spirits are still there. But I kept getting other thoughts. Someone's gonna be in big trouble soon. Have you been getting the same thoughts?"

Ric frowned.

"Yeah, big trouble." said Uncle Wilbur.

As he spoke, Ric felt a sudden pounding in his head. He assumed he was about to see what Wilbur was seeing. Instead, the headache worsened, and no scenes entered his mind.

"Cassie, you'll have to drive back," said Ric, handing over the keys. He raised his arm and cradled his forehead with his elbow. "Ahh! I will get Uncle Wilbur to sit in the front with you, so I can rest in the back."

"Are you alright babe?"

"Not sure."

"Cassie, Ric is right. You must do the driving now and let him rest. And maybe you could put your foot down," said Wilbur.

The drive back to Cairns in the gathering dusk was even bumpier than the drive out. It was punctuated by wild swerves to avoid kangaroos, and furtive glances into the back seat.

Ric's head lolled about, only the seatbelt keeping him upright.

As they arrived at the hospital, Wilbur said, "Drive up the ramp where the ambulances go. I'll stay with him, you go and ask for help, real urgent. Something's happened inside his head."

Cassie stopped the car and found Ric to be unconscious. She ran into the Emergency Department, calling for help. Wardsmen rushed out, bundled Ric onto a stretcher and wheeled him into the resuscitation bay.

In another part of town, Cecilia received the message and called Nadine.

Nadine came straight to the point.

"I met up with my old boyfriend today, he's turned up in Cairns."

"Wow, how did that go?"

"Yeah, pretty good at first but then he told me something terrible. He said on the weekend Ric was born, there may have been a mix up with the babies' name tags! He thinks Ric doesn't know. But that means either one of us could be Ric's mum!"

"What? Oh God, you're right. But it could still be the other woman too. And you have to decide whether to meet your son. Hey, could we meet up today and try to get our heads around all of this?"

"I'll come over straight away."

When she arrived, Cecilia came to the door, trembling. "Thank goodness you're here. I don't want Ted to see me like this. I'm staggered to think I could be Ric's mum."

"Hey sister, that wouldn't be so bad, would it?" asked Nadine.

"I just feel so guilty, and so bloody stupid that I never worked it out before."

"Well, if the department gave you an assurance your baby was adopted elsewhere, how *could* you have worked it out?"

"I know, Nadine. But since I spoke to you, my mind has thrown up so many other things. You know that nephew of Uncle Wilbur's, the one he called Jamayl?"

"Yeah, he was my cousin."

"Well, I think that guy was my boyfriend. I called him Jimmy."

"Ah," said Nadine. After a long pause, she said, "So that could be why Ric has Murri features, and it fits too, because Jamayl was seeing things like Ric is now."

"No, no it can't be. I was just so stupid," said Cecilia, pacing around the room.

"We were all stupid, weren't we? Hey, you know we said earlier, even if one of the babies was swapped with mine, it needn't have been your baby."

"No, I've remembered. Although the other woman's baby was very cute, he didn't look at all like ours. Your baby and mine looked very similar, don't you remember? That's why we started getting on so well that weekend."

Nadine thought for a while. "Yeah, that's true. So, he has to be your son, or mine."

"Why did I betray Jimmy, I just feel so guilty," said Cecilia with a faraway look.

Nadine made soothing noises.

"My baby wasn't Jimmy's baby."

"Huh?" said Nadine with a frown on her face.

"When Jimmy wouldn't come back to me, I picked up a job at a coffee shop, and tried to get on with my life. One of the customers had just been dumped by his girlfriend. He kept coming back every day and flirting with me. Even though I knew he was on the rebound, and he mightn't be serious about me, I was so lonely, we had an affair."

"And he was the one who got you pregnant?"

"I think he was. Then I heard Jimmy's van had gone over the range. Some of his mates thought it was suicide. I knew that wasn't in his nature."

"Yeah, that was a terrible shock to everyone. You must have felt awful then."

"I was so shocked, I got into the alcohol rehab program, and decided not to keep the baby. I wanted to make a clean start on my life," said Cecilia looking up and wiping away tears.

Eventually she calmed down, and they tried to plan what to do next.

"Hey, did I tell you I've received a form saying my son wants to meet me, yet Ric has just assured me he didn't submit a form?'

"I can't remember you telling me that."

"Yes, if he had been the one who put in the form, one of us would most likely be his mother, but now it's all confusing again. Of course, he could have done it then changed his mind, I suppose."

"We should both keep our feelers out and see if Cassie will give us a hint."

"Good plan."

They agreed not to tell anyone else about their pregnancies, and to keep in touch if there were any further developments.

At exactly that time, the doctors advised Cassie that Ric was critically ill.

Chapter 63

Maybe

Cairns, October 1997

In the Emergency Department waiting room, Cassie phoned Margaret, and Wilbur phoned Nadine, then Ron. They all arrived at the hospital at the same time. Ron brought Phil who was staying with him, Margaret brought Cecilia and Nadine came with Nora.

Cassie said she was grateful to have them all by her side as she now feared the worst. The looks on the faces of the two doctors offered no comfort at all.

Ron and Phil asked Cassie to go through what had happened in the hours and minutes prior to Ric falling ill. After some delicate probing, Cassie hinted about why they had taken so long to return to Wilbur. Ron looked at Phil, his lips pursed.

"Ric may have experienced what is known as a thunderclap headache. It's a sudden pain which comes on after sexual activity. Sometimes this happens before a cerebral aneurysm bursts," said Phil.

"Oh," said Cassie. "You mean it could be my fault?"

Ron gently touched her forearm. "If it is an aneurysm, it could have burst at any time. It was good that Uncle Wilbur was with you. He knew how urgent the situation was."

Cassie's head bowed. She remained sitting close to the two doctors.

Phil phoned Matthew to tell him about Ric's condition. Ron and Phil spoke with the Emergency Department doctors, who then decided to call the neurosurgeons.

"Does this mean Ric could die?" asked Cassie.

Ron and Phil both pursed their lips and nodded.

Cassie's eyes turned to Uncle Wilbur. He walked over and sat next to her.

"Ric's spirit is strong. There are many more things for him to do. When he's ready, he will know all he wants to know."

Cassie looked into Wilbur's eyes. He said no more.

The senior doctor came out to speak to Cassie and Margaret. "We've consulted the neurosurgeons. If the scans confirm their suspicions, they want to operate if his level of consciousness doesn't improve soon. The surgery could save his life, and he could have a good outcome. On the other hand, he may *not* have a good outcome. He could develop complications, and he could even die on the operating table."

Cassie and Margaret both gasped.

"We can't ask Ric to make the decision because he's unconscious. Would you like some time to discuss this with your family and friends before you make a decision on his behalf?"

Margaret and Cassie nodded.

"We can allow each of his friends and relatives to go into the treatment room and spend a few minutes with him. No more than two at a time. And you must all stay calm. Then when you've all had time with him, we will need to know your decision."

Margaret couldn't restrain her tears. She whispered the news to Cecilia and then called John. Cassie told all the others, barely holding back her sobbing.

Cecilia and Nadine consoled each other, reaffirming their decision to keep their secret to themselves.

Once she had sorted this out, Cecilia went over to comfort Margaret. They went in together to see Ric. They sat on either side of the bed, each holding his hand. Neither woman said a word and neither looked hopeful. As they left the room, Cecilia murmured, "At least he looked peaceful."

While Margaret and Cecilia were in the treatment room, Ron motioned Wilbur to come over and sit with him and Phil.

"I've told Phil you were at the hospital that weekend," said Ron to Wilbur. "And I've told him you thought the tags might have been on the wrong baby."

"I did."

"So, we didn't manage to reverse the swap?" asked Phil.

"No, I don't think so," said Wilbur. "And I reckon us three all know which baby was swapped with Nadine's."

The two doctors agreed.

Wilbur's eyes engaged the two senior doctors.

"Before Ric collapsed in the back of the car, he swapped seats with me. As we passed, he whispered that now he knew everything. He said,

You have to make sure no one ever tells my aunties. I think we should all respect his wishes."

Ron looked directly at Phil and said, "We *will* all respect his wishes."

Margaret, Cecilia, Nadine and Nora huddled together, crying and hugging each other. Wilbur walked over and sat with them.

"My nephew used to tell me he had a girlfriend called Sissie … yeah, that's right, ay," said Wilbur, looking at Nadine. "I never had a chance to meet that girl, but he was always talking about her."

Cecilia and Nadine looked anxiously at Wilbur.

Margaret and Nora looked puzzled.

Wilbur didn't enlighten them.

Cecilia took control.

"Uncle, I once had a boyfriend named Jimmy. Like that nephew you were telling us about, my boyfriend died at a very young age. He had a car accident on the range road."

"Yeah."

Now only Margaret looked confused.

"Uncle, you told us your nephew used to see things," said Cecilia.

"Yes, he was troubled by what he was seeing, and he tried to make it all go away. And just in case you were wondering, he never intended to harm himself. It really was an accident."

Cecilia couldn't hold back any longer.

"My Jimmy, he was also called Jamayl, wasn't he?"

"Yeah."

Margaret looked even more confused.

Nora turned to Cecilia, wide-eyed. "Fancy you being Jamayl's girlfriend!"

Margaret drew Wilbur aside. "There's something I want to ask you about Ric." She asked Wilbur about how he'd been helping Ric deal with the things that came into his mind. Also, whether this sort of thing was common with Aboriginal people. Wilbur said it was only a small number of people.

"Lately, I've noticed that Ric seems drawn to the Aboriginal community. Do you think there is a connection there?"

Wilbur took a long time to answer the question.

"There is definitely a connection."

"I think I've remembered the name of a man one of my great-aunts told my father about. She claimed his father was not the man who married his mother. She claimed he was an Aboriginal man. When I told Ric this story, he asked me the man's name, but I couldn't think of it at the time."

"And you know it now?" asked Wilbur with a gentle smile.

"I've remembered something … it was a long name … It started with Jamba … or Jambul … or something like that."

Chapter 64

Is This the End?

Cairns, October 1997

There was now a steady stream of people going in to see Ric. Unlike Cecilia and Margaret, most of them could not sit in silence.

"Well Ric," said Phil in a strained voice. "If you ever wake up, you'll find I've decided not to broadcast what I've done. And I'll ask everyone else to keep it quiet too." He leaned over and squeezed Ric's shoulder and walked out, shaking his head saying, "Why am I talking to him, he's unconscious, for heaven's sake?"

Ron was the next one in. "Well, my young friend, we will respect your wishes, however if you recover, and if you and your mum ever want to meet each other, I can help you with some information ... of course, only if you both want to know."

Nora went in with Nadine. She hugged Ric, then started weeping.

"I can't stay in here Nadine, it's too sad," she said as she left the room.

Nadine had no hesitation in talking to Ric. "Well Ric, you certainly stuffed up my life when you linked me in with Matthew again. Hey, did I just see your eyelids flicker?"

There was no response from Ric.

"Matthew blurted out to me that two babies' name tags may have been swapped. Cecilia and I figured it would have been our two babies, so one of us would have had to be your mum, for God's sake! But I've received a form from my son, and you've assured me you didn't submit it. Hey, did I just see you frown?"

Again, there was no response from Ric.

"Maybe not. Oh, and Cecilia said her boyfriend might have been our cousin, Jamayl. So that would have explained why you see things and why you look like a Murri, but bloody hell! Now she tells me it may have been a white fella who got her pregnant."

Nadine looked to the ceiling, rolling her eyes.

"Gees Ric, it's a good thing you can't hear any of this. Anyhow, Cecilia and I have made a pact not to tell anyone else we were pregnant. And I've torn up the form from my son, just in case it was from you, and you lied to me about that. And Ric, you better pull out of this coma, because I've got big plans for you. You hear me?"

Ric didn't answer.

She was silent for a few moments, then she leaned over and kissed him on the forehead.

She didn't notice the faint smile on his lips.

When Nadine came out, Wilbur ambled in and sat down.

"You been playing my tricks," he said, before lapsing into silence.

After a few moments, Ric's eyelids flickered, although they remained closed.

"I reckon some of these people have been telling you things, thinking you can't hear them."

Ric's mouth twitched.

"Err, ahh … is that you, Uncle Wilbur? Where am I? I think I must have blacked out. I'm coming around now … what happened?"

"I reckon you've been coming around for quite a while, Ric. I reckon you heard every word they said, you cheeky bugger. And I'm sure you know exactly what happened to you."

"I had already figured out a lot of things, Uncle. I suspect you have too."

"Yairr, you've come a long way. There's not much more I can teach you."

"I do need your advice on one thing."

"Hmm."

"Cassie hasn't been in yet, should I tell her everything, or not?"

"I reckon you've already worked out neither of them aunties wants to know definitely that they are your mum."

"Yeah."

"And you already know which one it is."

"Yes. I do. And I think Jamayl knew Cecilia was pregnant. I think the shock of it caused him to lose control on the range road."

"I think so too. And if he was your father, that would've explained how you look, and why you've been seeing things," said Wilbur, now watching Ric carefully.

"It would have."

"And?"

"There was one thing I took a long while to work out. It was about Jamayl."

"He wasn't your dad."

"You knew! I *do* still have things I can learn from you."

"Ric, the main thing I can teach you is how to handle what you see. I think you should share everything with Cassie one day, but not yet. She's in a terrible state, she thinks you're gonna' die. You need to give her time to understand you will survive this thing. Then you both need to get to know each other better. If it all works out, you can tell her then."

"Thanks Uncle. That's good advice. Okay, so Nadine was the one who received a form, and she swears I'm not her child. If she's right, that means I am Aunty Cecilia's child. And if the father of Aunty Cecilia's baby was a white man, and I think I know who he is, then her baby wouldn't be Aboriginal."

"Well, he may be, if there were other Aboriginal people in one of their families, even way back," said Wilbur. "For instance, that old man who talks to you in your dreams. He may have been one of our Mob from way back, like the one your mother just told me about."

A cold shiver worked its way from Ric's neck down to his spine.

Images coursed around Ric's mind. He held his palms to his temples, willing them to go away. His mind cleared slowly.

"Well Uncle, whether I'm Aboriginal or not, I would like to work as a doctor with your community up here, if you'll all have me."

"I reckon our community will welcome you. Maybe I could take you down to meet the people at Wu Chopperen."

Ric frowned.

"It's our own Community Controlled Health Service. It's been going here in Cairns for almost twenty years."

Wilbur sat by the bedside in silence for a few moments longer.

"I'll go and tell Cassie you're starting to wake up. We don't need to tell anyone we've had this talk."

Wilbur walked out of the room, and whispered to Cassie that Ric might soon be waking up. As she went into the room, Ric opened his eyes and smiled.

She rushed over and hugged him. "You're going to get better babe, at least Uncle Wilbur thinks so!"

"I think Uncle Wilbur's right, Cassie. And it's so good to have you hug me again."

"All the others have already been in to see you. They said you weren't looking good but now look at you!"

"It may be a long road ahead, Cassie. I know I will get there one day. I think you and I will get there too."

Cassie hugged him again.

At that precise moment in the waiting area, everyone's eyes looked up. Matthew had entered the room.

Nadine scowled at first, then her face relaxed. She rose and embraced him.

Wilbur was sitting next to Cecilia, watching her out of the corner of his eye. She gasped.

"That's Mattie!"

Wilbur squeezed her arm and said, "Well bub, now you know."

She responded in a whisper. "Ah yes … you're right Uncle Wilbur, now I know. But, as you can see, he and Nadine look so happy with each other, I'm definitely not going to spoil that."

Nadine introduced Matthew to Nora and Margaret, and then pulled him to the other side of the room to meet Wilbur and Cecilia.

Wilbur was sitting alone. Cecilia was nowhere to be seen.

"Good to see you again, young fella. It's been a long time since you worked up here."

Nadine scanned the room, frowning.

"Leave it for now, Naddie" said Wilbur. Then, in an uncharacteristically loud voice, he said, "I have a surprise for you all. Things have changed in there."

As he spoke, the door of the treatment room opened to reveal Cassie striding out, her face beaming.

Thanks

My heartfelt thanks go to my wife Sue, who not only encouraged me to write, but also provided honest and forthright critiques of my writing almost on a daily basis, and tolerated those many times when my mind was in another world.

I thought it was important to present this fictional story thoughtfully and sensitively. For this reason, I consulted a Sensitivity Reader recommended by the Queensland Writers Centre. Venessa Curnow not only reviewed and advised on Aboriginal and Torres Strait Islander issues, but also contributed most of the text for the Glossary of Terms used by contemporary First Nations people, for all of which I am extremely grateful.

I also wish to thank both Joseph Murphy, whose ancestry is Jinibara, a friend and colleague for almost fifty years, and Sharon Barry, an Aboriginal women reviewer, living on Kabi Kabi (Gubbi Gubbi) land in the Sunshine Coast, whose ancestry connections are to the central west Queensland area. They have both read the entire manuscript in its earlier drafts, and provided advice from their own experiences and perspectives, virtually all of which I have incorporated into the text.

My sincere appreciation also goes to my three non-Indigenous beta readers, Graeme Smith, Ineke Hodalin and Barbara Glass, without whose patience and persistence in painstakingly checking multiple drafts, this story would have remained in the bottom drawer of my desk.

Thanks also to my son, Andrew, and daughter, Michelle, who read the manuscript and provided many useful suggestions on the plot, the characters, and the dialogue.

I have been fortunate to work with Ian Mathieson (ianmathiesonediting *iEdit*), an editor who has an incisive eye for detail. I have appreciated Ian's advice, and his willingness to work with me to develop the best possible version of my story.

And lastly, thanks to Donna Munro (Donna Munro Book Design - donnamunrobookdesign.wordpress.com), for the final book design and layout.

Glossary of Terms

Used by Contemporary Aboriginal and Torres Strait Islander People

Bora Ring – ceremonial place used by Aboriginal people in Eastern Australia. Some are circular shapes on the ground.

Buliman – commonly used term to describe police.

Cat – term used by some Aboriginal and Torres Strait Islander people in north Queensland to describe a gay male.

Cleverman – commonly used in many parts of Australia to describe special Aboriginal and Torres Strait Islander people, not gender specific, who have supernatural abilities. They are often consulted by community members to assist with spiritual and cultural services, and support in safeguarding Indigenous Cultural and Intellectual Property.

Country – a term commonly used across Australia to describe land and ecology, but it also has more broader meanings including knowledge, spirituality, culture, language, social and familial relationships.

Creation Spirits – supernatural entities from Aboriginal spirituality.

Deadly – Excellent, awesome.

Elder – a revered person, not necessarily referring to their age, this term recognises their role amongst their community. They are often called Aunty or Uncle to denote this respect.

Gammin/gammon – pretending, kidding or joking.

Gammy – a descriptive term to describe a body part or limb which is not functioning properly.

Grannies – grandchildren.

Medicine Man – term used in many parts of Australia to describe special Aboriginal and Torres Strait Islander people, not gender specific, who have special roles in safeguarding Indigenous Cultural and Intellectual Property as well as providing spiritual and cultural medicinal treatments, advice and care for community members.

Migaloo – term commonly used by Aboriginal and Torres Strait Islander people across Queensland to describe non-Indigenous Australians.

Mob – term identifying a group of Aboriginal and Torres Strait Islander people associated with a particular place or Country … it is used to describe who they are and where they are from. (Australian Indigenous HealthInfoNet).

Murri – term used to describe Aboriginal and Torres Strait Islander people from Queensland.

Murri grapevine – a description of the way news travels in the Indigenous community.

Myall – a term commonly used by Aboriginal and Torres Strait Islander people in Queensland, to describe someone displaying ignorance, backward thinking or not of the right mind.

Old People – term used to describe older people within community and also people who have passed to the spirit world.

Picaninny – commonly used by Aboriginal and Torres Strait Islander people to describe children.

Tidda – girl, female friend, sister.

Womba – commonly used by Aboriginal and Torres Strait Islander people in Eastern Australia to describe a mentally unstable person.

Yarndi – marijuana, term used by some Aboriginal and Torres Strait Islander people.

Yidaki – unique wind instrument from East Arnhem Land, Northern Territory, Australia. Didgeridoo is the English name for the instrument.

Yufella – you people.

Rod Davison is a retired doctor who has had an unconventional medical career, with stints in General Practice, Public Health, Medical Administration and Aboriginal and Torres Strait Islander health services. Rod has always been a passionate reader of Australian novels. Reading was an escape from the pressures and traumas of medical and public health work.

Throughout his life, he has worked with many complex and challenging characters in both urban and rural locations. In this novel, he has created a fictional story to bring such characters together and to delve into their personal stories, their backgrounds and their history.